KARRIE AND THE ROCK STAR

DIANA KNIGHTLEY

For my daughters...

I AM SO OVER YOU

Karrie

I had my rolling suitcase parked beside me, my oversized, fur-trimmed parka folded over the handle, and I was dressed for a funeral: a simple elegant black dress, and high-heeled shoes. I glanced down at my phone and caught a glimpse of my face, grief-stricken, stressed out. I tried to relax, looking down at the text from Jayden, the friend I was bringing with me to the funeral:

`Almost through security!`

I texted back:

`Hurry!`

I tapped my foot and looked around at the mostly empty gate area, wondering why the hell I was still here when everyone else was way down the tunnel and nearing the plane. I couldn't miss this flight. I would be going directly from the airport to the church.

Jayden better not screw this —

The television above my head began playing a song by Finch

Mac. I glanced up to see a news story: Finch Mac climbing from a limo, pushing through a crush of people, covering his face from the photos, escaping into an airport.

Closed-captions read:

Finch Mac in downward spiral since the death of his son's mother.

I sighed thinking about how I got to this moment: bringing a date to a funeral.

I had been in the kitchen a little over a week ago, pulling the turkey from the oven when a quiet had descended on the outer living room. A moment later, my friend, Blair, crept into the room, sheepishly.

"What?"

"Have you seen your notifications?"

"No, what happened?" I placed the turkey on the counter, shoving aside the potatoes and stuffing, and blowing upward to dislodge my long bangs from my steamed-up forehead.

She grimaced. "I don't want to ruin Friendsgiving."

"Seriously," I tossed the oven-mitts down, "I'm going to pick up my phone and look — is it my boss? Did something happen with the premiere next weekend?"

"No, it's Finch Mac, his baby-mama passed away. I thought you would need..."

I couldn't hear the rest of what she said because blood was rushing to my head, noise in my ears — I grabbed the counter, swaying, my knees buckling.

"Shit!" Blair rushed over.

I came back to focus a moment later, sitting on a kitchen chair, a bag of frozen peas on my forehead, *why?* My dog, a little yorkie named Zippy, was sitting on the table, eye level with me. He barked. My friends, Blair, Vi, and Dani, were crowded around me. Jayden and Sam watched from the couch in my living room

"She died?"

They nodded.

"Where's my phone?"

Blair hunted for my phone, finding it closed up inside the Sunset Magazine recipe section. She passed it to me wordlessly. I had missed-calls from my mother and a text from my sister:

```
Thinking about you.
Call me.
```

I dropped my phone to the side. "I'm going to need to make some calls, but... the food is all ready."

Jayden said, "And I'm hungry."

Dani said, "Shut up, Jay-Dog, Karrie is going through something."

Blair said, "I'll cover the food with aluminum foil, go on..."

———

After the calls, red-eyed and devastated, I joined my friends for the feast.

To say I was fucking depressed was an understatement.

My childhood best-friend, practically a sister, had passed away, and I for sure, definitely, would need to go home to go to the funeral, and probably, the love of my life would be there.

Probably.

Since they shared a child together.

And yes, this was why we broke up, why we were estranged, why...

Blair said, "This green bean casserole is delicious, by the way, and..." She finished chewing. "So you'll be going to the funeral, and he will be there?"

"Yeah, probably, I mean... right?"

My friend, Dani, shrugged. "Why would he? He's a freaking rock star, he's not going to go... where?"

"Orono, Maine."

"Finch Mac is not going to go to a funeral in Orono, Maine. He's too freaking hot, famous, and way too fabulous."

My other friend, Vi, asked, "So you're serious, you grew up with Finch Mac, but he's Scottish — isn't he Scottish?"

I picked at the turkey on my plate, completely unhungry. "He moved to my hometown from Scotland when he was twelve. We fell in love with each other and... it was very serious. We dated through high school and then through two years of college. I haven't seen him in years."

Blair said, "I told you guys, this is why we don't talk about Finch around Karrie, you know this — that's how she gets her mailbox money."

Vi said, "I guess I forgot it was Finch Mac mailbox money. What did you do to earn it?"

I said, "I'm listed as a writer on like, five of his first songs, I got a pile of contracts, and now I get money. I only have to deal with his management." My chin trembled.

I thought about Finch and me in our first year in college. He was playing shows, he had just released his first song on Soundcloud and we had been watching the views rise all week, and now we could officially call it a viral hit: over one hundred thousand listens. We had popped the cork on some champagne, and were Googling Finch's name, and then had devolved into some really hot sex on the rug of our living room and now we were there, naked, our feet under the coffee table. I wiggled to the couch and dragged a pillow off and stuffed it under my head.

He tucked his cheek to my breast. I wrapped my fingers through his hair. "You've done it, Finch, this is it, finally."

"I ken, I am really blown away..."

"Me too. This was almost easy."

He chuckled. "Do ye want tae be a singer, too, Ree-Ro?" He joked, "Now that I hae it all figured out."

I chuckled. "Now that you have this fabulous music career, you want to get one for me too?"

"Ye hae such a beautiful voice. Sometimes I wonder if I am being unfair. We focus on my music all the time."

I wrapped a lock of his hair around my finger. "You aren't being unfair, you want this so bad, you are driven. I've never known anyone to work at something as hard as you do, and when you're on stage I just see your power, like you were born to be up there."

He kissed my breast.

"I do think about it, you know, wondering — I love singing, really truly, and when you pulled me up on the stage at the show last weekend, I loved that, singing with you... I love sitting with you at the piano helping with the songs. I love writing with you, we work really well together."

His hand trailed down my body. "Aye, I couldna write without ye."

I considered it for a moment. "I don't want to sound fearful or self-deprecating, but I don't have that drive."

"But—"

I put my finger on his lips. "Shush, you beautiful boy."

He chuckled and sucked my finger into his mouth.

I asked, "Scale of one to ten, how much do you want to play?" I pulled my finger free of his lips.

"Ten, easy. I winna rest until it happens."

"For me, the scale of one to ten is a two. How am I going to start a music career from a two? That's singing in the choir, tops. That's not even *running* the choir."

"I canna imagine ye a chorus director like Mrs Hart."

"I like being listed as a writer on the songs. I really like that part, maybe when you're a rock star I can be part of your management team so I can keep everyone from bothering you. I can be your guard dog."

"Good, and frankly, I am glad tis yer answer, I daena ken how it would work for us both tae follow music careers, but I would try, ye ken I would, but I want this tae work and I need yer help."

"I know you need me," I teased, "You need me so so so hard. "

His hand trailed down my body. "I just daena want ye tae feel like ye missed out."

I pulled his chin up and kissed his lips. "Are you going to marry me, Finch Mac?"

"Aye, yer parents are makin' us wait, but aye, as soon as we are finished with school," he plunged his fingers between my legs, bringing me to a moan of pleasure. "I am going tae make ye Mrs Finch Mac, so so so hard."

I laughed. "Exactly, we've been together for so long, it's always been me and you and when I see you perform I feel proud, like this is something *we* are accomplishing together because we will always be..."

I shook my head of the memory and added, "Whatever," to make it sound like I considered it unimportant. It had used to break my heart whenever I got a check in the mail, but now that money from Finch Mac deposited directly, I didn't have to think about it.

Sam said, "Super cool, we know someone who helped write Finch Mac's early stuff," he raised his beer to Jayden. "...and *dude*, you dated Karrie *after* Finch Mac, how's it feel?"

"I'm not gonna lie, pretty awesome. Jay-Dog was a step up, am I right, Karrie?"

Blair rolled her eyes. "Karrie also broke up with your ass, I don't think you get to be the 'step up' when you were left on the curb."

Sam cracked up. "Burn!"

Blair said, using her fork to punctuate the words, "So, Karrie, you probably won't see him, but you might, maybe, so you need to be ready. By ready I mean, you need to signal to Finch Mac that you have moved on. By moved on I mean, you have a fabulous life, a great job as assistant to one of the best agents in Hollywood—"

I said, "Do I still have a job? Blakely is going through this divorce, leaving the agency, I might not have a job anymore."

Sam said, "What do you care, you wrote Finch Mac songs, did you write 'Endless Future'?"

Blair waved that away. "Sam, you are off topic. Karrie, at this funeral, in front of Finch Mac, you have a great job, you have friends who adore you, you cook a mean Thanksgiving feast. — where'd you learn it, by the way...?"

"My mom would always invite people to Thanksgiving if they didn't have anywhere else to go. She once cooked a feast for twenty-eight guests, and it was always an 'all hands on deck' kind of thing because she doesn't really like to cook. Alison and I would..." My voice trailed off.

Blair said, "So zooming past the realization that my friend Karrie is just like her mother, collecting all of us strays for the holiday — Alison Parker, Finch's baby-mama, spent Thanksgivings with your family?"

"Alison Parker lived with my family, full time, from sixth grade on. She was in every way like a sister, except we were best friends too."

Vi said, "So he slept with your best friend? Dude, celebrities suck."

Blair shook her head. "Karrie, this is a freaking tragedy.

There is a chance you will see Finch Mac, and you have got to signal to him that you have moved on. It's the only way you survive."

Dani laughed. "That's overdramatic, but I agree, you have to signal."

Vi said, "I think better, she just doesn't go. I think seeing him is a huge mistake."

"I have to go."

Vi said, "Then you should make sure not to see him, but if you do... I agree, you have to signal."

I swirled my fork through my potatoes. "How? What do I do?"

Blair said, "First, you look great. But I think you need some sexy layers in your hair, long blonde layers, so you've got that gorgeous California-girl thing going on. Men can't resist that."

Vi said, "Oooh! And you need to practice the doe-eyed look, you know, the one where you look super sleepy?" She tilted her head forward, widened her eyes, and looked like she was bored of it all. "He'll be—"

"I'm not trying to win him, I'm trying to signal that I moved on."

"Oh, right. Don't see him. I recommend dividing the town in half, make him look on you from afar."

Blair said, "Still, I think the long-layers haircut."

"Okay, don't see him, but get a haircut in case he sees me from afar."

"And if he sees you for the first time in, how long...?"

"Six years."

"First time in six years, you need to amp this all up. You need to signal success. Your wardrobe has to be on point. If you're home for three days, all three days you need to wear designer, with costume changes."

I pushed my plate away. "Okay, shopping. Will you take care of Zippy? I'll be gone at least a week, maybe two."

Blair said, "Definitely. He can stay at my house, anything to help."

Vi said, "You ought to take a date."

Blair said, "I agree."

"A date to a funeral? Who takes a date to a funeral?"

Dani said, "Everyone. Especially if their ex will be there."

"But I'm not even seeing anyone, I don't know if that's..."

Blair leaned on the table. "What about Jay-Dog?"

He had just shoveled in a forkful of potatoes. "Huh?"

Blair said, "You'll go with Karrie to the funeral, right? You're an actor in between gigs."

Sam said, "He's always in between gigs."

Jayden said, "Shut up," with his mouth full. "Where's the funeral?"

I said, "Orono, Maine. Next weekend."

"Sure."

He looked around. "Is there pie?"

Blair said, "Maybe you don't understand what is happening. You're going to go to a funeral in Maine with Karrie."

He shrugged. "Sure, I said, 'Sure'. Why not? We have to fly? I've got no money for a plane ticket."

Vi said, "Do you know where Maine is?"

"Of course I know where Maine is!" He jokingly shook his head at Sam.

Sam said, "You'll get to meet Finch Mac."

Jayden raised his brow, put his beer bottle to his lips. "I'll be like, 'Hey dude, I tapped that ass after you, how's it feel?'"

I groaned. "Jayden, that is... Oh my God." I looked around incredulously. "This is the dumbest idea in the world, I am not taking Jayden to a funeral."

He laughed. "I'm sorry Karrie, and no worries, I got you. Seriously, I'm an actor, we used to date, I can easily play your 'man'. What do I wear?"

"A suit. Do you have a nice suit?"

He scoffed, and then shook his head. "Nah, I've got some nice pants."

Blair said, "Karrie will buy you a suit, she'll buy you a ticket, right Karrie?"

"Really? Is this really necessary?"

Vi said, "Yeah, it's absolutely necessary, he cheated on you, you can't be single, that means he wins."

LITTLE SELF-RESPECT

Karrie

And that was how it was decided.

And how I was in LAX waiting for Jayden to get through security.

I was signaling to Finch Mac that I had moved on, after six long years.

I groaned. I should have moved on ages ago. If this was 'moving on' it was at a slug's pace.

In my defense though, he was famous, and news of him was everywhere, his hot self—

Wait.

As Blair would say, no *buts*.

Once I signaled (from afar) to Finch Mac at the funeral that I was so completely over him, totally, completely, so so so over him, *then* I would move on.

We could ignore each other, agreeing to disagree, and live a life where we didn't ever, ever have to see each other.

But now I was irritated that the plan involved Jayden because he was dumber than burnt toast.

I thought I had a little self-respect, but at this moment it became apparent — not *enough*.

I checked the time on my phone, boarding was almost done. I tapped my foot. The group decision of this plan had made it seem a perfectly reasonable thing.

While outfitting myself with a new wardrobe, I had bought Jayden his suit, a plane ticket, and promised him a place to stay and all his meals.

His job was to be 'hot' and to act like he adored me.

That was all he had to do.

I stared down at my phone wondering if he could pull off this basic, very basic task when he couldn't even get through security—

Jayden was running toward me, his suitcase careening behind him.

He was wearing a green t-shirt with 'Gucci' emblazoned across the front, gray sweatpants, bright red Nikes, and around his neck an inflatable neck pillow, pink with cats, oh, and a blue eye-mask up on his forehead causing his hair to stick up. He looked like he had gotten dressed in the dark.

I grabbed the handle of my suitcase and turned to the sky-tunnel. "Why the hell aren't you dressed?"

He looked down at his shirt. "I'm dressed! You don't want me to rumple my suit, I got you, babe, it's in my case, no worries. You wanted me to look hot, I've got hot—"

"Jayden, this is not hot." The flight attendant scanned our tickets and waved us through. "I told you we were going straight to the funeral. You haven't shaved! You—"

"Karrie, don't worry, I got this. I'll suit up in the taxi, if you're lucky you might even catch a sight of Dear Dongly, I bet you missed him." He grinned, wiggling his hips, making it pretty clear that he was commando under those sweats.

"I regret all of this."

"It's going to be fine."

I tried to match his stride down the gateway, but he was tall and my shoes were so high.

He added, "I'm going to sleep on the flight. Got in way late last night, that party was fucking mayhem, and when I wake up, I will be your perfect escort."

"Oh my god, I hired an escort."

He asked, "This is the first you thought of that?"

"Where's your coat?"

"In the suitcase, like I just said."

"I mean, your *winter* coat, I told you it would be cold, really, really cold."

He blinked. "I forgot, but hey, how cold can it be?"

I stopped mid-stride. "It's Maine! In late November! It's going to be freezing!"

He kinda shrugged.

"Do you even know where Maine is?"

"Not really, but from the way you're freaking out, I guess it's up north?"

A flight attendant came up behind us, "Continue toward the plane please, we'll be closing the door in a moment."

We continued in a rush.

But then we met with the end of a long line of passengers inching along into the plane.

I sighed, "Why did they make it seem like we were late?" I looked him over. "Okay, you'll dress in the cab. I'll have my mom bring an extra parka to the funeral so you won't freeze. I suppose there's no chance of you shaving?"

"Nah, scruff is hot, Karrie. Girls love it. He'll be jealous, promise."

"It's not jealousy I'm looking for, just a signal: I'm doing great. I don't even think about him—" I brushed off Jayden's shoulder. "We'll need to do something about your hair. I've got some product in one of my checked bags."

He asked, "You checked your bags?"

"Yeah, I bought so many new outfits—" My eyes went wide. "Jayden, is that all the luggage you brought? A carry-on? Is your suit folded up in that carry-on?" My chin trembled. I was going to cry.

I was going to a funeral, I was stressed out, and I did not have time to parent this man-child.

He said, "It's all good, Karrie, don't worry."

No amount of blinking could keep the tears from coming. They rolled down my cheeks — the loss of my old friend, who, though estranged, had at one time been my best friend, combined with the stress of going home, the anxiety of seeing the man who once broke my heart.

I dug in my pocket for my package of tissues and dabbed at my eyes. "Why are we moving so slowly?"

He said, "Remember what we talked about the other night?"

"Yeah." We passed the flight attendant welcoming us on board.

He said, "Do it."

I said, "Here in line? In front of First Class? There are people everywhere."

He said, "You need to do it."

"Fine, step one: deep breath." I took a deep breath and closed my eyes.

He said, "Step two: wiggle everything to get the blood flowing."

I wiggled all over, accidentally jostling the woman in front of me. "Sorry."

He whispered, "Step three: mutter, 'fuck him.'"

I said, "Fuck him."

He laughed.

I added, "Not that it matters, I am not going to see him. He might be at the funeral, but I will be across the church. He will have to see me from afar. This is going to be fine."

The flight attendant bellowed, "Move to your seats, there will be time for autographs after the flight."

What? My heart dropped as my tear-filled eyes swept First Class and landed on *him*, Finch Mac, one of the biggest rock stars in the world.

He was dressed in a dark funeral suit, a bit of tattoo on his neck coming up from the collar, his beard the perfect blend of overgrown and trimmed, his hair tousled and excellent. Oh. His eyes looked full of grief. He was the man who was, once upon a time, the love of my life. And he was about three feet away.

Jayden whispered, probably loud enough for Finch to hear, "Shit, he's right there, holy shit, he's checking you out, be cool."

Finch looked away.

LONG LOST LOVE

Finch

Och, she was right there.

Karrie Munro, the woman who I had always loved. Her mother had told me she was comin' tae the funeral and here she was, dressed in black.

She was traveling with a man.

I looked away.

I had written a song about this moment. Seeing m'long lost lov
She had once been...

A part of m'self
A windin' through,
wrapping around,
rending my heart, part...
My fingers drawin' down her skin,
where did I start and she begin...
The problem started with m'brutally broken and frightened heart...

I exhaled.

Our history was long and complicated. This funeral was goin' tae complicate it more.

It made sense she would be with a man, it had been six long years. She was bound tae be with someone else, havin' moved on. Long moved on.

I hadna seen her in forever.

She looked good. Beautiful.

Flashes in m'mind of my fingers drawing down her skin, her body risin' tae meet my mouth, I remembered her taste, though it had been years — why was it? How could the memory run so deep, how come I remembered her so well?

She had been m'education, I supposed, all of m'firsts. The bumbling beginning and then as we grew accustomed, the exploration and practice... her skin against mine, her breaths in m'ear, her pleasure moans, the smile that beamed upon me, the grip of her hands on me as she climbed tae climax, her legs around m'waist, pullin' me in... She had allowed me tae do things...

We had grown up taegether and it had led tae trust, tae hae a woman who ye trusted so much that ye could touch her in need and for pleasure and she allowed ye, and tae in turn, tae ken she was yers, only yers, I had never known someone so trustworthy since — what had I done?

I had sabotaged our life... och, I missed her.

She disappeared down the aisle behind me.

I looked back tae watch her headed tae coach and when I turned back around the flight attendant was right there. "Hi! Can I get you anything?"

"Nae."

"A drink, a snack, would you like me to plump your pillows?" She touched her hair, they always touched their hair and laughed louder than they ought.

"Nae, I daena need anythin'. Just sleep."

She winked. "Not allowed to help you with that, but if it was my day off..." She laughed, loud enough for people tae turn.

"Nae, just need tae rest, daena need any help."

"Of course! I'll come check on you in a bit."

She left. I dropped my seat back and closed my eyes.

She returned. "My apologies, Finch Mac, you can't put your seat back until the light goes off, so sorry, so so sorry, can I bring you a drink?"

"Nae." I exhaled and pulled my seat up. She backed away, leavin' me alone tae m'thoughts: shame, sadness, loss. I had been carryin' them for so long. Too long.

Ever since that night, six long years ago.

Karrie and I had been home for Christmas, we were headed back tae school the next day, tae the apartment we shared.

The trouble was one of m'songs had hit. It had hit hard.

I had received, days before, big news, the band and I had an offer. We were goin' tae... I scowled and shook m'head. If I had told her, the day the call had come, it all might hae been different. But I dinna want tae ruin the holiday, the holiday was a big fucking deal for her, for her mum, her whole family.

My mum hated Christmas, she went tae Scotland and dinna care what I did. Karrie's mum had decorated the house, had every moment planned, and I had been young, I dinna want tae upset Karrie, I dinna tell her. I met with the band, made plans, and dinna say it.

Then the last possible moment I said it, "I'm nae goin' back, the band and I need tae devote the next few months tae m'music," and she lost her shit.

I couldna blame her, not really.

But we couldna even talk about the details, the specifics, we couldna plan, because we had tae argue over whether I was a shite person for nae sayin' it before.

I sat with my elbows on m'knees, she standing over me, "You didn't tell me? You were just lying to me?"

"Nae, I wasna lyin', I just—"

"You were not telling me, making plans without me, aren't we happy together?" Before I could answer, "We were going to get married!"

"Please, Karrie, it's just for a few months, we are goin' tae be in the studio, working on—"

"You're dropping out of school? Seriously, dropping out and leaving me with the apartment?"

"It's a chance I canna pass up, Ree-Ro, ye gotta understand—"

"I don't have to understand anything." Then she said, "I mean, I'm happy for you, congrats, this is everything you've ever dreamed of, hope you have a great fucking life, since you obviously want to do it without me." And she left her room, slamming the door on me.

I stood, opened the door and looked up and down the hall, I went down the stairs, no one there. I stood at the top of the stair to the basement. That was probably where she was, but I—the tv down there turned on, loud.

I left the house.

And Ree-Ro and I were no more.

I MOVED ON

Karrie

In our seats back in coach Jayden got comfortable leaning on the window with his neck pillow positioned just right, his knee in my space. He said, "I can't believe it, you actually *do* know Finch Mac."

I said, "First, I told you all about it, the whole long story."

He said, "Well, none of us really believed it. Not only am I your escort, I'm also a spy. That's why I took this photo just now." He showed me the photo, Finch glaring in his seat.

Jayden wrote a text while talking to me. "They all want me to report back about it." He pushed send, then asked me, "Do you think I'll get to meet him?"

I groaned. "How? I hate him and we do not talk to each other. After that whole fiasco up in First Class I will make sure to not see him again. How would you meet him?"

"I don't know, I play a little guitar, I could strike up a conversation—"

"Jayden! You are not here to meet Finch Mac, you're here to wear a—"

"I know, I know," he shifted to get more comfortable. "Jay-Dog is here to look hot."

"Exactly! And wait, Finch Mac didn't acknowledge me in any way. How did you get proof that I actually know him?"

Jayden grinned. "Karrie Munro, he totally acknowledged you, he was fucking acknowledging the hell out of you. He was completely jealous of me," He put in earbuds and closed his eyes. "Your plan is working perfectly."

I said for the tenth time that week. "I'm not trying to make him jealous, I'm trying to signal that I moved on. From afar."

He said, "Can't be easy to move on from that Scottish hottie." And then, "Nudge me if I snore."

LAST TRULY HAPPY MOMENTS

Karrie

I closed my eyes but couldn't sleep, replaying through my head all the memories of my childhood friend. At the age of ten, holding hands and jumping off the dock into the lake. At fourteen propping up our bedding like a tent so we could whisper about Finch and other boys of merit without my little sister, Tessa, overhearing. At the age of fifteen, both of us learning to drive in my dad's car.

Occasionally I cried, trying to hide it from the man sitting to my right.

The flight attendant brought drinks around. Jayden slept, snoring through it.

I ordered a coffee and sipped it remembering growing up alongside Alison. She had been my best-friend, and had lived with my family once my mother discovered that her mother and step-father were abusing her.

On her eighteenth birthday she had asked my parents for only one present, "I have given it a ton of thought, I know they're expensive. I just don't want anything else... I would really love a t-shirt launcher."

Finch, who had come for dinner, like most nights, asked, "What is a t-shirt launcher?"

"You've never seen one?"

"Nae."

"Remember, at the Warp Tour? The t-shirt launcher, *remember*?"

Finch and I held hands on the dinner table. He said, "The wee man on the stage flingin' the shirts intae the audience — one of *them* gadgets?" He shook his gorgeous head, his dark hair, always tousled, perfectly hanging in his eyes. His teenager face had gained the chiseled cheeks of the hotness he would become. "I daena think I understand."

I said, "Alison, you didn't even catch one of the shirts!"

She collapsed on her arm on the table, dramatically. "I know! But I can't stop thinking of them, wasn't it thrilling?"

I laughed. "Alison, what on earth are you talking about?"

"Think of it, Karrie, if you're at a concert, a festival, a school event, *anything*, anything in the world, what makes it better?"

Mom, her hair dark and spiky, said, "Mosh pit."

Dad gave her a high-five.

Tessa, my little sister who was thirteen at the time, said, "I don't know, a cotton candy machine?"

Alison pointed at her, "Ooh, good point, that is also a good thing for an event, but think of it, a t-shirt launcher makes everything better! When a t-shirt launcher shows up it gets so freaking exciting. It's the best part of *anything*."

Dad said, "Well, this was not at all what I expected you to want for your birthday. There's nothing else you need, something — and I can't believe I'm asking this — more practical?"

"Nope, I honestly, completely, totally, have everything my heart desires thanks to you—"

Mom and Dad gave each other another high-five.

"Except a t-shirt launcher."

Dad said, "That is very hard logic to argue against."

. . .

The flight attendant came by with a trash bag. I scrolled through the choices for in-flight entertainment, but nothing looked interesting. I needed distraction, but didn't want to put in the effort to be distracted. I received a text from Jess, Blakely's best friend:

```
I'm helping Blakely get ready,
what's the name of the spa?
```

I sent her the name, the location, the details, and the order number for the package that I had already arranged.

I texted:
`Do you want to go with her?`

Jess texted:
`Yes please!`

I spent the next few moments arranging Jess's spa visit and then checking in with Blair:

`How's Zippy?`

Blair texted:

```
Zippy's great.
How are you and Jay-Dog?
```

Jayden snored so I nudged him and he shifted up against the window.

I texted back:
`Just great.`

I closed my eyes and tried to rest, but kept remembering Alison's birthday, a painful memory because we had been so happy.

She had ripped the paper off our gift and discovered the t-shirt launcher and with it a bag of twelve multicolored shirts. We all stood on the grass in the backyard, while she was up on the back deck, holding the launcher to her ear. "Hear that?"

Finch said, "Nae! We canna hear anythin'!"

She said, "It's the sound of awesome!"

Dad started a chant, "T-shirts! T-shirts! T-shirts!"

We all joined in.

Alison patted her heart and said, "This is the greatest moment of my life!" And launched a green t-shirt end over end toward us.

Dad lunged for it, Mom leapt, Finch tried to catch it, Tessa grabbed it from under Finch's arm. "I got it!!!"

Alison launched another. Dad caught it and danced around, tall and wiry, in his jeans and Doc Martens. "I caught the t-shirt!"

Alison launched another and another with us catching and tossing them back to go again. It was the stupidest thing in the world, but it was also the greatest, and that made it the funniest and we were falling all over the place laughing hysterically about how idiotic it was, but also, brilliant.

Finally we lay all over the yard, surrounded by t-shirts, spent by the joyous leaping and running.

Our laughter died down. Alison said, "Best present ever," and we started laughing again.

Finally she sat up. "Well, family, I have to go visit my mother."

My mom sat up and looked at her phone. "Right, yes, I think she expects you at six so you ought to head out."

They walked to the house, Mom whispering to her as usual: advice on how to protect herself from the anger and abuse of her real family. I overheard Mom say, "Don't forget, you're an adult now, you can leave if it gets rough. If your stepfather is drunk, you just call us, we'll come get you."

"Thank you, Lydia." They hugged and Mom said, "I love you dear, be safe."

I shook my head.

I hadn't thought about that memory in so long, not really, not the happiness part of it. The laughing-til-we-cried part. How after she left, Finch and I had remained on the lawn. I had my head resting on his arm, and how he kissed my hairline, a t-shirt laying half on his forehead.

He had been the love of my life.

She was my best friend.

In the scheme of things it was one of the last truly happy moments, all of us together: Finch and I would go off to college. Alison would stay in town. Finch and I were following our dreams, while she was working a job. The three of us meant to always be friends, but the world conspired...

DISMAYED

Finch

It was impossible tae sleep on the flight.

I got up tae go tae the restroom and as I returned, through the drawn curtain separating first class from coach, saw Karrie's head a few rows back. I slid intae my seat as the flight attendant leaned on the row, makin' herself comfortable. I was versed in the body language, a fan planned tae speak tae me, wanted tae strike up a conversation, nae considering that I might nae want tae speak tae them. "So where are you going?"

"I would like a drink, a beer, now that I think of it..."

"Oh sure, of course." She laughed, loudly, turned, and rushed away. I put in my earbuds so when she returned I could ignore her.

When she returned with the beer, she poured it into a glass. "When does your tour start?"

I pulled an earbud from m'ear. "What?"

She was called away to deliver more drinks afore she could answer.

I was in nae mood. I couldna be expected tae chat with strangers when I was headed tae the funeral of Alison. Och. I wished I had remembered m'eye covers, like the ridiculous man Karrie had been with. I guessed the flight attendant would have one for me, but I dinna want tae ask.

I closed my eyes and was transported back tae the scene that day. My old Subaru had a hatch that went up and I was sitting on the tail of m'car, staring down at m'phone, texting and erasing texts, trying tae decide what tae say. I needed tae say I was sorry, but for what, for nae telling her in time? I couldna go back, I made a mistake I—

A text from Alison:
`Can you come get me?`
`Hurry!`

"Shit."

Another text:
`Karrie won't answer, help!`

I texted:
`On my way!`

I jumped off the tailgate, closed the hatch, dropped intae the driver's seat, started the car, and headed tae Alison's house.

I pulled up in front. I couldna pull up in her driveway as I dinna want tae block her step-father's car, he had once lost his shit over that.

I texted her:
`Here!`

It was cold outside, I kept the heat going. I waited a minute, looking up at the house, then I opened my door. From the house I heard a man yelling, then Alison screamed.

I swept the car door open and raced to the house. I slammed open the front door. Her step-dad was looming in front of the door, Alison was down the hall.

It took one second to see, he wasn't letting her out.

I said, "Alison, come on."

"The hell she is, the little bitch lives here with—"

I plowed into him, knocking him into the wall.

Alison's mom, Sheryl, rushed out of a back room, "Don't you come in here brawling, Finch!"

Alison's step-dad shoved me back. Then swung, and hit me with a right hook against my eye, an instant blinding pain.

I touched my cheek then looked down at my bloody hand.

I charged him, swinging, and connected a left, connecting, hard on his jaw, knocking him stumbling back onto the stairs. "Ow! You little fuckhead!"

Alison grabbed the back of my coat, pulling me away. "Stop it! Stop it, Finch! He's going to kill you!"

We made it through the front door. She yelled, "Run!" We ran across the lawn to my car, I started it and we drove away.

She was overwrought, shrieking, "No no no!"

Blood dripped down my cheek. I looked in the rearview, *yep, totally busted*. "I'm going to pull over at the park."

"Don't let him find me, please don't let him find me!"

I pulled over at the end of the parking lot, near the trees, opened the glove compartment, and fished out a napkin. I dabbed at my cheek. "Why the hell do you go back there?"

She sobbed, "I didn't have anywhere else to go!" She clumsily climbed from her seat, across the console, bumping my chin, and jostling my arm, into my lap and curled there.

My heart was racin' from the fight, my adrenaline pumping, and I was shocked by this, she had never climbed in my lap before. This was definitely crossing some kind of line. I had on a big parka, unzipped in the front, she had on a small sweater, and was crawlin' intae my coat, nestling against my chest.

"Are ye cold?" I pushed my seat as far back as it would go, I held my hands up, refusin' tae touch her.

"Yes," but she said, "I really just need you to hold me."

I patted her shoulder, awkwardly. "It'll be okay, Alison, ye ken, twill be okay."

She sobbed intae my shirt, clutching the front.

"I don't have anyone!" She grasped at me, holdin' ontae me. Then she looked intae m'face. "Your poor poor eye, I am so sorry, Finch!" She pushed my hair back from my face. "I'm so sorry!" She nestled her face against my jaw. "I'm sorry."

"I ken, it's nothin', ye ken, Alison, but ye canna keep goin' back tae them—"

She pressed her lips against my neck and kissed, up and down my neck, she licked and sucked, her breaths in my ear, her mouth against m'skin, then her lips pressed tae mine, she kept repeatin', "I'm sorry," and it lulled me intae a calm. I lost m'sense. My breaths grew shallow as her hand went tae the zipper on m'pants and she was pressing and pulling and rose up and pulled her pants down her legs and sat down astride my lap and she was kissing and my hand was between her legs and she was ready for me. The parka I was wearing was big, shielding, a barrier between us, it was as if I were separate, encased in the coat, as she was unbuttoning my pants and then we were both pulling them down and it was funny, how we were strugglin' tae get undressed in the carseat with m'big coat, trying tae get undressed enough, in the cold, without talking or thinking about how there was nothing funny about this at all.

She sat down on me and fucked me, her tear-stained cheeks pressed against my sore face, nothin' felt okay. It was nae a pleasure, nor a pain, an uncomfortable release, as if we needed tae relieve the pressure, and it was thoughtless. Twas brutally thoughtless.

And minutes later we were done. She drooped weighty against me, a last kiss on my cheek, that felt verra much... pleased.

My hands out tae m'sides, I was fucking dismayed.

My voice a croak I asked, "Are ye on the pill?"

She nestled against my throat. And kissed there. Then drew away, nude from the waist down tae sit in the other seat, pulling her pants along she drew them up her legs. "No, I'm not—"

"Fuck!"

Panic swept over me. "Fuck." I buttoned my pants, and zipped them up.

A tear rolled down her cheek. "It's going to be fine," she concentrated on her clothes. "It's going to be okay, Finch."

"Nae, it winna be all right, nae, never again."

I looked down as m'phone lit up, it was Karrie, m'notification showed the first line of her text:

```
I love you, can we
...
```

I flipped the phone over so I couldn't see it.

And I sat lookin' out the window of the car wondering what the hell I was goin' tae do.

It grew dark, I ran the car engine tae keep the car warm. Alison textin', then Alison's voice after a long time, "Can you drive me to Dylan's?"

"Dylan, from school? The football player?"

She nodded, starin' out the window.

"I dinna ken ye were friends with him, he's a jock."

"You and Karrie left, I have new friends, just drive me, please."

I started the car and drove her tae Dylan's. M'phone buzzed on the console between us. She said, "I bet that's..."

"Aye."

I pulled the car up in front of the house. She said, "What are you going to say to Karrie about...?"

"I daena ken."

She pushed open the car door, lettin' a blast of frigid air into the car, stepped out, and walked up tae the house.

"Fuck!" I banged the heel of my hands on the steering wheel, a sharp pain up my arms. It was a relief, I banged again. "Fuck fuck fuck!" I beat the shit out of my steering wheel. Then roared tae the sky and then dropped my head against the wheel and breathin' heavy, said it again, "Fuck, what am I goin' tae do?"

I leaned back and ran my hands down the wheel. I picked up the phone and turned it around, notification after notification, all from Karrie:

```
Have you heard from Alison?
I'm worried about her.

Now I'm worried about you too.

Look I know we had a fight,
we need to talk,
will you come over?

Where are you going to sleep?

Finch.

Finch, answer me!
```

I texted:

`I'll be there in a minute tae talk.`

I tossed the phone down and drove.

It took a time tae talk myself intae walkin' up tae the house.

Longer tae actually put on m'mittens, zip up the parka and leave the car.

I entered the mudroom and sat down tae take off m'boots.

She stood in the doorway tae the kitchen, her arms crossed out of anger and tae warm from the cold. "Hey."

I looked up.

"Oh, oh no! What happened, who hit you?"

"Alison's stepdad."

"Where is she now? Is she okay?"

"Aye, I dropped her over at Dylan's, that jock from school."

I put my feet out in front of me, starin' down at m'wool socks.

She went tae the freezer, and called intae the mudroom, "I've got an icepack but you'll need to get in where it's warm."

"Are yer parent's here?" I stood and walked tae the kitchen and dropped down in a chair at the kitchen table.

"No, they went to the pub, I was in no mood." She passed me the ice pack which I dutifully placed against m'temple. She dropped down in a chair. "I suppose we need to talk about our fight — what are we going tae do?"

I shook my head.

Her chin trembled, "Are we okay?"

I drew in a long deep breath. "Nae we arna okay, Ree-Ro. We arna."

Her eyes went wide. "But we can fix it, right? We can, we can make it better— we just need to talk this through—"

"Ree-Ro, somethin' happened, somethin' happened between me and Alison."

She blinked, slowly.

"What do you mean? Like something, something you...?"

"We fucked." I dropped the ice pack tae the table.

"You fucked. You fucked Alison, when? Finch, when did you fuck Alison?"

"Just now."

She stood so abruptly her chair rocked and then tipped and crashed tae the floor. "No no no no no."

"I am sorry Ree-Ro, I—"

"Don't you... don't you dare..."

I clamped my mouth closed.

"So that's it...? We had a fight earlier, and you're going to go off with my best-friend? Perfect, just perfect. You know what, bro? Good riddance, good riddance to you and her." She grabbed up the ice pack, yanked open the freezer, tossed it in, and slammed the freezer shut. She spun back around. "I knew it. I knew she wanted you, I saw this coming. I just didn't see you wanting her."

"It was nae like that, we —"

"You what? Is this that moment where you make excuses? When you beg my forgiveness? You know I am your fiancée, and for how long were you making plans to start your music career without me...?"

"About three weeks."

"Yeah, for about three weeks, you were too scared to tell me that you were going to work on your music career, why wouldn't you tell me? Because apparently you think I'm the biggest bitch in the world and—"

"Nae, Ree-Ro—"

"You know what? I don't want to hear any more of your bull-shit. You're a liar, I thought I knew you, a liar and a cheat."

I sat silently.

She said, "I want you out of my house. Out of my life."

I nodded. Stood. Dressed in my coat and boots, and left her house.

HIS EYES WERE FOLLOWING YOU

Karrie

It took forever for us to get off the plane, and there in the gate stood Finch, surrounded by people clamoring for photos and autographs.

I had to skirt the whole gate area, trying to make it look casual, winding around a column.

Jayden pointed past Finch. "Why you going that way? Baggage claim is over there."

I jerked my head. "Follow me!" And muttered under my breath, "And please just ignore him, go go go..."

But I was unheeded by Jayden, who turned and gawked as we walked by. "What do you think that's like, Karrie, to be swamped by fans everywhere you go?"

"I have no idea. I imagine it might be a pain in the ass."

"Or the greatest thing ever." He looked back over his shoulder. "Have you heard his latest song, *Famous Like You*?"

I shook my head. I didn't listen to Finch's music. I didn't watch his documentaries. I didn't stay up to see him on late night television. I turned it off. For self preservation.

"He might be the most famous person Jay-Dog ever flew with."

"Can you please not gawk? And please, please, whatever

you're doing with that, talking about Jay-Dog in the third person, please stop it. Women hate it."

He said, "Do they?"

"Yes, it's a total red flag."

"Fine, but look, you want him to notice you, you look great, you need to be more..." He put his hand on my back. "Laugh! He just glanced up, pretend like I said something funny."

"Jesus, Jayden, I'm going to a funeral."

He shrugged. "His eyes were following you."

"They were not, he's just wondering why the man in the inflatable pink kitty neck pillow keeps gawking at him."

A LIMO SLID UP

Karrie

I went down to baggage claim while Jayden changed into his suit in the men's room. I stood there at the carousel, waiting for my bag, over-heated by the stressful situation, trying to stand as far away from Finch Mac as I could.

He remained surrounded. Either people wanted to talk, touch, or get a photo with him, or they wanted to stand a few feet away and furtively take videos of his every move.

It seemed like every phone in the baggage claim area was out and pointed in his direction.

He was tall so he was able to look over heads — a glance, at me.

Jayden's voice echoed around baggage claim, "Karrie!"

Finch's eyes darted away.

I said to Jayden, "Hey, well, that looks better..."

He did look much better, though his suit was very wrinkled, but there was nothing to be done about that. I just had to hope the wrinkles would fall out while we rode from the taxi to the church.

I lugged my three suitcases off the carousel and Jayden and I moved toward the exit where he began shivering before we even got out the door. "Fuck, it's cold."

"Stay here, I'll hail the taxi."

I went out into the cold — the wet, raining cold, as a limo slid up to the curb, there for Finch.

A taxi right behind it for me.

Finch left the throng of fans, and headed straight for the limo, climbing in, sitting inside while the chauffeur placed his luggage in the trunk.

I tossed my suitcases in the trunk of the taxi waiting for Jayden to finish filming Finch's limo as it pulled away from the curb.

GREAT DEAL TAE FIGURE OUT

Finch

Och, it had been so hard tae see her like that. After all these years tae hae her be so close, we were both traveling tae the same place, tae mourn over the same person, but we were so distant we were lost tae each other.

I scowled. I hadna liked the man who was accompanying her. The asshat dinna even help her put her case in the taxi. Stood back like a pretty-boy in his inflatable neck pillow, without a coat. He was in Maine without a coat. An idiot. How had she ended up with an idiot?

The familiar landscape rolled by my windows. I had grown up here, but truly had only lived here for about six years. I supposed they would be called m'formative years. All with Karrie. Now, I stayed in a hotel when I came home, because my mother had moved back tae Scotland. I had been stayin' in the hotel so often while Alison was in hospice that it had become a kind of home. If an impersonal room could become a kind-of-home. Our son Arlo liked the indoor pool.

I checked my phone. Arlo was already at the funeral, waitin' for me in the conference room. I hated I had tae leave him, I had had a photoshoot that I wasna able tae cancel but I had arranged everything else, I would be able tae stay for a few days while I figured this out.

My son had just lost his mother.

There was a great deal tae figure out.

I looked down at my phone. On the screen was a photo of Karrie's hands taping up my first concert poster, many years ago. I had kept it on m'phone all these years, not because of the poster, but because of the hands... they belonged tae her.

TOO MUCH FOR ME TO BEAR

Karrie

In the taxi Jayden asked, "Tell me again whose funeral this is?" He had a small shoulder bag and he was organizing his things in the pockets.

"She used to be my best friend, but more like my sister. First, she spent every summer with me, but then, when she was ten, I noticed she had bruises. I figured out that her stepfather was beating her and I told my mom and after that she lived with my family mostly full time."

He held out a piece of gum. "Then she slept with Finch Mac and they had a kid together?"

"Yeah, we were home from college for Christmas, and they... yeah. So we had a massive falling out, haven't been speaking to each other, and now she's gone."

"That sucks, big time. I don't get it though, why are you going to the funeral? You could have skipped it, saved yourself the grief."

"Because my family was still a part of her life... I don't really know..." I watched the wet, chilled-through landscape of Maine go by. "I think I'm just exhausted by having been angry all these years. I just... I think I just don't want to be angry about it anymore."

I remembered back to the last time I had seen him. It had started with a phone call. "Ree-Ro, can we...?" His voice trailed off.

What?"

"Talk about it."

"No, not really..."

He had sat quietly, then he said, "I'm no' goin' tae make excuses, ye deserve better than that."

"I do, you treated me like shit."

He exhaled.

I said, "You need to come get your stuff."

"Aye, I was thinking I could come next weekend, nae this one, I hae somethin' I hae tae do, but next Saturday mornin'."

"You mean in like, ten days? Perfect. Fine."

"Will ye be there?"

"I don't know..."

"I wish ye would be there, I would like tae..."

"You know, we don't get what we wish for. The world isn't magic."

"It's sad tae hear ye say it, ye always believed the world tae be verra magical."

"Well, I'm having to grow up a lot these days, the world is a lot different than I thought. And seriously, Finch, no one cares what you would 'like'."

He said, "I ken, Ree-Ro."

Oh how I loved his voice, it had always been his voice that had gotten me through everything, I felt sometimes like his voice matched the beat of my heart, and when he sang to me... when he said my name like that... *I ken, Ree-Ro*.

I had sighed, and said, "Yeah, well... I will be here."

"Good, thank ye. I will see ye next Saturday, Ree-Ro."

We had broken up, just a little over a week before.

I had been home now for well over a week, alone in our apartment.

Having lost my best-friend and boyfriend in the same day.

I had entered the phase: Was I wrong? Maybe I had overreacted. Maybe this loss was too much for me to bear. Maybe my expectations were too high.

Should I let him grovel?

All day long my brain was just twisting around recriminations and blame, I hated him and I loved him, and I missed him so much.

I would never ever forgive him, but...

And I stared at the ceiling in our bedroom all alone in our bed. The pillow still smelled like him. I tucked it against my face and thought about all the ways that I might be able to ignore it, to pretend like it never happened, and I wept.

I didn't know what to do.

NAE SECOND CHANCE

Finch

I arrived at the apartment that Saturday morning and awkwardly knocked.

She opened the door, said "Hi," and went and stood in the kitchen. She gestured toward a stack of six boxes, and my instruments. "I packed some of your stuff, but I'm sure you want to go around and look, it was really hard to do and... your music stuff is there, I..."

"Aye." I shifted m'keys from hand tae hand then dropped my keys and phone in our tray on the kitchen counter.

I wanted tae say the right thing, the thing that would make it all go away. I kent I was going tae be movin' out, but I thought it would be temporary, that I would be living in New York until she finished school and then she would meet me. But I couldna think of what tae say tae make it right. "I'm sure tis fine, ye got..."

"No seriously, look around, make sure I got it all — you don't want to have to come back." She glared at me.

I looked away and said, "Aye."

I went through tae our bedroom and opened m'drawers, all empty. I looked in the closet, my clothes were gone. I walked tae the bathroom and looked through the drawers, mine were empty as well.

I returned tae the livin' room, my eyes settlin' on an empty shelf. "Ye dinna keep the turntable?"

"No, it's yours."

"Some of the albums were yers, I gave them tae ye as gifts."

Her voice was cold. "Without a turntable? Why would I want to keep an album that reminds me of you?"

I chewed my lip. "Ye daena want me tae leave a keyboard?"

"No, I don't want a keyboard, besides you'll need them, right?"

I shrugged. "The label has bought us some new — we have a good setup, Karrie, I wish ye could see—"

"Great." She tossed her hair, irritated. "I suppose you're enjoying New York? Your new place?"

"I am nae enjoyin' any of it, but I am trying tae carry on. We are in the studio every day..."

"Poor Finch, he got everything he ever wanted and fucked up at the very last minute, but hey, look on the bright side, you're a free man, you can be a true rock star. If you think about it, it's for the best. You needed to be single to get the full experience."

I said, "Karrie daena—"

"Right now I just want you to get out, this is too much." A tear streamed down her face. "Say something, just fucking say something, anything, to explain why you did this to me."

"I canna explain it, Ree-Ro, it's the worst fucking mistake of m'life and I daena hae an excuse for it."

She glared at me, her breath ragged in her chest.

"If I could do or say anything tae make it better I would, I daena ken what it is tae—"

"Are you seeing her?"

"Nae, nae at all, tis nae like—"

"Because she called once, left some long rambling apology voicemail, she texted a bunch with apologies and—"

"Ye ken she canna deal with—"

"Don't you dare take her side."

"I'm no' takin' her side, I daena see her, I winna ever see her again, she and I are no'—"

My phone vibrated on the counter. Her eyes settled on the screen and then rose tae m'face. She said, "*Alison* is texting you."

I picked up the phone and glanced down. "She wants tae ken if I've seen ye."

"You've seen me. Tell my best-friend that you're here now and moving out. She should enjoy it."

I texted Alison:

```
                              Ye ought tae call Karrie,
                                             I am here,
                             ye ought tae talk tae her.
```

Karrie's phone rang.

She answered and left the room. I picked up the first box, and carried it down tae the car. Then I returned for the next.

I heard Karrie cryin' in the bedroom.

I strapped tape across the top of the next box, patted it down, and lifted it.

Karrie walked out of the room, her face pale, as if she had seen a ghost. She said, "What did you do?"

I said, "What?"

She shoved the box, makin' me take a step back.

"What, Ree-Ro, what happened?"

"You know what happened! Don't lie to me!"

"Nae, I daena ken, tell me!"

"She's pregnant! Alison is having your fucking baby!" She grabbed a box up from the pile, tipping it, the side ripped, my albums slid out. "I want you and all of your things out of here, now!" She began taping the box, like a madman, around the sides, shovin' albums intae the box. She hefted it up and charged past me tae the door, shoving the box outside on the stoop. She returned for the next box.

I stood there, dumbfounded, watchin' her grab boxes, lug them past me, and shove them outside, pushin' them intae a tumbled pile outside the door, makin' it near impossible tae get through tae m'car, and then she went for m'instruments.

"Nae, daena touch them! I will get it."

"Yeah, good, get it, get out, I never ever *ever* want to see you again. You better stay away, Finch, and I mean it, you stay away from me."

She went down the hallway tae our room, her room, and slammed the door.

Alison was pregnant.

She hadna told me.

I had thought, if I just worked on it, kept my head down, that over time I would win Karrie's forgiveness. If I proved tae her that I was worth it, worth a second chance, it might be possible.

But now I kent, there was nae second chance.

It took thirty minutes tae complete the move from our apartment, a small amount of time tae move m'life away from her's.

My limo pulled up in front of the backdoor of our church. I took three deep breaths and went in.

SOUNDS LIKE A LOT

Karrie

Jayden and I arrived just as the funeral was scheduled to begin. I hugged Mom and Dad and Tessa, and our tears flowed, and I was crying so hard it was difficult to introduce Jayden. Then we all tiptoed down the aisle to take our seats in our pew on the front row, left side.

I glanced over at Alison's mother, on the front row, right side. She looked older, but still like a big giant bitch.

I felt terrible for thinking it while inside a church.

But it didn't make it less true.

Jayden was looking all around. He whispered, "Don't think I've ever been to one of these before..."

I asked, "What, a funeral?"

He said, "No, a church."

I saw my mother purse her lips as she sat down beside my dad.

My mother and father were old punks — she had spiky hair, he had bushy gray hair and a mustache, and they both wore vintage, handmade and decorated, odd-looking clothes, but they had long ago left city life, protests, and wild parties for this small town where Dad had become a history professor, and Mom worked on her art.

But Mom, through the years, had also embraced church, becoming a regular in the congregation and one of the women that ran everything and whom everyone counted on. I had been in the choir. We had been sitting in this pew, every Sunday, most of my life.

My whole family looked dignified in their black funeral clothes. Dad's hair was slicked back. I had really really missed them. I had missed being home.

I sat between Jayden and Tessa, dabbing my eyes and looking around — Finch hadn't arrived yet. Not that I cared.

I asked Tessa, "Do I look as exhausted as I feel?"

"Truth?"

I nodded.

"You look like hell. Did you have a coffee? Because it did not take."

"On the plane. It was too uncomfortable to sleep, and my time is all upside down."

We grew silent again.

I glanced at my phone. The agency I worked for had a big movie premiere tomorrow, for our star actress. My boss, Blakely, had a million things to do to get ready for it. This was the worst possible time for me to leave for a funeral. I set up a group text with Blakely and Jess with three texts: her appointments for hair, makeup, and the fitting for her dress.

I scrolled through my twitter feed, and froze on a photo of Finch.

I glanced at the headline:

Finch Mac, in the arms of Natalie Strong.

I scanned the article, he had been out partying, hooking up with women.

Great. Glad his life was completely unaffected by Alison's death.

I turned on my selfie camera and groaned.

Jayden shook his head. "You look fine."

"I do not, there is mascara all over..." I licked my finger and tried to get the eye makeup from looking like I had black eyes. My nose was bright red. I tried to smooth down my hair.

Tessa whispered, "There's nothing you can do, but it's a funeral, once everyone starts crying you'll blend right in. Besides they all know what you look like, you grew up here."

"Yeah, but I'm returning, I wanted to look..." I let my words trail off. I sounded like a self-centered creep, but then I couldn't help asking, "Why isn't Finch here yet? We arrived at the same time."

"You saw him at the airport?"

I nodded. "And on the plane."

She looked past me at Jayden. Then whispered, "Well, at least hottie was wearing a suit. He's really hot, by the way: do you really like him?"

I said, "Shhhhh, he's right there."

"And anyway, nothing you can do about Finch. He'll be here, Alison was his baby-mama."

Mom said, "Tessa!"

"It's the truth."

Mom said, "Alison was also practically a member of our family, I won't have you showing her memory any disrespect."

I made sure my phone was on silent and took a deep breath, closed my eyes, and tried to calm myself for the ceremony.

It had been almost six years since I had heard that Alison was pregnant. My parents had flipped out. Finch had upended all of us.

No one would see Alison, no one saw Finch. Mom only learned about what was going on through the grapevine.

She only told me if I asked.

. . .

Finch had listened, he had stayed away. Except for once, months later, he had texted:

Hey, I am playing a show
near school.
I ken I'm no' supposed tae
contact ye
...
but I thought,
maybe ye'd want tae come out
...
we could
...

The endless three dots as he considered what to say next.

I texted back:
Nah,
you didn't hear?
I don't live there anymore.

Och nae,
I dinna,
where are ye?

Quit school.
Moved to LA.
Got a job.

More of the three dots.

`I come tae LA next month.`

I stared down at my phone, thinking about all that I wanted to say, I miss you, I'm so lonely, I hate you, but how are you, are you okay?

I really really wanted him to ask if I was okay.

The three dots danced on my screen, and kept going, on and on...

He didn't ask if I was okay.

And what would it have meant anyway? What would my answer have been?

I'm fine. I ran away to LA and now I'm working at a restaurant, don't know a soul out here, spend every day alone. Miss my parents and even my little sister. Miss my dog.

What would I truly say? I miss *you*.

But there was no solution. He and Alison were having a baby together.

Finally I texted:
`You know what?`
`You have a baby on the way,`
`don't contact me again.`

The three dots stopped.

And he didn't contact me again.

Then, years later, my mother came to LA to visit. She took me out to dinner. "I want to talk to you about something."

"Sure." I looked over the menu. I could tell it was her Alison voice. I knew she had seen her, their paths crossed. I knew it.

It had been many long years and I had heard the voice many times and honestly didn't care.

Don't get me wrong, I wasn't a saint. I hated them both, but I could see Finch become a world famous rock star without absolutely freaking out.

I could hear my mom mention Alison without crying.

And mom had been mentioning them more and more.

I had relaxed, mom had relaxed.

I knew Alison went to church.

I knew her son was cute.

I knew that she had an apartment that Finch paid for.

I knew that they shared custody, but they didn't live together.

. . .

Finch was off fucking models, or whatever it was that rock stars do.

Funny how his rock star life had included everyone but me, and I had once been his... *everything*.

So, whenever mom brought it up on the phone, or when I visited, or when she came to visit me, she tentatively mentioned Alison and her son. I was used to it.

I said, to put her out of her worry, "Mom you know I don't mind, I know you see Alison occasionally, you don't have to worry about me. I'm so totally over Finch. I don't even think about Alison, what*ever*—"

She interrupted with, "Alison, has been diagnosed with cancer."

I dropped the menu.

"She... what?"

"Alison has been diagnosed with cancer."

I blinked. "I know, I heard you." I asked, "What kind, like the *cancer* cancer?"

"It looks like it." Her hand shook as she raised her glass of water to her lips. She placed it down and shook her head. "Shit, she is so young."

I said, "It's like *that* kind of cancer? The shit-she's-so-young kind? Mom, what are you talking about?"

She reached across the table and patted the back of my hand. "I'm talking about how your best-friend from high school is battling cancer. I didn't know how to break it to you."

"But she's going to be okay, right?"

"There's a chance." She sat up straight. "This is what's going to happen. She is very tired, desperately sick, I can't believe she waited so long to tell me. But I am going to help her. I do not want you to be upset, I am not picking sides. But I have to help."

"Oh yes, of course. Of course you do."

"She doesn't have anyone, Karrie, and her son..."

"Yes, I totally understand. I mean, she was a bitch, she slept with... and she has barely spoken to me and I mean she said she was sorry, but she did not say it well enough... but it's really fine, I'm just not being dragged into a friendship with her. I have principles, she and I are not friends, at all, and we can't ever be and... this sucks."

"I know, I just want you to know, this is not me choosing her over you."

"No," I nodded, tears welling up, "No I get it, she needs someone and her mom is useless. I'm not a monster." I dabbed at my eyes with my napkin. "Is she going to be okay?"

"I don't know."

"What is... what is Finch doing...?" I didn't really want to know, but it was impossible not to ask. "Is he... is he helping her?"

"He sees his son. He pays for everything, he does what he can."

The waitress took our order.

I fiddled with my fork and said, "So by helping, what will you need to do?"

"Her boy needs someone to help him get to school and pick him up at the end of the school day, things like that. Driving, grocery shopping, she will need rides to the doctor."

"Sounds like a lot."

"It needs to be done."

"It does sound ordinary and necessary, and I understand why you would want to help."

I took a drink of my wine.

She said, "But that was all I wanted to say, we do not need to dwell on it, and it doesn't involve you, I am just doing my part to help. It is not something between us, it's separate, right?"

I nodded.

"So how is your work, tell me all about it!"

THIS ROCK-STAR BOY

Karrie

I brushed my hand through my hair as another image flashed in my mind:

Alison and I were lying on her bed, covered in one of my mother's band shirt quilts. This room had once been the guest room but had since been converted into Alison's room. On this particular day... it was... when? Tenth grade?

And I had fallen in love with Finch. Honestly, truly, without hesitation — I loved him and I was going to marry him. And I was talking about it with her.

She was so excited for me. "You truly love him?"

"I do, I know a lot of people think we're too young, but I just know." I clutched my heart. "A heart knows what it knows, it doesn't care about age — you've heard him — when he sang 'Waiting on the World to Change' — I love him, I will never *not* love him."

Alison grinned. "He was singing it just for you, I could tell." She pushed some of my hair off my cheek. We were curled up facing each other, almost nose to nose. "You're not worried about deciding when you're so young? I mean, there are so many boys in the world, aren't you worried you might miss out?"

"Miss out?" I scoffed. "Every other boy sucks, and you know it."

"I wish all of us could go off together and see the world—"

"Absolutely, Finch said he's in. He wants to show us Scotland, and then we'll move to LA."

"That would be really fun."

"Okay, ask me questions, I bet you can't talk me out of it."

"How about... he knows when you got your period — remember when he went in your bag for some gum and pulled out a tampon and threw it across the room like he had gotten shocked?" She giggled.

"That was mortifying, but I don't care. I *like* that I know everything about him and he knows everything about me. I still love him. Next."

She said, "I can't think of anything else. I'm convinced."

"Good because when he says 'aye' to me it breaks my heart open with happiness. I will love him my entire life."

She said, "You are such a glorious nut-job."

I sighed, remembering what a little nut-job I had been, with my delusions of never-ending love. How much heartbreak would I have been spared if I had just been more realistic?

I glanced at my mother, who noticed and gave me a sad smile.

I bowed my head and thumbed through the funeral program, shifting because my ass was sore from the thin cushion on the wooden pew. I couldn't believe her name was on the program: Alison Parker. I couldn't believe she was gone.

All I had been thinking since I heard she had passed was, "But she was so young," and, "It's not fair," and these things were all true but they did not help. I was devastated but putting it into words felt too casual and light for something so deep and horribly wrong.

Cancer sucked.

I hated it with a white hot fury for taking her.

And she hadn't even been a part of my life for a long long time — because she had broken my heart and I had been a self-righteous bitch about it for years.

It had always been easier to ghost her than to deal with the reality of it.

So here I was, screwed over by my best friend, and then she *died*, and now I was full of guilt: deep, consequential, possibly-needing-a-therapist, conscience-riddling guilt.

Ugh.

I wiped my eyes, seeing a smear of more mascara on the tissue. *Well, that had to be the last of it.*

Jayden nudged me in the ribs. I followed his eyes across the room to see Finch, fucking Finch, finally entering the church — late, caring about nothing and no one but himself.

I scowled and whispered to Jayden, "Our plane got in so long ago, what's he been doing...?"

"Must have been important, we've been waiting for fifteen minutes."

Finch looked so damn sad as he crept down the aisle, being as quiet as possible, but too tall, too handsome, to be unnoticed — the most famous person our town had ever produced, and we hadn't truly produced him. He and his mother moved here when he was twelve. But he had sung in this choir and the school chorus and had gone on to a big recording contract, and sold-out stadium shows. Everyone in the church was watching him as he slid into the pew beside a young boy, Alison's son. Her heart-breakingly young son.

His son too, but I couldn't fucking think about that or my heart would break in that old way, that young way — this was a time for grown up heartbreaking, because of the loss of an old friend, gone too soon.

Too young.

It wasn't fair.

I had long ago stopped thinking about this rock-star and his charming ways.

Long long long ago.

Tessa nudged me. "What are you thinking about?"

"Nothing, no one."

I raised my chin and turned my attention to the minister as he began his sermon at the front of the church. My little sister and I held each other's trembling hands.

NOW OFFICIALLY GONE

Karrie

The funeral was long. Alison had been well-loved. Two of her teachers spoke, then her softball coach. Her mother refused, but not my mother: my mother loved Alison like a daughter, and she planned to speak about it.

She shook as she walked to the front of the church, and along with my guilt for the distance I had taken from Alison, came guilt for how I treated my mom too. She was devastated — all our hearts had been broken that day six years ago.

It hadn't been just me, though it had felt like it at the time.

I had tried to make my mother choose between us, between me, her daughter, and the young woman she had opened her heart to, and I felt burning shame rising in my cheeks.

Ugh. This was really really hard.

I glanced at Jayden, his eyes glazed, looking bored.

Why in hell did I bring him?

Only a psychopath brings a date to a funeral.

My mom's speech brought me to tears, again, quiet tears of rage and shame and sadness and loss. She graciously thanked Alison's family for the privilege of having Alison live in our home. Alison's mother scowled. Because that's how she was.

My mother said Alison had been a great girl and someone who she was grateful for having known and she gave a sad smile to Alison's child on the front row and spoke directly to him about how great his mom had been — that's when my tears really poured from me and the whole church was full of sniffling and sobbing people.

And then there was another prayer, a few more somber words, and then the organ played, signaling it was over. I glanced at Tessa with tears running down her cheeks — she sort of laugh-cried and we both sadly laugh-cried at how we must have looked: mournful expressions, swollen puffy lids, red shiny noses.

I hadn't seen Tessa in person in a year. She looked older, grown up. It washed over me how much I had missed her. I had convinced myself I was too busy in Los Angeles and had barely checked in.

My phone vibrated as if on cue. I glanced down at the screen. My boss wanted to know how I was holding up.

I texted:
`Good,`
`the funeral is`
`just now over.`
`Need anything?`
`Can't really talk.`

She texted:
`No worries,`
`just making sure you're okay.`

Yes, kinda.

Except for all this pain.

I shuffled along our pew to the middle aisle, with Jayden just behind me, and then realized there was a receiving line in the foyer. I had to make a decision: Alison's awful mother on the left side of the door or... Finch standing on the right.

Great, I had had one plan: *Don't see Finch; if I had to see him, see him from afar.*

And it was clearly not working.

I was steps away from having to talk directly to Finch. He was holding the child, an incredibly cute little boy, too old to be held but needing it all the same, his little pudgy arms around Finch's neck. He must have been what — almost six years old?

Finch put him down and the little boy stood stoically, hanging back beside Finch's leg, while Finch shook hands with people as they passed.

Everyone wanted to be on Finch's side of the door.

I felt frantic, and slowed down, people filing past me, jostling around me. I stepped into a pew.

Jayden ducked into the pew beside me. "Um, the doors are that way."

"I know, I just... I'm not supposed to see him. This is too much 'seeing him'! You're supposed to be better at your job."

"We're signaling that you've moved on." He put an arm around me. "You're doing great."

The church was near empty.

Tessa realized I wasn't beside her anymore and came back. "What's going on?"

I said, "I needed a moment, before..."

She followed my eyes to the door. "Oh, right."

I said, "Don't let me keep you though..."

She said, "That's all right, I'll see him all the time anyway, and I don't want to talk to Alison's mom either. I'll wait with you."

We waited for the last people walking up the aisle. I asked, "How come he was in LA?"

"I don't know, he had a big photo shoot for a magazine or something."

Jayden said, "Yeah, TMZ said he was in LA for a shoot for Vanity Fair."

"Figures, he would think photos are more important than his son." I huffed. "I mean, come on, just take some time off from your fabulous career."

Jayden said, "You need to take a deep breath and wiggle this shit out."

I did both, barely.

He said, "Now repeat after me: 'fuck this dude.'"

I said, "Right, you know what? *Whatever*, let's just go. Why am I the one hiding?"

They followed me into the aisle.

Jayden whispered, "So what did you decide, which side?"

"Ugh, left, I think...except she scares me, but she probably won't even speak to me, so it will be fine. I'll probably survive."

Jayden said, "Can I go down the Finch Mac side?"

Tessa and I both said, "No."

Three steps away from the door, the little boy saved me by tugging at Finch's leg and bursting into tears. Finch picked him up, grabbed an umbrella, and swept down the stairs, and out into the rain. Then it was easy, Alison's mom and Alison's sister were on the left side of the receiving line, my mother was standing on the right. I went there, where Mom was nodding awkwardly as the rest of us left the church.

The funeral of Alison Parker, my once greatest-best-friend, the one who lived with my family because her step-father was a drunk and she wore his bruises on her body, and who broke my heart by sleeping with the once great love of my life, was now officially gone.

OUR TEN DIFFERENT VERSIONS

Karrie

I stepped from the doors of the church. The sky had turned steel gray, thick and heavy. My dad passed Tessa an umbrella as the cold rain continued to fall. Alison's mom, Sheryl, pushed past me, charging down the steps toward Finch, who was forlornly holding the little boy in one arm, an umbrella in the other, out in the rain. She looked furious.

Mom muttered, "Dear me, she is in one of her moods."

Jayden shivered, huddling beside me under the umbrella. I asked Tessa, "What is Alison's little boy's name again?"

Tessa said, "Arlo."

"Yeah, I don't know why I can't remember that." Sheryl was angrily yelling at Finch out in the rain.

"You never met him though, right?"

"Yeah, yeah. I never met her son."

I shook my head, dazedly staring out at the scene: the boy, Arlo, crying, clinging to Finch, a despair that shook me to my core. Sheryl screaming, "Give me that boy! You don't get to carry him away!" That awful woman pulling the boy from Finch's arms. The boy holding onto Finch, wailing, begging and pleading for Finch, and—

Jayden nudged me and jerked his head toward the parking

lot, where a photographer had a long lens camera sticking out of the back of a van. All around the churchyard stood people, filming, their phones recording the argument between Finch and Sheryl in the rain outside of Alison's funeral.

Sheryl finally freed the boy from Finch's arms, but Arlo struggled to return to Finch. And Finch, the man I had once loved for almost my whole life, was trying to say goodbye to the little boy, as the grandmother carried him away. And this was the grandmother who hadn't protected her daughter from the abuse, forcing that wailing little boy into one of the cars to ride to Alison's burial. And all I could think was *oh, oh no, this is all so very complicated.*

What had happened, six long years ago, had been a very simple story: Young woman loves young man, young man breaks her heart with her best friend. But here I was watching the aftermath, still unfolding, all these years later, and thinking — *this isn't a story, this is a very very real and tragically complicated life.*

And I hadn't realized when it had shifted from the story to the life.

When the black and white of wrong and right had become this, a family tragedy.

And I was watching it from afar.

THE MOST BEAUTIFUL GIRL

Finch

I was in the back of the car, numb tae the world — a funeral, that fucking bitch, Sheryl, she had made Alison miserable her whole short life and had ruined the memorial service. I banged my fist against the seat.

Fuck, I was all alone in this now.

A single father.

I thought about those long hours, holdin' Alison's hand, with my mouth pressed tae the top of Arlo's head as he held ontae his mother and wept over her as she died.

God.

Tae hae known so much pain in such a young life, m'heart broke for m'son.

I closed m'eyes.

Karrie had been standing at the top of the steps.

My eyes couldna help but draw tae her, she had always been the most beautiful girl I had ever seen.

And she stood there watching me fall apart, she was like a ray of light, coming through the crack of a long closed door.

THE ENEMY CAMP

Karrie

There was a bustle of activity around me as my parents opened their umbrellas to usher us out in the rain to our own car, but I couldn't get my feet to move. I was frozen watching the scene continuing on the lawn, Finch, standing under an umbrella in the freezing rain, watching his son driven away in Sheryl's car.

And oh how I hated him with a white hot searing fury… but…

His eyes met mine, across the distance of the lawn from where he stood, under an umbrella in the pouring-down rain of late fall in Maine, brisk and cold and wet, and there was a moment of static charge in the air between us, a flare of anger, a surging rage in my breast and then his eyes darted away. He turned and stalked toward his car.

My family urged me into motion and I rushed across the grass following them. Keeping up with the umbrellas, we made it to dad's SUV and opened the doors.

There was a flurry of motion as we climbed into our seats, the umbrellas down, our coats situated. Jayden, way in the back, lamented, "It's so cold here, why would anyone live like this?"

Dad shivered and joked, "What, this? This is paradise!" He

ran his fingers through his bushy gray hair causing it to stick up all over. "My hair was too somber for too long."

My mother said, "It's still got to be somber longer, my dear, it's not time for your bushy hair, there's a meal to get through, yet." She looked out the window at the gloomy weather. "I hope Finch and Arlo are okay."

Dad patted his hair back down.

Tessa whispered to me, "Is today the first time you've seen Finch?"

My father's car rolled away from the curb. I watched out the window at the rain streaking down the panes. "It's been six years."

The reception was held at a local restaurant, with food placed out buffet-style, and it was packed. Finch stood in the corner of the room in his funeral suit, with a press of people trying to get close and talk to him. There was a young man who buzzed around him, and Tessa kept watching the young man, and blushing, so I whispered to Tessa, "Who's that guy?"

She said, "That's Mitchell, he's Finch's assistant." She blushed again.

"You know him?"

"Yeah, um... we're friends from school, I got him the job."

My brow drew down, trying to understand what she meant — how did my little sister have any influence with Finch?

I watched as my mother, and later, my father, found a chance to push through the crowd to speak to Finch, but I stayed away. I could not do it. I would not deign to do it.

Not that I still hated him. I would never give him that much power, the *privilege* of being in my brain, because I was uninterested — *whatever*, he was the past.

Frankly, I didn't think about him at all.

Instead, I talked to Jayden, signaling, of course, my having moved on.

Sheryl glowered and glared. I overheard my mother whisper to my father, "It's like she's drinking again, you can see it in the way she is holding her mouth."

My dad shook his head, "Poor Arlo."

Then Jayden leaned in and whispered, "Introduce me to Finch Mac?"

My eyes went wide. "No way, that is not, no, Jayden, no, I'm not talking to him, this is too close already—"

"But you don't mind if I talk to him?"

"I mean, it doesn't matter to me, either way, but why would you...?"

He ignored me and sauntered over to introduce himself, while I hung out with my family off to the side, stealing glances — *what the hell were they talking about?*

Finch glanced at me, then looked away.

I wanted to look normal, but I couldn't remember what normal looked like. I posed awkwardly. Tessa raised a brow. "What is that?"

"What?"

"The thing you're doing with your hands?"

"I don't know, I can't remember what hands do."

She thrust a drink toward me. "Hold something, because you look maniacal."

I rolled my eyes. "Great, that was exactly what I hoped to look like." I looked around the room. "Why's it always so weird at things like this?"

Tessa said, "Because we were Alison's chosen family. She ran away from that lady's house and preferred us, so it's going to be weird. There's no escaping it."

Mom added, "We wouldn't have come if it hadn't been for um... Finch."

My eyes traveled over to where Jayden was talking to Finch.

He was using his hands to explain something. Finch's brow was drawn.

Tessa said, "They're hitting it off."

"They are not hitting it off. Jay-Dog is hitting him up for..." I pretended to be Jayden, "'Hey, Finch dude, how about you let me tour with you? *Why?* Because I'm an *actor*, oh and I know how to play a couple of covers on the guitar.'"

Tessa pretended to be Finch. "'Well, um... nae, and who are ye again?'"

I chuckled. "Good Scottish accent."

She nodded and we went quiet. She said, "The good news from all of this, we won't have to spend any more time with Sheryl. We never have to deal with her again."

My mother said, "That is one blessing of this entire debacle." She pursed her lips as she often did after speaking ill of anyone, a rarity. My mother saw the light in every soul. *Usually*.

Finch's assistant sidled over to talk to my sister. He was kind of nerdy looking, like a Maine college student, which I supposed he actually was. He had light brown curly, close-cut hair, and was handsome but in a 'cutest guy in the dorm' kind of way. He was wearing a new, really nice suit, but looked like he had never worn a suit in his life. The expression on his face of 'just lucky to be here' was not the classic assistant expression of: 'I am so over all of this.'

Tessa introduced us, "Mitchell, this is Karrie, my sister. Karrie, Mitchell."

His brow drew down. "You're... um... *the* Karrie, Karrie?"

Tessa nudged him. "My sister, you know, I told you all about..."

I saw his eyes glance over at Finch. "Yeah, of course, I just didn't remember... we just weren't sure she would come."

My brow drew down. "Who's 'we' in that sentence? *Finch* didn't think I would come? That's rich. Alison was my best friend."

His eyes went wide. "No, that's not what... That wasn't what

I meant. Ugh." His eyes went wide and he glanced at Tessa for help. "I don't know what I'm talking about, at all, most of the time. Ask Tessa." He crossed his eyes, stuck out his tongue, and sort of grooved his shoulders back and forth.

I squinted my eyes. "How long have you been working for Finch Mac?"

"Um... about five months."

"So you've been working for the biggest rock star in the world, as his personal assistant, at a time when there are stories coming out everywhere about his downward spiral and you're just going to tell me that you don't know what you're talking about?"

He gulped. "I'm sorry, I think we got off on the wrong foot. I do that sometimes, it's part of what my mom calls my 'charm'."

Tessa said, "Karrie, chill out, that is none of your business, and, I'll have you know, Finch appreciates Mitchell and gave him a raise. It would be so much worse if Mitchell wasn't helping."

I nodded. "Okay, yeah, you're right, I'm sorry, Mitchell, I didn't mean to get so... I'm an assistant too, to a talent agent, and so I've got some advice: Don't tell the exes anything, it just stirs up trouble."

He gulped again. "Yes ma'am, you're right, I won't do it again. I was just worried about him, I just..."

I looked at Tessa wide-eyed.

She shook her head, telling me to 'leave it'.

After a few minutes of their conversing while I did my best to not overhear, Mitchell left to go back to Finch's side.

"What is going on? Has the world gone upside-down? How is *that* Finch's assistant?"

She took a sip of her drink. "I like him. He's really funny."

I huffed. "So basically my whole family is in the enemy camp? That is totally uncool, unless you're trying to sabotage Finch by helping him hire an incompetent assistant, then you should not be anywhere near his camp."

She said, "That's not what this is, we're in your camp, or

rather, we're in no camps, there are no camps, Karrie. It's just... Finch needs help, and Mitchell's trying. Finch trusts Mitchell, it's not easy finding people he can trust."

"That's rich, poor Finch, can't trust anyone."

Her brow went up. "And guess what, this is new — Karrie is worried that Finch's assistant might be incompetent? Why do you care?"

"I don't care, at all, not one bit. Not one tiny bit."

My mom walked over, balancing a plate of food. I asked, "You spoke to Finch?"

She nodded.

"What did you say?"

Her brow drew down. "I've spoken to him quite a bit, Karrie. He's been regularly at the hospital since..." Her chin trembled and I let it go.

Jayden sauntered over. "I met him, he seemed great. Cool dude."

"Great," I said. "All of this is really, great."

We stood there for a bit longer and ate a bit of the meal, but then my father thankfully said, "We should let the family... um, go..."

Which seemed necessary under the circumstances. And the most truthful thing that had been said the whole day.

My family had to let Alison's family go.

I watched the side of Mom's face as we drove home. Her skin was splotchy from crying. The four earrings on one side looked out of place against a face that was so drawn and sad. I wished I had listened to her more. I sighed, remembering the time she had asked, "Are you sure, Karrie, like *really* sure? Because somewhere between the ages of fifteen and twenty-five a person is supposed to move through ten different versions of themselves. The chances of your going through ten different versions and Finch going through his ten different versions and ending up the same version are—"

"I know the chances are slim, Mom, but Finch and I are different..."

What would that youngster think now, when the only thing Finch and I had in common was a hate-filled scowl?

SUCH A HUGE MISTAKE

Karrie

We were downstairs in the rumpus room with hot cocoa-filled mugs, a fire blazing in the hearth. Mom and Dad and Tessa had changed into sweats, and sweaters, basically their pajamas, with thick socks and fuzzy slippers. I was wearing a very expensive pair of uncomfortable pants, that were too tight to get truly relaxed in, and the warmest shirt I had brought, also too tight. I hadn't brought comfort clothes. I had purchased a wardrobe to impress, entirely forgetting everything about my life in Maine.

My mother loaned a sweater to Jayden, an orange vintage wool sweater that she had embroidered across the front in purple yarn, Green Day. I patted the couch, beside myself, so Howard, our yellow lab, could curl up beside me. I scratched him behind the ears, "Hey old man, I missed you so much."

Dad said, "You talking to me? I missed you too."

We laughed.

Dad put down his cocoa mug and rumpled his hair all around so it poked up everywhere. He rubbed his hand along his mustache too, getting it to poke out at the sides. "Now I get to relax."

Tessa said, "Your hair has to look like you asked the salon for

'The Einstein, please,' or you can't relax? That seems like an issue, Dad."

He chuckled. "I'm on sabbatical, I gotta keep it real."

Jayden said, "This is great, I love a fireplace that we get to use un-ironically." He shivered. "Karrie, you did *not* tell me it was going to be this cold."

"I did, I totally did."

Mom said, "So, we know nothing about you, Jayden."

"I'm an actor."

"Oh! Have you been in anything we've seen?"

"I was in a show called *Clark's House*, have you watched it? It's a psychological thriller kind of..." Everyone shook their heads. "It got canceled after the first season, but it was received well."

"And how do you know Karrie?"

"We've been dating for a really long time."

Mom said, "Oh...?" She glanced at me. "I go to visit Karrie about every three months, I don't think I've met you yet...?"

I said, "Mom it's been almost six months since you were in LA."

"Has it been so long?" She sighed. "The um... hospice took a lot of my focus. I will come, really soon. It is lovely to meet you, *finally*."

Dad got up to tend the fire. We were all quiet for a moment. It dawned on me that the music playing was one of Finch's songs. I glanced at Jayden with his head bopping to it.

Tessa said, "Today fucking sucked."

My dad said, "A-yup."

I said, "I can't tell what time it is. I'm jet-lagged, I'm worn out from crying, and it's dark outside."

Jayden glanced down at his phone. "It's almost dinner-time in LA." His stomach growled.

Mom laughed. "And we did not eat enough."

She got up to go get some snacks. Dad said, "Come on, Tessa, let's go help."

"How come Karrie doesn't have to help?"

"Because she has a guest."

They followed Mom up the stairs.

As soon as they were gone, Jayden said, "Cool family, but… artist mother, history-teacher father, both a little old school punk, now I see where you get your nutty streak."

"Nutty streak? I'm not nutty!" I fished a marshmallow from my cocoa mug and slurped it into my mouth, dripping a bit on my shirt. "Shit!" I dabbed at it with a napkin. "Dammit, this cost so much money."

"Yeah, how long have you been stressing over coming home to see these wonderful people? You're totally nutty. Most people would kill to have such a cool family."

"My family is great, but it's still stressful. Those two things can both be true."

He grinned. "Anyway, I talked to Finch Mac for you. You're welcome."

I paused in mid-spill-dab. "What did you say? You talked about… me? I didn't tell you to talk to him about me. You had one job — to wear a suit."

"I told him that I was going to ask you to marry me."

I muttered, "Jeez Louise, what are you doing? Are you trying to kill me, because I think you're trying to kill me."

"Trust me, if you're trying to make him jealous—"

"I'm not, I'm trying to stay on one side of town and keep him on the other, and how the hell did that even happen? You wanted to meet Finch Mac, I gave you the chance, and instead of saying something good, something you ought to have planned out, you made up some bullshit story about marrying me? You walked up to Finch Mac at a funeral and said, oh and by the way, I'm marrying Karrie Munro?"

He grinned. "I'm not going to lie, Karrie, he looked shocked. It was something to behold. Again, you're welcome."

I dropped my head back on the couch with a moan.

Mom returned carrying a tray with crackers and cheese. Dad brought a beer for Jayden. Tessa brought some popcorn. Everyone settled back into their seats.

I looked around at the lighting set up in the corner. "So this is your photo studio, Mom?"

"Yes, when I have the time again, this is where the magic happens."

My dad squeezed her hand. "You'll get back to it, you just needed to be present for Alison."

Tessa said, "Yeah, Mom, no worries, your Insta fans will be there when you're ready."

Mom laughed. "Don't forget theTikTok fans, too. I'm going to have to retrain the whole algorithm, it's probably totally forgotten about me. As soon as Alison went into hospice I closed up my Etsy shop."

Jayden asked, "What do you make?"

My mother smiled and gestured to his sweater. "I make and sell punk rock-inspired embroidered sweaters, household goods, and gifts. What old Gen-X punk doesn't want a paper towel holder with their favorite band's sticker decoupaged to it?"

Dad was wearing a vintage green sweater, with leather pads on the elbows, and embroidered across the front, in poorly spaced running-downhill stitches that looked unplanned: Sex Pistols.

I held up my cup. "I follow you Mom, of course, but seeing them up close is something else. I'm really proud of you, they're great. "

Mom said, "It's post-punk, DIY, what I'm learning is that there's a *huge* market for it. We Gen-Xers love this stuff."

I said, "And your TikToks are hilarious."

She grinned.

I said, "So what's up with you, Dad?"

"I'm still writing the big one, medieval Scotland. It's mind-blowing." He pretended like his brain was exploding, then fished a marshmallow from his mug and popped it in his mouth. "But I am closer to figuring out some main details and then..." He shrugged. "I'll be done with the preliminary stuff."

My mother sighed and jokingly rolled her eyes. "The preliminary stuff? You've been writing this book for a year now!"

He stretched his arm along the back of their sofa and Mom put her head on his arm. "True, it won't be done as quickly as my last book."

Tessa said, "Dad, your last book took you my entire childhood to write."

"Not that long," he joked. "What are you forty-five?"

"Twenty-one. I wrote a thesis paper this semester that took a week."

"Well, my last book was about the Earl of Breadalbane, as you know. A lot of *that* book wrote itself. There were good records, only a few mysteries, but it still took considerable time. You cannot rush a thoroughly researched biography. I have to be cautious. I have to pay attention to details and write slowly. If I put something down, I have to be willing to stake my reputation on the truth of it. With this new book, thirteenth century Scotland is considerably older. There are many mysteries." He grinned. "It could take decades."

Mom said, "Dear God."

He said, "Aw honey, you know it was my methodical record keeping and long winded stories that made you fall in love with me."

Mom smiled. "I suppose that's why we gave up our city life to live out here in the country. To go slow, to take a tenured position at the university, to take up shabbily-done punk embroidery, to write your histories—"

Dad said, "With no one to bother us but the moosies."

Jayden said, "Are there moose here? Do you think I'll see a moose?"

Dad said, "I've only seen a couple, they're elusive. Speaking of living in the backwoods with gigantic hoofed beasts, Karrie, how is LA?"

"It's good, I'm incredibly busy, but the kind I love. My boss, Blakely, is great—"

Mom said, "I met her, she was lovely. The big premiere is tomorrow?"

"Yeah, because she's going through a huge divorce and there's a lot riding on her hair and makeup, I'm sure she's going to have ten emergencies between now and tomorrow afternoon. I'm trying not to look at my phone..."

Tessa's eyes went wide. "So much could go wrong! What if she got a pimple?"

I groaned. "I know! The tragedy!"

Tessa said, "You better watch your phone, you might need to get an emergency flight for pimple-popping!"

Dad said to Mom, "You know these drama queens are your fault."

Mom feigned outrage. "My fault? How?"

Dad said, "Yes, your fault, you named them after your favorite tragic heroines, that's why it's nothing but drama, tragedy, and catastrophe with these girls."

"That is not how it works, naming them after a tragic story didn't make them over-dramatic, you can't blame me for any of it. But you heard about the divorce — a pimple at the premiere would be an absolute tragedy. If Karrie has to rush back to LA with zit cream, Tess and I might have to go with her to whip up some face masks."

Dad jokingly rolled his eyes. "Yeah, their over-dramatics has *nothing* to do with you."

Jayden said, "I always assumed Karrie was named after um... that show about the ladies in New York."

Mom said, "Sex and the City? Oh no, definitely not. Karrie is named after Stephen King's tale, with a slight lettering change. Tessa is named after *Tess of the D'Urbervilles* by Thomas Hardy. Both Tess and Carrie were total tragedies."

I chuckled. "The truth is, I'm not going to get dragged into any emergencies or dramas because there are plenty of makeup artists in LA, and besides, I already arranged for everything. Blakely just has to focus, get her hair and makeup done, put on the dress. She just has to do it."

Jayden took a sip of his beer, "So is this the night life in Maine?"

I laughed. "Kinda, but we also just had a funeral today, in case you haven't noticed. Why, are you needing a dance club?"

"Yes." He rubbed his hands together and clapped one down on my knee. "How about this, I go stay at a hotel tonight — are there hotels here, one with a bar? I don't want to put your family out any more, and in the morning I'll take an Uber to the airport. If I get back to LA in time, do you think you can get Blakely to give me a ticket to the premiere?"

"I'll see if I can transfer over mine. But honestly you can stay in the guest room."

"No, I think there's a drink in a hotel bar in Maine with my name on it. I've got jet lag and I might as well lean into it and stay up all night."

Dad said, "Oh, to be young."

Mom said, "Well, Jayden, you can keep the sweater."

"Awesome, and you can call me Jay-Dog."

Mom said, "Awesome, Jay-Dog, it was lovely having you, even if it was just for a few hours."

I helped him gather his things, ordered him an Uber, and paid for the hotel because I had promised meals anyway, and honestly, this had been such a huge mistake I just wanted it over with. It was time for Jayden to go home.

As I headed back downstairs, my phone vibrated in my pocket. It was Jayden texting our friend group:

Just left Karrie's house,
Operation Make Finch Mac Jealous
was a success

I stood on the stairs texting:
I'm not trying
to make him JEALOUS!

He texted:
Right.
Either way it worked.

Blair texted:
Lol

I texted:
All y'all suck.
I'm doing the best I can
to signal having moved on.

Vi texted:
You're seeing him?
He's there?

I texted:
He's everywhere.

Dani texted:
Stop seeing him!
No good comes of seeing him!

I sighed.

I texted:
I'm trying.

Blair texted:

We know you are,
just remember how long
it's taken you to get over him.
Years.
Don't be weak.
Hugs.
Call me if you need to talk.

MY CHILDHOOD BEDROOM

Karrie

I went back downstairs and collapsed onto the couch.

Tessa said, "So what the heck was that...? Did you seriously bring a date to a funeral? Were you trying to make Finch jealous?"

My mother pursed her lips.

I groaned and put my head back on the sofa pillows. "No, it wasn't that at all... Jayden was a signal that I do not care, that I have moved on. He wasn't about revenge, he was about... being mentally healthy if you must know."

Dad said, "Mentally healthy. Is that what they call it out in California?"

Mom said, "So you weren't actually dating him?"

"We used to date, now we're just friends."

Mom said, "Well, whether you are dating or signaling or revenging, I need to point out that *everyone* has a lot going on right now and none of that should be a priority."

"I know, I know, I'm sorry. He's gone — I think, honestly, I hadn't come home in so long that I thought I needed... like support, but now that I'm here — why did I think that...?"

Dad sang a line of a song, "... Standing up and then you fall, who is gonna take care of you..." Then he added, "That was old

Quarter Riot, I love that song. Remember when Finch played with them at Coachella? Hey honey, make me a Quarter Riot scarf?"

"Of course." Then she said, "I'm so glad you were able to come home, even with Jayden along, even with the funeral, we are so glad to have you here, Karrie. I hate that it was for these terrible circumstances..."

She looked over at the far wall, blinking away the tears.

I gulped down the wave of shame and regret I had been drowning under for days, ever since I heard that Alison had passed away and it came to me, like a rubber mallet to the head, that one quick phone call was all I would ever have. I had let six years go by, in anger, and hadn't resolved it, not really, just one phone conversation, and now my old friend, like the friendship, was gone.

More shame of course, that my thoughts on the day of the funeral were that the woman who died had left me without letting me feel better first.

I was a terrible, terrible person.

Tessa said, "You want to talk about it, Mom?"

Mom shook her head. Then she said, "Alison was once an important and loved member of our family, shit happened, now she is gone and regardless of the shit happening, she was loved, and she will be missed." She raised her mug, we all raised our mugs.

I rubbed my eyes.

"I think I'm overwhelmed by the day and lack of sleep, I need to head to bed, you know?"

I put down my cocoa mug and moved around the room, hugging everyone and saying good night. Then I went up to my childhood bedroom to toss and turn trying to sleep.

KABOOM!

Karrie

The next morning Tessa bounded in and plopped down cross-legged on my band-shirt quilt. "I need to talk to you."

I opened one eye. "It's like five a.m. where I'm from. Is this something that truly needs me awake?"

"It's important."

I opened my other eye. "I love your hair, by the way, that is very cute, like a shaggy bob? You look like a college student, smarter than before."

She laughed. "I am smarter than before, so smart, that's why I'm about to tell you something, some truth bombs, and you need to listen to me."

I fluffed up my pillow and sat up. "Before coffee?"

She rolled her eyes. "Would it kill you to think about someone else for a moment?"

My eyes went wide. "Whoa, that was harsh."

"Yep, and it's going to get worse."

"Are you sure? I mean, I already feel like shit."

"You, my wonderful older sister, 'feel like shit' about all the wrong things. You need to think about Mom, *Mom*, the mom who took in your friend Alison all those years ago. You came home from school and told Mom that Alison had bruises on her and she didn't even flinch, she opened our house to her, she fed and clothed and cared for her, like a daughter. She loved her, and then you and Alison had a falling out and then you left — you went to Los Angeles and you only came back a couple of times because of 'work'." She made finger quotes when she said it, which was true, I did blame work a lot. "And if they want to see you, Mom and Dad have to visit you in Los Angeles. Nobody likes LA. Then Alison came down with cancer and Mom needed to help, but she had to be careful. She didn't want to take sides, and she couldn't talk to you about Alison and she suffered. Mom had to visit her and visit you and she was stuck in the middle of all of it, and now Alison is gone. Mom went through all of that all by herself — you didn't help her."

I opened and closed my mouth a couple of times, then said, "Dude, that's really really harsh."

"I told you."

We looked at each other for a long moment. I asked, "How'd you get so smart?"

"I've been growing up while you were gone."

"At home, in your childhood bedroom?"

"Just because you moved three thousand miles away doesn't mean you grew up. It's just as likely to mean you ran away." She gestured, an explosion.

I chuckled. "You going to keep going with the truth bombs?"

"Hell yeah, this is fun. You've been gone too long." She acted like something exploded again. "You're being self-centered, Kaboom! You need to make amends, Kapow!"

I sighed.

"How come *my* heart was broken and *I* have to make amends?"

She said, "You've had six years and you haven't fixed that broken heart yet? That's on you. Kablam!"

I used my feet to dislodge her backward off the bed.

BE OLD-SCHOOL PUNK

Karrie

I came downstairs to the kitchen.

Mom had paper spread on the kitchen table, a decoupaging brush dipped in a cup of water, a jar of glue, a stack of stickers, and a wooden paper towel holder that had been spray painted black.

"That's cool, you're going to put the stickers on it?"

She sighed as she appraised it. "Eventually. I gathered everything, ready to get started, but it's not really in me to make anything right now."

"Paper towel holders?"

"It's a new product line, I think they'll love it, because no one knows what the hell to do with their paper towels. My heart just isn't in it."

"That's okay, Mom, Alison's funeral was yesterday, it's okay to give yourself time."

She gestured with her head. "Coffee is in the pot. Cereal in the pantry. Or frozen waffles in the freezer."

"Where's Dad?"

"He's writing, which probably means he's taking Howard for a walk. He's been blocked for weeks, I suppose he's having trouble dealing with all this, too."

I glanced out the window over the kitchen sink. "He's walking Howard in this weather?" It looked freezing outside, gray, and sleeting.

"He's brooding. With a warm coat he can brood anywhere."

I poured a cup of coffee and sat down across from her. "Wait, is this... is this Finch's new song? Are you listening to his new album?"

"Oops!" She opened her laptop and clicked the music off. "I didn't think you would be up for a while."

I was horrified. "God, Mom, I am so sorry."

"What on earth for...? Because I don't want to listen to Finch Mac's songs while you're eating breakfast?" She waved her hands. "I'll be fine. How about Willow, or she's on tour with him, better yet..." She turned on Eddie Vedder's new song.

"No, it's not that... I'm sorry because I..." I clamped my mouth shut. "I've been..." I stopped. "Because you lost Alison, you loved her, she was like a daughter, and you should be able to mourn her — and for the part I played in complicating that, I'm so so sorry."

She frowned, "I don't blame you for anything, dear."

I sipped from my coffee, blinking back tears. "Well, you would be wrong. I never meant to make you choose sides— wait, that's bullshit." I put down my mug. "I totally meant for *everyone* to pick sides, because I was so horribly wronged, but now she's gone and I feel like an ass." I added, "I think I got used to being the victim and I think... if I really consider it, that I bullied you."

She said, "I am a grown assed woman."

"I am too."

"True. I just mean, I've managed it, but... thank you. That means a lot."

"I just can't believe she's gone. I thought there was still time."

"That's the thing about life, sweetie, it's fleeting... When we're teenagers we think we have all the time in the world. Then we grow up and every year is another year that we didn't do all we should have." She grinned. "But look at you, my love, a grown woman of twenty-five, a powerful assistant to an agent, living the grand life in LA, and apologizing to her mother. You're going to be okay."

I chuckled. "It was Tessa's idea."

She teased, "Well, Tessa has always been the grownup of the family. I never worry about her."

I said, "I worry you?"

She looked at me long. "Yes."

"I'm doing okay, I'm successful... I have an apartment without needing a roommate, that's a big deal in LA. You just met my ex-boyfriend, um... Jay-Dog, he's totally hot. I have a career. My boss is in her prime," I decided not to mention that after Blakely's divorce she was no longer at the agency, and that meant I was probably out of a job. I finished with, "I'm doing really well."

Mom shrugged. "These are not the things that keep me awake at night. Or rather, they are, but not why you think..."

"Well, tell me what does, maybe I can set your mind at ease."

She narrowed her eyes. "You are devoted and loyal to a fault, my love. You love fiercely, but when you are crossed you can be..." She tapped her chin. "What's the word...? Ah yes, *unforgiving*."

"Ouch."

She smiled kindly, then pulled the paintbrush from the water and wiped the bristles with a paper towel. "I always believed I was chill, but on reflection I realized that you get your sense of justice from me. It's the thing that gave me my righteous indignation in the early nineties — I was furious about that Iraq War, the first one, and look where we are now — so far past it, so so so far." She shook her head. "That's why I worry, because being a hard-ass is not good. It's unhealthy. It's—"

"I wish I had had more time with Alison, to talk about what happened. She called me, did you know?"

"Yes, she told me. She said you had a good conversation and

that she really liked hearing your voice and that it felt like the good old days."

"It did for me too. I just didn't realize that was going to be our last conversation. I wish I had known she..."

"You did know, honey, I told you. I told you she had been diagnosed with cancer, she was in the hospital. I told you when they moved her to hospice, and... I told you. You were plenty warned, but the thing is, you were busy, right? Your job kept you away. But you took the call, she was happy about it, and that's good." She put the paintbrush away in a small box. "The truth is, if you had come back, while she was dying, expecting a perfect resolution, I don't know if you would have gotten it. She wouldn't have been able to handle it, you know? And she had moved on. I hate to say it, that she had moved on from her mistake, but she had a child to say goodbye to, people who loved her that were there for her. I don't want to sound harsh, my love, I really don't, but she had already said goodbye to your friendship long ago. Your bad blood had gone on too long. I don't know, maybe this is part of the lesson, that you can't let things drag on and on, you shouldn't suffer. You can't wish suffering on others. Stop it. And I'm sorry about the 'shoulds'."

I nodded. "Okay okay, I'll try. And that would make a good design for a shirt or something: 'Sorry about the shoulds.'"

She chuckled. "Yes it would. And no to your 'I'll try.' Just stop doing it. Be old-school punk and don't waver. Throw that shit out. And thank you for the apology, that really means a lot to me. I feel seen, that's nice."

"I do see you. I'm glad I came home."

I wiped my eyes and got up to make some frozen waffles.

Tessa came down, freshly showered, grinning.

I jokingly glowered. "Thanks a lot, Tessa, I've been back less than a day and already been lectured by you and mom."

She said, "I live here, I get lectured all the time. What was it last week, Mom? Oh yeah, 'You're twenty-one, why haven't you moved your clothes from the washing machine to the dryer yet?' I just wanted you to feel welcome."

CONFUSED EVERYTHING

Karrie

Tessa ran some errands while I read a book, played a few rounds of Bananagrams with Dad, and had a cup of coffee with Mom in the afternoon. Then, as it was getting dark and close to dinner, Tessa said, picking up her phone. "By the way, your boss is all over Twitter, she's on the red carpet."

"Oh, I forgot to look!" I scrolled through my phone. "She looks beautiful, right? I helped her pick out that color."

Tessa and I both looked through our phones and then turned to show each other photos. She asked, "Who's the hottie?"

"That's... I'm not sure, but I think it's this guy she's seeing... yeah, look this one says it, this is the Scottish guy she likes. I'm so glad he went to visit her."

Tessa showed mom the photo.

I said, "He's a rugby player."

Mom and Tessa fanned themselves. Mom said, "Rugby players are the hottest of the players. And Scottish, whoa nelly, Outlander has ruined me for anything else."

Tessa said, "True that, like Finch, just hotness."

Mom opened her eyes wide. "Except Finch is like a..." She didn't finish then added. "Too young for me."

Tessa scrolled some more. "Look! Here's Jayden!"

The photo showed Jayden about ten feet behind Blakely, posed perfectly.

I muttered, "Nicely done, Jayden, always turn your best side to the camera."

Tessa looked at the photo for a few moments. "Are all the boys in LA that hot? Maybe I need to come visit without Mom and Dad."

"You do need to come visit without Mom and Dad, but you do not need one of the LA boys. Jayden is so pretty, but he is not the sharpest tool in the shed. And what, there aren't any college boys, someone smart and just a little handsome here? The pretty ones are just a lot of trouble, so much trouble, just heartbreaking trouble."

I sent a text:

`Blakely you look great,`
`have a fun premiere!`
`Wish I could be there.`

I scrolled for a minute and said, "I sure do hope it goes well."

Mom said, "I was wondering, after this big divorce, will you still have a job?"

I said, "Oh, yeah, of course. I mean, yes, I'm irreplaceable. Yeah, I totally have a job."

Then I added, "Absolutely."

Mom patted the back of my hand. "Good, I'm sorry you're missing the premiere, my love, I really appreciate that you came home in the middle of it."

"Well, it's not nearly as important as a friend's funeral, it's ultimately just a job. I just really like it." I chuckled, "Look at this photo, that's her friend, in the background, she's pretending to wave at someone. She's hilarious."

Tessa said, "And you've met Ainsley Potter? What's she like?"

"Exactly how you'd expect, she's an amazing actress, but off screen she's dumb as a box of rocks, and such a diva, you wouldn't believe the snacks and drinks I have to stock when she comes to a meeting. If my boss asks, 'Would you like a drink?' and Ainsley asks for something like, 'I'd love a cucumber spritzer with a dash of rosemary,' and we don't have it she goes all sullen, and then it's hard to get her to agree with anything— make sure you don't repeat that to anyone."

Mom said, "Not my first time at the rodeo with a famous person."

Tessa said, "Yeah, we have to keep all of Finch's dramas hidden from the..." She let her voice trail off. "Sorry."

I shook my head. "No worries."

As if on cue a headline about Finch appeared in my newsfeed. The photo was of Finch in the rain holding his struggling son in his arms.

I showed it to Mom and Tessa.

Mom pursed her lips. "I thought they were bored of talking about him and had left, now that photo will probably renew interest. I expect the press will be all back up in his business."

Tessa said, "Maybe Pete Davidson will do something insane to take the heat off."

"How long has Finch been here?"

Mom glanced at the calendar, calculating.

Tessa said, "When did she get the diagnosis?"

Mom counted on her fingers. "They knew it was terminal months ago. He came as soon as he was told."

"Oh." I frowned. "I kind of thought you would say a week or two."

"No, it's been months."

Tessa said, scrolling through her phone. "That's why he hired Mitchell, because he needed someone nearby. And this all sucks, I had tickets."

Mom said, “He’ll give you new ones, once the new tour is rescheduled.”

I watched them discuss Finch as if he was just an easy part of their normal everyday life. I said, “I heard they paused his tour, I didn’t know why... I guess I thought it was something else.”

Tessa screwed up her face incredulously. “Of *course* it was Alison’s cancer treatment.”

“In my defense the press never gave the reason — Finch and Alison never married, I knew they weren’t a couple, I just... I didn’t think they were involved. You both never mentioned it.”

Mom said, “She was the mother of his son. Finch has been taking care of her,” as if that explained everything. Though it confused everything I thought I knew...

THIS HOT, FAMOUS ROCK STAR

Karrie

It grew colder and colder.

Dad emerged from his office. “We ought to go to McLoonie’s pub for some grub.”

Mom said, “Thank heavens, I had not one ounce of interest in cooking.”

I said, “I would love to go to McLoonie’s, I missed it soooooo much.”

Tessa said, “Need to change, first? Put on something more casual?”

I glanced down. I was wearing a long-sleeved, Prada crop-top, with fur lapels, and black flared pants. My outfit would have fit dinner in LA, but here in Maine, not so much. “This might be the most casual thing I brought.”

She laughed. “We need to take you over to Goodwill and get you some proper flannels and a pair of jeans.”

We went out to the mudroom, bundled up in our scarves and mittens, and drove, mindful of the ice, at five miles per hour into the tiny town, then Dad dropped us off at the door while he parked. A few minutes later he slid in through the door, blustering with the wind. “My mustache is frozen!”

We were already seated at a big table in the middle. My

family had been coming here for years but mostly on special occasions, but now Mom and Dad talked to the owner, the cook, the bartender, and the waitress as if they were regulars. Tessa explained, "They come all the time now that I'm so busy and you're not around. Mom hates cooking."

Mom overheard and said, "I do, I hate it, I hate it so much. I used to do it when you were all young, out of necessity, but now I can't seem to be arsed to bother. I'd much rather make things."

Dad, looking over the menu, said, "Cooking is making things."

Mom said, "You are welcome to cook, whenever you want."

"I hate cooking."

Mom's brow went up. She muttered, "Careful, I'm going to shave my head and start printing out my feminist manifestos again."

He chuckled. "I prefer you with this Joan Jett vibe." He kissed her cheek and went to the bar to order pints for us.

The door opened and in blew Finch.

It was sudden, but also slow motion, one two three...how the recognition swept through the pub.

First, all eyes turned to him.

Second, mine followed, then I averted, then I got hot and warm because for the briefest moment he had seen me looking at him.

Then, furtive glance, he was clench-jawed, color rising on his chiseled cheeks, running a dismayed hand through his hair, as if he would turn around and leave.

My mom waved.

Finch raised a hand in return, then looked away.

All eyes turned to my mom, because if you didn't know Finch personally, you at least knew he was famous — if you didn't know my mom you'd wonder, *how did the lady know the rock star?* Not realizing that she had known him since he was twelve.

Mitchell entered behind Finch, they went to a table across the room, sadly within sight of ours. I was on the wrong side of the table, facing his. I picked up the menu to block my view and remembered that conversation with Alison, a month ago:

"Hi."

"Hi Alison, how are you?"

"I'm doing good." Then she chuckled and said, "Bullshit, not doing good, not overall, but today has been one of the better ones."

"Good," I said, though it wasn't at all what I meant to say, "and... Mom was telling me."

"She comes to visit every day, I tell her she doesn't have to, but she still comes."

"You know Mom, she is relentless."

"Yeah, I love her so much. Sometimes I think of her as my guardian angel."

Tears welled up in my eyes, I nodded.

I meant to ask about her illness, her son, her life, anything... but the whole conversation was so confusing, so emotional — in retrospect I didn't ask any of the things I should have asked.

She said, her voice breaking with tears, "I know I'm the last person who should be asking for you to do something for me, but..."

I gulped.

There was a long pause where she took a deep staggering breath, then choked out the words, "I need you to forgive Finch."

"Oh." It was all I could think of to say.

She paused, then plowed on, "He is having trouble processing what's about to happen, and he is trying to take care of Arlo, um... and he needs help. He needs a friend, and you're... you're the one he needs."

Tears streamed down my face.

She said, "Anyway, I know you have a life, friends, and things going on, a fabulous life in Los Angeles, and I don't mean to... I don't want to guilt trip you... I know it's hard... but I was thinking if you could find it in your heart... it doesn't have to be about me, I know what happened and I'm not going to be around for long, it doesn't have to be about me, it's about Finch. I wish you would forgive him and it would... it would help him."

She sat quietly, while I cried, over the request, over Finch, over Alison, over being so separate that I had to take a phone call with a deathbed wish. Finally, I said, "Yeah, I... I will try."

She exhaled. "That's all I ask."

I said, "How is... um, your son?"

"He's great, Karrie, so cute and crazy smart, it's really... I know it's... so complicated, he's my bright spot, the love of my life."

"Yeah." I closed my eyes.

"Anyway, I'm really tired now... I probably should go."

"Will... what if I called you next week, we could..."

"I would love that, thank you, Karrie. I love you."

"I love you too."

That was the end of our call. And there hadn't been another one, because...

I shook my head to clear the memory and gulped to try to rid my throat of the cry stuck there and asked, "So, Dad, how was writing today?"

"Not so good, I got caught up in a question, how did dogs arrive in Scotland? I only have one book that even addresses it. It took most of the day. Unfortunately the library wasn't open, but I'll be there first thing tomorrow."

Tessa teased, "Dad, you could look it up on the internet. On your phone. On your computer. Or you could call the librarians and they could look it up for you, I can think of eight ways for you to research Medieval Scottish dogs without waiting for Monday or having to drive somewhere through snow."

He gasped, then went back to looking over the menu, jokingly mocking Tessa with a high voice, "'You could look it up on the internet,' I'll have you know, young lady, that for that travesty of an opinion, *you'll* be buying dinner tonight."

I said, "But I agree with Tessa, you ought to consider stepping up your research game—"

"Et tu, Brutus? My eldest daughter is going to promote Wikipedia?" He pretended to retch.

"I'm not saying that you should replace researching in old books, I'm saying keep the old books, but maybe include the occasional Google search, too. Anyway, I'm buying dinner tonight, it's my first time being here when I have enough money to buy."

Dad joked, "All right then, everyone gets an appetizer."

Mom stood, said, "I need to use the bathroom," then she didn't even pretend, she went straight over to Finch's table.

My face went hot again as she sat down, leaned in, and patted his hand while talking to him.

Dad looked over the edge of his menu. "I heard you apologized to your mom today."

"Yes."

"Good, she wasn't asking for an apology, but I appreciate it, she needed it."

My eyes drifted over to Finch's table again. "What do you think they're talking about?"

Tessa said, casually, "Who knows, they're really close though. They've been spending just about every day with each other since Alison went into hospice. I don't know, like six hours a day, they're very close."

"Oh," I said, "weird."

Tessa's eyes went wide. "*This* is one of the things you apologized about today, it's not weird — you need to get on board. Mom is friends with your ex. Or ignore it. He's dead to you, right? So just stop thinking about it, don't look over there, pretend like she's in the bathroom. Don't pay it..."

She kept talking, lecturing, basically enjoying her newfound power, reprimanding her older sister, but I stopped listening — I couldn't ignore it, that was my mom, talking to Finch, and I had loved him for so long... and hated him for years and this was *all* in the past tense.

If the world was fair I would never ever have to see him again.

I blamed this small town.

I also felt such anguish in my heart that this burning hatred was still there. Shame and anguish. What had I been doing spending so much of my life hating him?

It hadn't been every moment of course. In LA there weren't many things to trigger my memories: except the radio, the news, Twitter, Facebook. I rarely thought about Finch. And I had dated some lovely young men, had even rather liked one for a time.

Hatred hadn't consumed my every moment, but the idea of dealing with it, or coming home and being confronted with it — I hadn't been able to bear it.

I still couldn't bear it.

I blinked back tears and tried to focus on the menu: *Chicken or salad?*

Mom returned. She sat down, her nose red, her eyes misted.

Dad said, "How is he holding up?"

Mom shook her head. "It's Arlo, it's nothing... what are you ordering?"

Tessa asked, "Is Arlo okay?"

"Yes, he's fine, I mean, as fine as a child can be when their mother has passed away, but we don't need to—"

I watched their faces. "Mom, you can talk freely, it's okay."

She put down her menu. "It's just... nothing. It's Finch's business, dear, I'm sorry but there's too much in the public eye anyway, I have to keep this all quiet, and a busy restaurant is definitely not the place."

Mitchell sauntered over. "Hey Tessa! Hello Joe and Lydia, hello um... Karrie."

I muttered, "Hi," along with my parents then looked over the menu again.

Mitchell said, "This is awkward, usually we're at the same table."

Tessa laughed nervously. No one else answered him.

He said, "Tessa, can I come see you tomorrow?"

"Sure, I'd like that." She glanced at me, "Just you though, um... right?"

"Oh yeah, of course, Finch won't... yeah, he's going to be too busy. But me, I want to... yeah."

He grinned, bowed, and backed away from the table continuing to bow all the way over to Finch's table. Tessa giggled.

I said, "He's going to be too busy? He would come normally?"

"Sometimes," Tessa said, "But he's not going to come while you're here."

"An enemy camp situation."

"Yep."

I muttered, "Hard to believe that's all we are now, camps on a battlefield."

So I decided to drink, and dinner consisted of three pints, a chicken salad, some fun banter with Mom and Dad and Tessa, comfortable and conciliatory, while the other half of me watched Finch in furtive glances, worried, quiet, slumped in his chair, going through a big thing, and doing it while everyone in the bar was watching, because there was nothing more human than going through a big despairing thing, and nothing cooler than watching a rock star, the kind of musician that sold out stadiums, be human.

I wondered why he was even out in public, but also, glad he had, because it seemed like a sign — I was supposed to deal with this now.

I saw him stand. He pulled his coat from the hook beside the table and pulled it on, and then wrapped the scarf around his neck. It drove me to stand and without thinking about it, head over. I had no idea what I was going to say.

He blinked when I approached. That boyish confusion he used to get whenever I spoke to him, before we had become inseparable and our love had become a fact.

He froze, mid-scarf-wrap.

His brow drew down, then he said to Mitchell, "I'll be out in a moment."

Mitchell looked from my face to Finch's. "You cool?"

Finch said, "Aye."

"I'll bring the car around." Mitchell left.

I opened my mouth but stalled at the up-close sight of him — his jaw, bearded, right where I used to kiss, the edge of his mouth drawn down in a frown. I choked out, "I'm really really sorry about Alison."

That broke his position, he finished the scarf wrap. "Aye, me too." His Scottish accent was just as hot as I remembered.

He checked his black peacoat to make sure it was buttoned up. "Did ye need somethin'... um, Karrie?"

Hearing him say my name about floored me, I said, "No, um, I just wanted to tell you, um, that I was..."

His eyes narrowed.

I floundered, "I just wanted to say..." *What did I want to say?*

I had no idea.

I suddenly realized that I had wanted to talk to familiar Finch about the loss of my best friend and standing in front of this hot, famous rock star was not the same thing at all. He asked, "Are ye gettin' the funds from yer part in the songs?"

"Every month and I..." I had no idea what to say, I didn't

come here to talk business, I hadn't struck up a conversation to chat about nothing... *why did I?*

He nodded.

"Aye, I'm glad it's gettin' tae ye... and it's good ye returned home, it means a lot tae yer mum." He glanced out the window, "M'ride is here. Did ye need anythin' else?"

"No, I just wanted to tell you I was sorry."

The color rose in his cheeks.

"It was good seein' ye, Karrie."

He left the pub.

SHAME AND REGRET

Karrie

That night I got stuck in a doom-scroll of Twitter, Insta, Facebook: it was research for work, it was important to be on top of all of this. I needed to know the public's thoughts on my boss, the actor, the premiere, the movie... on Finch.

Wait, not Finch — it wasn't anything to me about Finch.

But... I found myself looking at photos of him.

I sighed.

Dad came into the rumpus room where I was curled up on the end of the couch with a crochet blanket over my legs. Howard was lying on my feet. "Hi Dad. I thought you were headed to the office?"

"I tried, I think I'm drunk." He sat down on the couch across from me, Howard perked up his head, gave me a look, left my couch, and went to sit beside Dad.

I muttered, "Howard you were keeping my feet warm, you deserter."

"You girls would be proud of me — to be hip I went on Wikipedia like you urged me to, and guess what happened? I looked up medieval period Scotland, and... and..." He shook his head. "Everything it says is totally different from what I know to be true. It lists Mag Mòr, a name I've *never* seen before—"

"Who is Mag Mòr?"

"Exactly! It's a title for King Magnus, a whole new king of Scotland, further proof Wikipedia is not to be trusted."

I teased. "Dad, couldn't it just be new information? How current are the books you're using for research?"

He chuckled. "Probably the most recent one was written in the nineteenth century."

"Ha, so maybe we've learned something new in the past hundred and fifty years."

"Yeah, that could be it, but also, Wikipedia can be altered by anyone at any time. That's why I say—"

"*Endlessly*, to never trust it."

"Never *ever* trust it." He ran his hand through his hair, causing it to go even poofier. "But it's such a strange feeling, it's as if history has changed. That's why I might be too drunk to write tonight." He scratched Howard behind the ears. "How are you?"

"Good."

He said, "Nah, I don't believe you, it's more like shitty and miserable because an old friend passed away."

"Yeah, but she wasn't a friend for a long time so I feel weird claiming the feeling."

Dad said, "'Friendship is constant in all other things, save in the office and affairs of love.' That's Shakespeare. Your friendship might have broken, but you had a deep long love with Alison, a childhood together. Go ahead and let yourself feel shitty. It's okay."

"Thanks, Dad."

"Want to talk about it? You talked to Finch, what's it been, a couple of years?"

"I didn't really talk to him, I just sort of stammered, and it's been six years."

"Phewie," he said, "that's a long time. That's practically stranger territory... you know what that is — that's history.

That's too bad." He shrugged. "Good thing is, that's ripe ground for a do-over, starting afresh."

I gave him a small frown. "I don't want a do-over." Tears welled up, almost without my noticing, and a sob erupted from me as I burst into tears. "I want my Finch back."

He passed a box of tissues across the coffee table.

I grabbed one and wiped my face. "I'm sorry, I didn't really mean that. He wasn't ever mine, I know that now. I just... it's like I thought the whole world was one way, I believed that some things were true, like if I loved someone they would love me back, and that everyone would be nice, and when it all blew apart it felt like I couldn't trust anyone again."

He nodded.

"And then Alison has a baby, then she gets cancer, then she is in hospice, and now she's gone, and I'm the girl that was still over there on the side saying, 'I can't trust anyone,' like that's a big problem, spoiler alert: it's not, it's mid-level trouble at best. I'm so deeply ashamed of myself."

Dad looked at me askance, "The human mind is a miraculous thing, you went from being wronged to feeling ashamed for how you handled it. That hardly seems fair."

"True that. And Mom is caught in the middle and Alison is gone and... what am I going to do?"

"You know what I think you ought to consider?"

"What?" I picked apart a tissue.

"Giving yourself a fucking break."

"Dad! If Mom heard you she would pretend to be furious!"

He acted frightened. "She's not here is she? Is she listening? My excuse is I had a couple of beers, feeling kinda wild."

I laughed.

"First, give yourself a break and give everyone a break, stop being all up in your brain."

"That's rich coming from you, all you do is dwell in the past. You're a historian."

"You got me there."

"And how? I can't stop thinking about Alison, Finch, what happened, and..."

"I don't know... I think Pastor Simon would advise you to be in service, that would get your mind off things. You could..." He looked around. "Your mother needs help with her business, everything came to a crashing halt months ago, what if you helped her get it back up and running? Or you could go to church, ask Mrs Hart if she needs any choir help, you have a voice like an angel, or... You could go visit some of the older residents, take some meals and gifts around... You could tell them stories about hanging out with Ainsley Potter, they'd love it."

I smiled. "Those are some great ideas, thank you. How'd you get so wise?"

"I'm an old punk. My youth was all outrage and insolence, followed by shame and regret. I had to learn early on how to move past it or I'd be stuck banging my head against brick walls."

I teased, "Someday I want to hear all those stories."

"There's no way you can handle how cool I was." He raised a fist and pretended to head-bang.

I laughed.

"Feel better?"

"Yeah. Tell Mom that I want to help her tomorrow."

"I'll let her know."

He departed up the stairs. After that my doom-scrolling deepened and got even suckier, so I went upstairs to bed too.

THIS IS A BIG DEAL FOR ME

Karrie

The next day, I woke up and sat at the table with Mom, with a notebook, making a list of all the things she needed to do to get her business going again. It was a massive list, but her heart wasn't in starting any of it yet.

So to help more, in the afternoon I offered to go to the grocery store, driving her car on a winding route through the neighborhood to see all the places that were strongest in my memories: the mailbox I brushed with the fender when I was learning to drive, my father screaming, Alison in the backseat, giggling like a maniac. The house on the corner where we could go play ping-pong in the backyard if we brought our own snacks. Slowly driving by the spot in the woods where we would bundle up with blankets and hang out with a couple of snuck beers. Finch would play guitar. I would sing.

The grocery store was fun, familiar, and again so full of memories that it was bittersweet. The produce department, where Finch would juggle apples for me. The candy aisle, where Alison and I would stuff bags into Mom's cart when she wasn't looking. The soda aisle, where we all danced when a song from *Hairspray* played throughout the store.

I struck things off Mom's list, piling them in the cart, adding some of my favorite comfort foods—

Suddenly Finch appeared at the end of an aisle carrying a bouquet of flowers. "Och."

I was halfway down the aisle, no escape, so I turned the cart to be between us.

"I was lookin' for yer mum. Is she here?" He looked left and right like he wanted to get out of there.

"I drove her car."

He ran a hand through his hair and looked at the flowers in his hand. "I was... Mitchell is goin' tae see Tessa, so I got these for yer mum. I was goin' tae send them with Mitchell but we saw her car and I..." He lowered the bouquet.

I narrowed my eyes, "You bought flowers for my—?"

There were groups of people standing at both ends of the aisle, phones up, filming our conversation.

Mitchell appeared, hands up, "Hey, ho! What's happening? You're not Lydia," he joked.

I said, "No, I am not."

Mitchell said to Finch, loud enough for people to hear, "So, this is your ex, and you're talking to your ex in a public place, don't think this is going to go the way it needs to go for you." He tugged at Finch's arm. "How about you back away slowly?"

Finch nodded. "I'll send the bouquet with Mitchell."

I said, "That will probably be for the best."

Mitchell came over in the afternoon. When I came downstairs, the bouquet of flowers was in a vase on the kitchen table. There was a card with it, enclosed in its envelope. And it was from Finch and not for me. And Mom didn't mention it.

It was upsetting to realize how much their lives were

centered on Finch. Not mine though, I had gone away. I shook my head to clear it and found Tessa with Mitchell listening to music downstairs.

Mitchell said, "So, Karrie, assistant to assistant, what did you think of my handling of Finch today?"

I nodded. "That was good, your instincts were spot on. That was not going to end well."

He nudged Tessa. "See I did good. I'm worth all the money he's paying—"

"There is an issue though."

"Uh oh, knew it."

"No one knew I was an 'ex' until you told them. Guess what? Now I'm a mystery. Now someone might want to dig into my story."

He said, "I did not think about that. That's why I don't deserve the big bucks."

I said, "It probably doesn't matter in the grocery store in Orono, but in LA... you gotta be careful what you say. You need code words. Like instead of 'ex', I would tell my boss, 'Dickhead on aisle three.' And then she will duck out of the way. Or if she's cornered by him, I say, 'Your appointment for a root-canal at eleven.'" I added, "Just please, when you come up with the code for me, don't let me hear it, just as a favor to me, as Tessa's sister."

He said, "Yeah, of course not, and that's a good idea. Codes. Like the Secret Service. And I wouldn't worry about it, he would never use something derogatory about you."

"Really, never?"

He shook his head. "And thank you for the advice, this is a big deal for me. I dropped out of school to take it and if I do well I'll get to go with Finch Mac on tour."

"Why did Finch send flowers to Mom anyway?"

"She organized it so he could see Arlo today."

BANG BANG BANG

Karrie

The next day, I woke up and convinced Mom to do one thing on her list. I helped her take photos for her Etsy shop. Then, since I was her employee, she took me out to lunch. I wore my tall, white, faux-fur hat, the big, padded, bright white parka with the fur-trim, and big, white fur boots, with pompoms hanging down from silver yarn, causing Dad to say, "I love the festive snowman look," causing me to roll my eyes.

I said, "This is very fashionable in Paris this year," but it was not lost on me that in small town Maine I looked a lot like a festive snowman and maybe this style was better worn, ironically, not in snow. Mom took me to a local diner and on the way home stopped in at the church to visit Mrs Hart, the choir director. I had known her since I was six and was shocked seeing how aged she was, and saddened because her hearing was going. I had to yell when talking to her. "Hello Mrs Hart, I missed you!"

She hugged me, her slight frame gripping and holding on for a long long time. Her eyes were misty when she looked me over. "I have missed you too, dear." She stroked a trembling finger down my cheek. "Did you come to sing for your old teacher?"

"I just came to visit—"

She moved behind me. "Let me help with your coat—"

The door suddenly opened and Finch entered, with his son, Arlo, beside him. He was tall, entering a room and filling it. His chiseled cheeks, with the lines that stretched back from his cheekbone, the sexiest kind of face, one that, as it had grown up had been so enticing, was flushed red from seeing me.

Oh.

Mrs Hart tugged at the back of my coat, I clutched the front, holding it on.

He mumbled, "I dinna realize ye would have company."

I said, "No worries, um... we were just leaving."

Mrs Hart said, "But you just got here!"

I looked at Mom with my eyes wide and jerked my head toward the door, but Arlo rushed over to my mother, stripping his coat and mittens off and tossing them on the floor. He climbed on her lap and threw his arms around her neck.

Mom said, "Karrie, this is Arlo."

My brain was malfunctioning, but luckily my mouth took over. "Hi Arlo, it's nice to meet you."

He waved, still hugging my mom.

Mrs Hart tugged at the back of my coat again. "Please don't go, Karrie, it's been so long since I had Finch and Karrie in my choir room! Will the two of you please sing for me?" I clutched the front of my coat.

My mother shook her head. "Oh, I don't think Karrie would want..."

Finch ran his hand through his hair, clearly upset.

Mrs Hart tugged on my coat again. "Is it still zipped, dear?"

I shook my head, but my coat was still zipped, I just didn't know what I was answering. Then she said, "Please, Karrie, it would be wonderful to hear you sing together once more. Do you ever practice together?"

I mumbled, "No, we don't."

Finch looked like he needed an escape route, but then again, so did I. Finch and I were both wearing our coats, looking from Arlo to Mrs Hart and then at the door.

Mom whispered, "What do you want to do?"

But the little boy was clinging to her, I couldn't make her leave when the little boy was desperate for her.

Finch relented first. "I suppose if ye want me tae, I could sing." He took a deep breath and unwound his scarf, careful not to look at me.

I was breaking all my rules of engagement.

The enemy was in my camp.

Sirens were going off in my head, and they made it impossible to think.

I unzipped my coat, thinking, *retreat! The enemy is right here.* I hung my coat on a peg as he hung his and for a moment we were awkwardly hanging our coats side by side.

The enemy was within touching distance!

He scooped up Arlo's coat and mittens and hung them from a peg, too, as Mrs Hart rushed to the bookcase to retrieve some sheet music. "Remember the songs you did together at graduation?"

I nodded, numbly, as she passed me the sheet music.

What the fuck was happening?

My mother silently mouthed, "I'm sorry!"

I muttered, "It's okay."

My mom, Arlo, and Mrs Hart, sat on the edge of the small practice stage, watching us.

The enemies are going to sing!

I stood close to the piano. "I haven't sung in a really long time."

Finch said, "I'm sure it'll come natural tae ye."

His voice rumbled through my heart, deep and low — oh when we used to practice together it had triggered so much desire in us. We would hold each other's eyes, my voice the high melody, his voice the low, the vibration and beat setting my heart, and though I practiced my breathing, it was difficult to stay on top of my breath, wanting him, wanting him so much. We would finish singing and fingers entwined, one of us would draw the other to the bed, or beckon the other to our waiting car, we were young after all, had to take it where we could get it, but then when we had our own apartment, Finch would sit at the keyboard. He'd play a couple of notes. He'd plead with me. "Ree-Ro? Would ye sing with me, please Ree-Ro?" He'd bat his eyes.

I'd laugh and come join him at the piano and we would sing and then he would pick me up, my legs wrapping around his waist. He would carry me into our room and drop me squealing onto the bed. He would crawl over me and we would make love, sometimes I would beg him, sing in my ear... and he would, my favorite a deep humming melody that made me breathless.

Then, after, wrapped around him, I asked, "Finch Mac, do you ask me to sing just because you want to fuck me?"

He chuckled against my throat, kissing there, "Tis nae like that, Ree-Ro, I ask ye tae sing when ye are wantin' tae fuck me."

I laughed.

He said, "I can see it in yer eyes, ye are busy about yer day but ye are thinking, 'Och, I do want tae fuck Finch Mac, because I love him so much.' I can tell what ye are thinking as yer thoughts are much like my own."

I kissed him on his ear, "You ought to write a song about that."

He kissed the tip of my nose. "I already hae, Ree-Ro, mostly, but I am tryin' tae come up with a proper rhyme for 'yearnin' vagina.'"

I laughed. Then said, "Just so you know, I have not given you permission to sing about my vagina on stage."

He rolled over onto his arm. "What about if I use metaphor, like I could call it yer yearnin' simmerin' stew pot?"

"My stew pot? I think, Finch, that all your ideas are grand and that your songs are beautiful, but this may not be your best idea. Perhaps talk about my heart instead of my vagina, your fans will thank you."

He chuckled, then looked off at the photo of the two of us,

in our graduation cap and gowns on the wall, "Ye hae always made me feel like I can do anything."

"I am your biggest fan."

He played a note on the piano and brought me out of the memory, he warmed up playing a song from Moana, grinning at Arlo, and then he peered at the music. "Did we decide on the Gershwin medley?"

Mrs Hart had her hands clasped. "Yes please!"

Finch met my eyes.

The enemy who used to be mine.

Time stood still, then... he played the first note, and we were singing together, about "Summertime," the way we used to do...

I swear to God I blacked out a little, it was that intense.

It was full of emotion, a little like time travel, how I was transported back — his voice rumbling, deeper than when he was young and when he used to sing it was meant only for me. Now his voice was for Mrs Hart, for the room, for his son, for fun, and when he sang in stadiums it was for his fans, but now, this one time, it was like being in the past, Karrie and Finch singing for each other, with each other.

And the thing about singing with someone was it required concentration, really listening. He had to pay attention to the sheet music. He watched the notes matching the moment with his fingers perfectly meeting the keys, except once or twice when he stumbled, and a smile spread, and his eyes sparkled. "I'm rusty," and then he picked it back up and his voice carried on. I only needed to sing. It was a song we had practiced so many times before our senior show. I knew the words, the beat, the notes, his voice, his smile, the side of his lips as he mouthed 'you' and I knew it all by heart.

We finished with "Someone to Watch Over Me" our eyes meeting as we held the last note, then he played the last few notes trailing along at the end.

My friends had warned me. Don't let him get close. This was so freaking close.

Mrs Hart, Mom, and Arlo all applauded.

I was so warm, I kind of thought I might faint. I wiped a bead of sweat from my temple.

He said, his voice low and rumbling, "It's like it was only yesterday."

I stood near Mom, fanning myself with the sheet music, then remembering that we weren't ever, ever, ever allowed to bend Mrs Hart's sheet music.

I flustered and placed it on the piano and pressed it flat. "Sorry about that."

Mrs Hart said, "It was so lovely, would you do it with the full choir? Could I please persuade you to sing after service on Sunday?"

The enemy was way up inside my camp, so far up inside my camp that I was overthrown — I accidentally knocked a paper cup off the piano. "So sorry," I picked it up and fumbled it back to its place. "Gravity is not working," I joked, "Oh, right, not supposed to put drinks on the piano anyway." I moved the cup across the room to the bookcase. Drinks were not supposed to be on the bookcase either, but it was also not a drink, it was an empty cup. I had just sung Gershwin with Finch and now I was obsessing over an empty paper cup.

I spun around. "I'm sure I can't be here to sing..."

Mrs Hart said, "You won't be here?"

"I will... I..."

She said, "Would *you*, dear Finch? I think if you would agree, I'm sure Karrie would. We have to get Karrie there. The congregation needs something wonderful after the loss of dear Alison this week."

It was disarming how she thought I was the one who needed to sing in front of the congregation instead of Finch, arguably the most famous person our town had ever produced, possibly our state.

Finch asked me directly. "If I agree tae sing, would ye sing with me, it means a lot tae Mrs Hart."

The enemy is calling for a truce.

I opened and closed my mouth two times before I managed, "Sure."

THE BIG TIME

Finch

This was such a hard thing within a long string of verra hard things. I had compartmentalized Karrie away and tried nae tae think of her.

One of the last nights we were taegether, I had performed at the Sinclair, a large venue, the largest so far. And it had been our best show — och, I had been on fucking fire that night. The crowd was rocking, chanting and cheerin', a pit opened up in front of the stage during "Outraged Thunder". The audience ebbed and flowed tae our beat and then clamored for an encore. We returned tae the stage and played two more songs, the first, I asked Karrie tae join in, her voice a perfect match for the song "Endless Future", then we finished with "Justice Frogs", buildin' tae a climax, the band hitting a groove and the sound roarin' through the venue. The audience went crazy as we left the stage.

My eyes settled on her. I grabbed her hand and led her intae a darkened back room and locked the handle. She said, breathlessly, "Oh my god, Finch, that was so... you were so fucking hot, that was awesome." She pulled her underwear off under her short dress and tossed them tae the side. She kent exactly what I had brought her there for.

"Och aye, they were crazed twas..." I undid my pants, and

pushed her against the wall, a hand at her jaw, holding her mouth up, meeting her lips, devouring her, she wrapped a leg around me, a Doc Marten pullin' my arse closer, her mouth opened and wanting. I hitched her up, balancing her pressed against the wall, I plowed intae her deep and fast. Her breaths panting against my ear, her moans as her head fell back against the wall, the roar in m'ears from the moments before, *Finch Mac, Finch Mac*, her whispered moans *—ohoooooohhhhh* — exposing her throat where I pressed my lips. I thrust and thrust intae her until I finally reached climax and we stilled. Consciousness returned. My forehead pressed against the wall, her arse heavy in my hands, her weight-bearing leg shakin' from the effort, the scent of her on me — she whispered, "Whoa, that was intense."

"Aye, I daena ken where it came from but twas necessary."

"I agree, that was... I wanted you so fucking bad, like desperately. That was adu*lation."*

I dropped her feet tae the floor. "Aye, twas...I am blown away, did ye hear them, Karrie? They were chanting my name."

"I did, but most importantly, that producer from XL was here, I saw him, he looked really into the music."

"Holy shit, really, you saw him?"

"Yeah, and you did great, you worked your ass off and you had to have blown him away." She pushed my hair from my sweaty brow. "Now, my love, it's just after-party."

I kissed her.

She pulled her underwear up, I zipped up my pants.

"Do ye think he will be at the party? What do I say?"

"I don't know, I think you say yes, I mean, that's the big time, right? But anyway, at least aim for a meeting, we'll figure out all the rest."

I missed havin' someone who believed in me.

CARRY HER SMILE

Karrie

I slumped down beside my mom, and she put her arm around me. I felt calmer and so I said we could stay for a bit longer. Finch played some songs for Arlo, and Mom and I sang along. Then Mom saw someone she needed to talk to in the hall.

Then Mrs Hart had to step out of the room and...

I was alone with Finch.

Thankfully his son was there to distract me from my dilemma: how to keep breathing.

Arlo swung his legs, bang bang bang against the stage. Then asked, "Did you know my mom?"

My breath caught. "Oh, yes, I um... I did know your mom, she was my best friend. She lived with me for a long long time. We grew up together."

"Do you know my Nan?" He pointed to the hallway.

"Who is your 'nan'?"

Finch said, "He calls Lydia, Nan."

"Oh, yes, sure, she's my mom."

"Oh." Bang bang bang went his feet. "She's kind of like one of my grandmas."

Tears welled up. I said, "That makes us kind of related."

Finch was watching us talk to each other then asked, "Arlo, ye ken this song?"

He played "On Top of Spaghetti", and Arlo sang at the top of his lungs, "...all covered with cheese, I lost my poor meatball when somebody sneezed..." Then he cracked up, "Ew, he sneezed! On his plate!"

I laughed.

Finch played a familiar tune on the piano and then sang, "Ar-lo, low, low, low, low."

Arlo said, "Again!"

Finch sang and played, "Next thing you know... Arlo go low low low low..."

Arlo jumped off the stage and began doing a low duck-walk around the room.

Finch sang again, "...next thing you know... Arlo go low low low low..."

I laughed more, "That song is so inappropriate for the choir room!"

Finch said, "It's why I'm changin' all the words!"

I laughed, Arlo duck-walking, Finch watching me while he played the song... It felt so good to laugh.

Arlo said, "You have a funny laugh," as he climbed back up on the stage beside me.

"Thank you," I said, "and I was noticing you have your mother's smile."

"Everyone tells me that." His feet banged on the stage some more. "She died," he added, his feet going bang bang bang.

I said, "Yes, I know, and am so deeply sorry for your loss, and I didn't mean that you have a smile that looks like her — what I meant is that I can tell that when you were with her you always made her smile, and now you have her smile here in your heart, and I can see that you carry her smile with you, everywhere."

He slid over and hugged me, a long friendly hug, and then he went back to his spot as Mom and Mrs Hart returned.

I wiped my eyes for the tenth time that afternoon.

Finch stood and said, "Okay, Arlo, I think we have tae get ye back now, yer grandmother and aunt will be wantin' ye back at five o'clock sharp."

"Will you stay for dinner, Daddy?"

Finch's jaw clenched. "We'll see."

And they were gone.

HIS STUPID FACE

Karrie

On the way home Mom said, "I'm sorry that you were put in that position, I know it must have been really hard on you."

"It was, I hate him so much. He is a horrible person. I'm not supposed to see him, at all, it's not fair."

Mom said, "I know, it's a lot to ask of you."

I stared out the window, dull gray sky, blustery cold, the street lights on, shop lights blazing, the occasional first Christmas lights, twinkling against the otherwise deep dark of evening in winter. "What time is it?"

"It's almost five."

I hoped Finch got Arlo back to his grandmother and aunt on time... I barely remembered Alison's sister, Angie. She was older, and had bolted, run off and gotten married, when Alison's stepfather started really kicking Alison's ass. Sheryl and Angie had both done absolutely nothing about Alison's abuse. I had been pretty furious about how she left, and how Alison hadn't been able to go with her. Alison had felt deserted. God, her family had been so awful, the abuse so dire. It was amazing that Alison had turned out so awesome. Then again, she had lived almost full-time with my mom from the age of twelve.

Mom asked, "Did you hear me?"

"Oh, yeah, sorry, I was thinking about Arlo. He lives with Angie and Sheryl now?"

"Yes, poor little boy."

"When does Finch leave?"

"He's supposed to leave on Monday, but he doesn't want to, not without Arlo." She pulled our car into the driveway.

I said, "It was nice seeing him, singing with him, even though I hate him, it was... I'm furious that it was nice."

"It was wonderful hearing it. I missed your voice. And the two of you together are..." She chef-kissed her fingertips.

I said, "Did I mention that I hate his stupid face with a white hot fury?"

She said, "Yes, you mentioned it."

THE WORLD JUST CONSPIRED

Karrie

The following morning I hung out with Tessa, playing games, and drinking coffee. Mom was padding around upstairs. Dad was in his office. Tessa was still in pajamas. I was in a pair of slacks and a cashmere sweater, wishing I had brought more comfortable hanging-out-in-the-kitchen-with-my-sister clothes.

She asked, "Have you seen that new story on TMZ about Finch?"

My eyes went wide as I picked up my phone to scroll for it.

She said, "Can't believe I'm telling you about it — aren't you an important agent's assistant? Aren't you supposed to check celebrity news first thing?"

"I've trained myself not to check on Finch's life, too much drama that has nothing to do with..." I found the article titled: Finch Mac spinning out of control. There were photos taken earlier in the week of Finch, obviously drunk, with a scantily dressed woman on his lap. Photos of him here in Maine, leaving the pub, and looking out of control, screaming at a reporter.

"This one is from the other night, I talked to him before he left, he wasn't drunk... what the...?"

"Half of what they say about Finch is wrong, no scratch that, all of what they say about Finch is wrong."

"I don't know if I would go that far, there must be truth to some of it."

Howard started barking, tail wagging, and then with a rush, the mudroom door opened, shocking me — a half second later, Finch entered. "Och."

Howard jumped and frisked around him, happily.

Tessa, without looking up, said, "Mom is downstairs."

"That's not why I came." He glanced at me.

I ran a hand through my hair, relieved I had put on makeup this morning. "Can I talk to ye, Ree — I mean, Karrie?"

My eyes went wide. "Like, um... *talk* talk? I..."

"Aye, can we talk talk?"

Tessa looked from Finch to me. "I need to go upstairs, to um... do that thing... yeah... that upstairs thing... I'll leave you guys alone."

She left.

Finch leaned on the counter. "Have ye been talkin' tae the press about me? Or that fella ye had with ye, the one who cornered me tae tell me he was going tae marry ye—"

I was shocked. "What... who, Jayden?"

"Aye, would he talk tae the press? He was clearly tryin' tae fuck with m'head when he came up tae me at the funeral."

"I don't think he would, he — he's an actor, he knows not to divulge anything, he..."

"Well someone *did*, Karrie, they're talkin' on me. There's a story that sounds like ye gave them the details, I mean... I ken ye hate me, but this is F-ed up."

"What the hell are you talking about Finch? I would never, ever ever, in a million years tell the press about you. God, that is one hell of an accusation. Jayden wouldn't say anything, he's been through media training..." I thought about how Jayden had wanted to meet Finch and how I had told him details that could be... *ugh*. My heart was racing with anger. And that terrible awful shame again. "I work for an agent, I would never try to use the press against someone, and another thing, I have other things to do. I'm a professional, and nothing in my life is about you anymore. Why would I...?"

"Because ye hate me..."

"Well, that is true."

"Great, okay, so... if no' ye, it must be Jayden—"

I stood. "Or check that ditzy actress, or the model that you had backstage the other night. I'm sure there are any number of people who don't give a shit about you and would be willing to—"

He leaned his head back and looked incredulous. "What? Karrie gives a shit? Call TMZ! This is news tae me."

"That's not what I mean, I mean you are a family friend. I'm not going to screw over — I don't even know why I'm still talking to you about this. This is bullshit. I will not stand for being accused. And what the hell would be my motivation?"

"I dinna ken, ye returned home. Ye hate m'guts. Ye are motivated tae make me pay—"

"Why would I, after how long, six years? Why would I still be *that* angry?"

"I daena ken, Karrie, ye've frozen me and Alison out of yer life for a mistake we made six years ago. Ye tell me what goes on in yer mind... I canna imagine what ye're thinking—"

"What I'm thinking! I'm not thinking about you at all, or Alison, I mean, I am now, but, but..."

"Are ye goin' tae marry that arse-wipe with the neck pillow?"

"No, not, never, not that it's any business of yours."

He just looked at me and shook his head.

I said, "Did you need something else?"

"Nae, no'at all."

"Good, and I'm not singing with you this weekend."

"Aye, of course not, why would ye, Karrie? Ye daena want tae sully yer good name, yer righteous position as the one who was wronged." He stalked through the mudroom for the door and yanked it open, then closed it.

I thought he was gone, but then he stalked back into the

kitchen. "Ye ken, this is yer family, and ye bolted on them, it's really a piece of work."

"Oh yeah, right, who are you to lecture me about anything?"

He stormed away, yanking open the door, and slamming it behind him.

I collapsed into a chair and immediately texted Jayden:

Hey, Jayden,
did you talk to the press
about Finch?

Three dots, then:
No, never.
What do you mean?

Me:
He just accused me
of telling stories about us
to someone,
now the press is running it.

Jay-Dog:
Oh.

Then there were three dots and three dots and three dots and...

I texted:
Did you talk to
anyone about Finch?

Jay-Dog:

Yeah, at the premier,
but I swear,
I didn't say anything incriminating,
nothing bad, just...
I don't know...
is it bad?

Me:
First, it goes against
all that training,
remember?
Loose lips sink ships?

Jay-Dog:
Yeah,
but it was just high school stories
no biggie...
not like I shared any fresh messes...

Me:
Finch's entire life
is a fresh mess.

Jay-Dog:
I'm sorry
was he pissed?

Me:
Totally, but it's okay,
we'll figure it out.
I'm sure it will be fine,
just shut it.

Jay-Dog:
Done.

The three dots again.

Jay-Dog:
```
You talked to him?
Was he jealous of me?
```

He sent a gif of a man kissing his biceps.

I sent a gif of a girl giving the middle finger.

He sent a gif that showed a girl pleading and batting her eyes.

Jay-Dog:
```
Don't be mad
with Jay-Dog,
Jay-Dog sorry.
```

Me:
```
Not mad, Jay-Dog,
I'll see you soon.
```

I looked down at Howard, sitting by my knee. "You're supposed to be a better guard dog, dummy, you just let him in, you greet him? You're a traitor."

I petted him behind the ears and because I felt bad, said, "I love you, you little traitor." Howard nuzzled against my hand, happily.

Mom crept into the room. "Whoo-whee, that was a fight if I ever heard one, wow."

"He accused me of talking to the press about him, some story, and I would never — but come to find out, *Jayden* was talking about Finch." I tossed my phone down on the table.

"Oh honey."

"Yeah. He didn't mean any harm. He was just at the premiere and it made him sound important to talk about Finch, like he knew him, and... Man, it was a mistake to bring him here."

"Well, it's all water under the bridge. Don't worry, I'll explain it to Finch."

"Make sure he knows that Jayden didn't mean anything by it, and that I would never want to harm him. I mean, I wish he knew that already, but make sure he knows."

She said, "He ought to know it already, but then again you're strangers to each other." She put her arm around me. "But, he's dealing with a lot, and he just vented on you, and I'm sorry. I'm trying to help him. He doesn't have a dad, his mom is in Scotland in the middle of nowhere. Finch is trying to be a dad and he has to deal with Alison's mom and sister and..."

"You're taking his side."

"Not really, I'm mediating with you. When I talk to him I'm going to take your side. He does not get to talk to you that way. Period."

"Thank you."

"But I think it would help *you* if you empathize with what he is going through. I'm sorry to make excuses, but..."

I wiped my tears. "But you're making excuses."

"Yes, well, I've always had a soft spot for Finch. I thought he was going to be my son-in-law."

"The odds were pretty good, either through Alison or me."

She frowned. "It was always going to be you, my love. The world just conspired against you two."

"How can you say that, Mom? It wasn't the world, it wasn't fate, it was Finch. It was... it was Alison. *They're* responsible."

"This is true, and they had to take responsibility and they had to do it together, and I'm really sorry that it didn't include you."

"I'm fine, my life is great."

She kissed my forehead. "I know. I'm really proud of you. I

mean look at you, every time I walk into the room you have a new outfit. It's like having Zendaya stay here—"

"You know who Zendaya is?"

"Of course! I'm hip, I'm down with the kids," she chuckled. "And I know you are a success and you love your fabulous job and I'm glad you came home. I hope you come home more often."

"Me too."

A PHOTO ALBUM

Karrie

I went to Tessa's room, shoved a pile of laundry away, and collapsed in her yellow velvet chair. "So… Jayden *did* talk about Finch. He *might* be the one who leaked a story about Finch."

"Ugh."

"Yeah, I told you he was too pretty and too dumb to be interesting."

"Consider me forewarned. Are you going to tell Finch that Jayden was responsible?"

"Yes, of course. Or Mom. She offered to mediate, since Finch and I don't talk to each other anymore. Did you hear him?"

"Yeah, he sounded like an ass."

"Thank you! Mom was making all kinds of excuses for him."

"Well, you know Mom, she has a heart bigger than her brain."

"Tessa! That is a terrible thing to say."

"It is not, there is no judgment there. Maybe having a heart bigger than your brain is a good thing — you got it from her, what do you think?"

I ran my hand along the smoothness of the velvet. "You think my heart is bigger than my brain?"

"Heck yeah. Heart's gigantic, brain is a little itty-witty pea brain."

I put my head back on the pillow. "So that's what my problem is...?"

She rolled her eyes. "The fact that you're asking it, proves the point."

Dad joined us for lunch down in the kitchen. "Did I miss anything?"

Tessa gestured all around, holding her roast beef sandwich. "Yea, a big fight. Surprised you didn't hear it."

He rubbed his forehead. "I didn't hear much of anything, I was so deep into my research, there's a whole king where he's not supposed to be — I feel sure of it... like *why...*? What did we discover...? Did I mention it to you...?"

I said, "Yeah, Dad, you mentioned there was a king of Scotland that was confusing, I thought you were drunk."

"No, it's a mind-bending, earth-shattering, time-twisting historical mystery — anyway, what were you saying about... ?"

"Karrie and Finch got in a fight."

"A sword fight? Do I need to lock up the broadsword? Don't go dragging the armaments out for your petty arguments — now, if we have a clan dispute then maybe, just maybe, we can break them out. If you see a Campbell, better arm yourself, they are dastardly."

Mom looked at him incredulously. "Are you going to just keep rambling on about Scottish history or actually ask why Karrie and Finch are fighting?"

He sighed. "I just hate it when they fight. I was rooting for those two kids — do I have to hear about it? It's like when parents get divorced. Can I just pretend it's not happening and get you to take me to Chuck E. Cheese?"

Tessa said, "Dad, you're the parent. You're supposed to take an interest in our dramas and advise us. Also, you can take yourself to Chuck E. Cheese, there's one about two hours away."

I said, "And actually, advice is not necessary. I hate Finch. I have for years. It used to be active hate, now it's passive. I don't need any advice about it. You can all have friendships with him, that's fine, doesn't bother me either way. Arlo is great. You can talk about Alison without worrying about me, it wasn't really her fault anyway. It was Finch who broke my heart, so yeah, let's talk about something else."

Dad said, "Perfect... so today I was researching the first canines in Scotland and found a connection to the new king I was telling you about, he wrote a great deal about his dog..."

That's where I tuned Dad out, thinking about Finch and the look on his face when he left. There had been a glimpse of the boy I had loved, combined with the man I now loathed, and more of that shame, this time for being someone who was actively causing him pain.

He had accused me of wanting to cause him pain.

I felt sick to my stomach.

I climbed the stairs and wandered into the guest room. Long ago this had been Alison's room. In the closet were drawers full of keepsakes from our high-school years. I slid open a drawer and right on top found a photo album. I pulled it out to sit on the bed and opened it to the middle to a big photo of us in tenth grade: Alison, Finch, and me, standing in the snow. I was in the middle. Our arms were slung around each other's backs. We had the smiles of kids who didn't think anything would ever change.

STICK WITH THAT PLAN

Karrie

I flipped to the front, finding a photo of Alison and me on a dock at the cabin my parents rented every summer. Our scrawny legs sticking out of our bathing suits, shivering, and smiling. I remembered that day like it was fresh; we were ten years old. She spent the summer with us, and at the time was completely quiet about her family issues. It wasn't until the following year that I saw the first bruises on her body.

A few months later she admitted what was happening and I told my mother.

Alison came to live with us, mostly full time, when I was twelve.

I was a kid so I didn't ever know what my mother went through to make all of this happen.

I remembered Dad driving Mom over to talk to her family. Alison coming in the middle of the night in her pajamas. The night that the police were at our door, my Dad telling us not to come downstairs. We were protected from the back and forth negotiations. Alison was safe. When she was older her mother manipulated her, persuaded her to come home. It was always devastating when Mom and Dad would drive her to Sheryl's house, and she would be there for a time, but then something would trigger her step-father, the abuse would begin again, and Alison would return.

Mom and Alison had long conversations about what happened. At the time, I was oblivious to the details. But Alison didn't need to talk to me about it. She just wanted 'normal'. She told me that it was the greatest thing in the world to know that our house was always open to her. That Mom always had her back.

I flipped to the final pages of the book. There nestled in the pages was a gold locket on a thin chain. I clicked it open to see another photo of Alison, me, and Finch with our arms around each other — a summer day, we were teenagers, best friends, this photo was taken just before Finch and I left for college.

There were more images from that photo shoot. We had been setting the camera on automatic and running back and forth taking random, hilarious shots. I ran my finger over one where we were laughing so hard we were blurry, falling on the ground — a big pile of Finch, Alison, and me. I pressed my hand to the page, the memory of the laughs, the warm sun, the smell of fresh mowed lawn, I had loved them so—

Then came the pain.

I had hardly looked at this album.

Alison gave it to me, full of photos, as a going away present. I was going away to college, she had been desperately sad.

I peered at the photos, it was as if I could see the deep sadness in her eyes.

I remembered her confiding in me that she was scared I was leaving. She was worried that she wouldn't have a place to live anymore. That Mom wouldn't want her there.

And I had promised her, Mom had promised her, that she would always be welcome.

But over the next year, while Finch and I were away at college, she drifted back to her mother's house.

We all came back together that first summer, but then fall of the second year I barely heard from her. My mom barely saw her.

At Christmas break it all came to a head. Alison's home-life was shit. We could see she was depressed, but she wouldn't talk to any of us about it. She pretended it was all fine.

The day I packed up to return to school for spring semester, she made up an excuse not to be there. In retrospect, I think she found it difficult to watch.

I was preoccupied with worry about Alison, enjoying the holidays, not paying enough attention to Finch, and what he had going on... an offer.

He broke it to me while I was surrounded by all our luggage and boxes, open, half-packed.

His second song had now blown up on SoundCloud. The band had an official offer from a label, and they wanted to take the deal. He told me that he had been negotiating a music contract and instead of returning to college with me, he needed to go to New York. They would record new music, they had come up with a plan. In one breath, while I blinked and stared, my heart-rate rising, he said, "It won't be long, just a month or two, in the studio," but then in the next breath, when I was able to ask some hurried flustered question, he admitted they would be touring, he mentioned they would be gone for months. He said, "I ken we were supposed tae finish school before I made a big move, but I... I had tae... I think I hae tae do it now and I really hope ye will..." He looked pained and worried, and somehow I was supposed to be proud of him.

"But... but... we're going to college together. We have an apartment together. We—"

He sat in my chair. I sat on the bed, and we talked about how I would be returning to our college apartment alone, while he started his music career. And I wish I could say it was a good conversation, but it was terrible — I was not happy enough for him. We had been a team.

He said, "This is why I dinna tell ye, Ree-Ro, I kent ye would be freaked out, I hae been worryin' about it for days, how tae tell ye..." and then that became our fight, how I wasn't handling everything going to shit well enough.

And so all those things that I meant to say, that he needed to hear, but I was too upset to be reasonable, and all those things he should have said, and I knew in my heart he would have said, except he was so afraid, went unsaid.

I'm sorry I dinna tell you.

I'm proud of you.

This is complicated, but we can work it out, Ree-Ro.

I might have said, We have a plan and I'm disappointed that it's changing, but if we lie here on the bed together, the way we do, I wrap around your arm and you press your lips to my hairline, we can talk it through.

We can make a new plan.

The important thing is that we do it together.

But we said none of that.

Instead I left my room.

Then he left my house.

And I knew in my heart that we would have gotten over it, that with some air and space for a minute we would come back to talk it out.

We had never not talked things out before.

But this time...

This time we never got the chance.

It was the last time he was ever my Finch.

Mom stuck her head in. "Looking at old photos?"

I closed the locket in the book and returned it to the drawer.

She said, "Finch had to go out of town overnight. I need to pick up Arlo from school and keep him until dinner. You'll be here to help?"

"Yeah."

Mom went and picked up Arlo and I helped her take care of him for a few hours. He was happy and generally well-adjusted but sometimes he would lose his shit over normal things, and then he would cry and we'd have to console and hug him.

One such time I was consoling him and he asked, "Where's my dad?"

"He had a business trip today, he'll be back first thing in the morning."

"I want to stay here with Nan."

I stroked his hair. "It's going to be okay, you can go stay with your... what do you call your grandmother?"

"She's Grandma."

"Well, Nan wishes you could stay too, but you are supposed to go stay with Grandma tonight, and your dad knows where you'll be. We should stick with that plan. Tomorrow your dad will come see you. He knows where you'll be because of the plan."

He looked down at his sneakers for a few moments. "Is my dad going to die?"

"What would make you say that?"

"I don't know. Because sometimes mommies and daddies do."

"Well, Finch won't. He's going to be okay."

"How do you know?"

"Because... because he's your dad and he knows you need him. He will be back tomorrow morning."

And then Mom had to drive Arlo back home and drop him off in time for dinner.

MOST OF THAT DRAMA

Karrie

When she got home, I asked, "Is that the hardest thing you ever had to do?"

"Yes, dropping that sweet boy off at Sheryl's? Definitely one of them. She's not supposed to be drinking, she's supposed to be going to AA meetings, but I got a distinct impression that she was..." Mom sighed. "But I've had many hard things. Remember when Alison first came to live with us? Her stepfather cornered me at the grocery store once — that was really scary."

She went quiet. "I made mistakes back then. I thought I could just be the groovy mom that took in the wayward teen, but then year after year she lived here, becoming a member of the family, she was deeply connected—" She waved her hand. "And then Sheryl and that wretched man would remember she was here and they'd demand her return and I'd have to drive her over there and... it was always hard. Remember that time when she was sixteen and she was gone for a whole month?"

"Yeah, but honestly, I don't think I really knew how bad it all was."

"Yes, we tried to protect you." She shook her head. "I guess it sucks that my worst things have always involved that family, but best things too, Alison was pretty great."

"I feel that same way, she was my best friend, but involved in my worst thing."

"I think sometimes trauma spirals out from people, like Alison tried so hard to start anew, again and again, a new layer of protection on her heart, a fresh smile, a positive outlook. She would shine herself up, but ultimately she couldn't keep recovering."

"What are you going to do about Sheryl?"

"I called Finch on my way home. He's on his way. He'll go get Arlo as soon as he's back. Looks like another night of worry."

"I'm sorry you've always had to deal with this."

"Who knew back when I was partying and shaving my head and wearing leather, that someday I would be mothering so many wayward children? First I fostered Alison, then I'm all up in Finch's dramas. I want to protect Arlo. And all of that is in addition to worrying about my own daughters."

"I'm responsible for bringing most of that drama to your doorstep."

"This is true. And it has been dramatic. But I don't blame you because honestly, I wouldn't have wanted any other life. It's mine. I'm happy to be someone who can be counted on. I really like that young people love me and need me."

"Is Finch going to be able to figure this out?"

"I hope so, I don't know how, but I always have hope."

IT HAD HAPPENED BEFORE

Karrie

In the middle of the night I heard my parents in the hallway outside my room, frantically whispering as they descended the stairs.

I lay there on the bed, eyes back and forth on the darkened ceiling, trying to work out why they would be up when they had gone to bed an hour before.

Then I flung off my covers and went downstairs.

Tessa was up, Mom had her purse over her arm, Dad was in his robe. "What's going on?"

Tessa said, "Whole thing going on — Finch got back, Sheryl won't let him see Arlo."

I slipped on my boots. "Do you have your coat, Mom?" I started grabbing coats off the hooks, handing one to Mom.

Dad said, "I don't need mine, someone's gotta stay home in case..."

I passed a coat to Tessa. "In case of what?"

"In case someone needs to make bail."

I looked from Mom to Dad. "Shouldn't Mom be the one...?"

Mom said, "I can *not* stay home, that is not my style. I've got to go help Finch and Arlo."

Dad said, "Any of the daughters of Lydia Munro willing to stay home while I go and handle it? No?"

Mom was already out the door, me following, Tessa still pulling on her boots.

I guessed he had his answer.

The cold air woke me up like a bucket of ice on my face.

Tessa offered to drive because Mom was too upset to function.

As we settled into the car and pulled our belts on, Tessa was already pulling us down the icy driveway. It was seamless the way they were coordinated. It almost felt as if it had happened before.

WHITE HOT RAGE

Karrie

Sheryl lived across town; It took about twelve minutes to get there. As we pulled up there was a huge scene: the house all lit up, a police car up on the lawn. Mitchell standing outside his car, looking lost. Finch in the middle of the grass, yelling. A police officer yelling at Finch to "Calm your ass down!"

Mom said, "Oh no!" as she jumped from the car.

Tessa pointed at a photographer snapping photos from across the street. "The press is already here. Damn." She rolled down our windows and waved Mitchell over to our car.

Finch's voice, yelling at the cop, "Nae, I winna! I need tae see m'son!"

Mitchell said, "I'm glad you're here, this is not something I know how to handle, this is nuts."

Tessa said, "It's good you called."

Sheryl yanked open the front door, stood on the steps of the house, and screeched, "You get out of here, Finch! You are not welcome! There is a restraining order!"

The police officer said, "Finch Mac, we need you to come with us down—"

A second police car and then a third pulled up in front of the house.

Finch was silhouetted in the headlights. "I winna leave, not without my son!"

My heart sank, I could hear Arlo wailing from the house.

My mom walked up with her hands out, placatingly. "Now now, officer, is there something..."

Finch yelled, "Fuck nae! I'm no' leavin' without Arlo! She's got nae right tae keep him from me!"

Sheryl shrieked, "I do! You're unfit! Out to all hours! Partying!"

I muttered, "What do we do?"

Tessa, her arms hooked over the steering wheel, peering out the window, said, "I have no idea, this is way more extreme than usual."

Mitchell said, "I hoped you would know."

"Nah, I never had to deal with the police."

Mom and the policeman got Finch calmed down enough for there to be a discussion instead of a brawl. We rolled up our window because it was so cold, but then it was hard to hear. Mom was talking, the first cop interrupting and explaining, more officers standing around watching, Finch waving his arms and belligerently arguing in the strobing blue lights of the police car. Neighbors were out in the street, gawking, their cameras recording. Even freezing outside, it was too good to miss — Finch Mac having a meltdown in the middle of their neighborhood.

The discussion seemed to take forever. I said, "Maybe you ought to go over there now, Mitchell? It looks like they're giving instructions."

"Yeah, sure." He walked over to stand by Mom and Finch.

Tessa and I ran the heater in the car, watching the scene unfold through the front window. The officer stalked back and forth to his patrol car, lecturing, filling out tickets. Finally, Mom pulled Finch by the arm, off the lawn and across the street. Then the conversation was much calmer. Finch was handed a ticket. Mom and Mitchell led him to our car.

She climbed in the passenger side.

Finch opened the back door and spoke directly to me, "Karrie, would ye mind drivin' me tae m'hotel? Mitchell has his own car and um... m'car is here and..."

Mom said, "He admitted to the officer that he had a beer, so now he can't drive away in his car. We could switch around and Tessa could—"

"No, no, that's fine, I will drive him. No problem." I was actually thrilled to have something to do, to help, and my adrenaline was pumping. I wanted to understand what the hell was going on. I climbed out of the back seat and followed him down the block to his car. "Keys?"

"Daena have keys, it's a Tesla."

"Oh," I climbed in the driver's side.

He climbed in beside me. His jaw clenching and unclenching, a high color on his cheeks, quiet fury fueling him.

I said, "What hotel?"

"The Hilton in Bangor."

We were quiet as I drove us out onto the main road and into town.

I asked, "What about Arlo?"

Finch said, his sentences short and clipped, "She filed a restrainin' order. I have tae go in front of the judge on Monday."

My heart broke for that little boy.

"She is such a bitch. Alison would be so upset if she knew."

"Aye."

As we neared the hotel I asked, "What if Mom called social services, told them about her suspicions, maybe..."

"Social services have been alerted a'ready. They'll be doin' a home visit. Och." He ran a hand down his face. "I daena want Arlo in foster care. This is insane."

We continued on in silence until I pulled the car into the parking lot and up to the front door of the hotel.

He said, "Ye can drive m'car home. I'll Uber over for it in the mornin'."

"That's okay, one of us will drive it back."

He unclipped his seat belt and brusquely climbed from the car. Then he turned around and put his hands on the roof, steam coming from his mouth. His jaw clenched, he looked hangry. "Ree-Ro, would ye like tae come up tae m'room?"

I was so shocked that he used his old nickname for me that I couldn't figure out what to say. Did he just ask me up to his room? What the hell? Just because I gave him a ride? "Um... no... What do you think this is? Did you think I drove you to your hotel to spend the night with the great Finch Mac?"

He winced. "Nae... that's no' what I meant. I meant, would ye... I daena really want tae be alone."

"Oh." I blinked, confusedly, then asked, "You need company?"

"Aye, I have a whole suite, with a lounge. There's a table and chairs. I daena ken... it was probably a daft idea."

"No, it wasn't, sure... I'll come up. But, don't be coming at me with 'Ree-Ro' this and that, I'm Karrie Munro to you."

"Aye, of course."

I parked the car in a space, met him at the front doors, and we stiffly walked through the hotel lobby with all eyes on him, and therefore, me. I was wearing my dazzlingly white puffy, fur-trimmed coat over my pink and red striped pajamas. My boots were white faux-fur. Now I probably looked like a festive snowman on candy cane legs.

His face was impenetrably stern as we stepped into the elevator, as if he were holding himself back, jabbing the floor button as if he was pissed at it. I was wondering what the hell I was doing, following Finch to a hotel room, having just this morning told him that I hated him.

I hated him with the white hot rage of an exploding star.

FINCH MAC'S HOTEL ROOM

Karrie

He opened the door to a large suite, and I felt relieved. There was, indeed, a table and chairs, a bar with stools with a tiny kitchen, and then a sitting room, and beyond it an ignorable bedroom.

He gestured toward a chair. "Beer?" He opened the fridge, pulled out two bottles, carried them to the table with one hand, the bottle opener in the other, and popped the tops off.

I said, "I'm wearing my pajamas."

"I hae seen ye in yer pajamas afore. Durin' finals week ye wore naethin' but pajamas the whole time."

It was true, but it still felt awkward to take off my coat and expose my pink and red striped long johns, so I sat down with my coat on, but then that felt stupid so I pushed the puffy coat off behind me, the arms wrapped around my waist.

He slumped down in the chair across from me. He was so freaking handsome in his black shirt and nice jeans and boots, his eyes dark and full of rage and sadness. He tilted the beer to his lips and chugged. Then, sprawled back in his chair, he rested the bottle on his stomach and looked down at it for a moment.

"I am sorry, Karrie Munro."

I took a sip of beer. "What for — this…? This is nothing, you need company… I don't mind."

"Nae…" He took a quick sip and put the bottle on the table. "Nae… it's no' what I meant. I'm sorry about what I did. I wanted tae beg ye tae forgive me, but I dinna ken what tae say, without makin' excuses and I am just verra sorry. I daena have any peace about it. It is always on m'mind what I did tae ye."

I nodded. "You broke my heart."

"Aye, I ken it."

"I thought you were going to marry me. I thought we were going to spend our whole lives together."

"Aye, me too."

I narrowed my eyes. "Really? I expected you to say something like," I lowered my voice, "'Karrie this is the imaginings of a little girl, the world is full of disappointments and ye canna expect tae have a fairytale ending.'"

A smile tugged at his mouth. "That's how I sound tae ye, Karrie?"

"You sound like your mom, your Scottish accent is more than I remember."

"I lean intae it. I'm told it's good for m'brand. But that is no' what I would say. The world is full of disappointments, aye, but lovin' ye was never one of them. We were a team, I ruined the best part of my life. I am far more likely tae blame fear about what m'future held, but I am no'excusin', nor askin' for understandin'. The time is long gone for these things. I was a bit of a lad on the edge of a career, ye were a dazzling girl who I had always known and loved, and Alison and I made a life destroyin' mistake, but now Arlo is here. I can beg yer forgiveness for the act of it, but I canna think on a world without him — how can I think on m'son with regret? I canna, I have tae look forward, ye ken? I am sorry that what hurt ye so much ended with such a fine lad, and I wished every day that ye were a part of m'life and that ye would ken him, that ye were friends once more with

Alison. I wished we could go back in time, tae before, when we were going tae be friends forever, but I want ye tae ken, I am sorry. I am verra sorry for it."

"Thank you Finch, that means a lot." I looked down at my bottle of beer. "I wish I could talk to her about it."

"I ken, she wanted tae talk tae ye as well."

"Was she happy? Was her life better than before?"

"Aye, I believe so. She had her own place. She doted on Arlo — until she was so sick she couldna."

"You went to hospice?"

"Every chance I could."

I peeled the label off my beer. "I've always wondered, why didn't you get married?"

"Tae Alison?" He looked me in the eyes, then shook his head. "We dinna like each other much—"

"Ugh." I said, "That sucks, that you destroyed me, our relationship, over someone you didn't even like, how little you must have thought of me to have done it to me."

He winced. "It wasna like that, I explained it a'ready — she had gotten intae a big fight with her stepfather, remember? She tried tae call ye, but ye were upset because of our argument. I was upset. She called me and I went tae pick her up, I got intae a row with her stepfather and he punched me in the face and Alison and I parked in the woods and she was comfortin' me and we just... we lost track of everythin' that was important tae us."

"God, you fucking dick." I shook my head. "Can I have another beer?"

"Aye." He got up and popped the caps off two more.

"We gave our virginity to each other, we were only ever going to sleep with each other, we promised. We were going to get married."

"Aye."

His eyes settled on me.

I sighed, then I took a long gulp of beer. "I walked in here, hating you, passionately, but you... and I... I just... I think with Alison gone it just feels so raw and upside down. Like I used to be full of righteous anger, but now I have a lot of shame, and sadness, and loss, and I used to want to wallow in it, you know? But now I want to do something about it, to turn it around. I was repeating to myself, 'I need to find forgiveness,' but it seems hollow and unnecessary. I think I must have forgiven you somehow along the way. I don't know... losing Alison, meeting Arlo, it's dawned on me that life goes on and love is hard and messy and—"

"What do ye mean, love, Ree— I mean Karrie?"

"Good save, you don't get to call me Ree-Ro, you lost all those privileges. But I um... I meant, love, like family, like those kinds of connections." I took another drink of my beer and put it down on the table. "Here I was building a family — it was going to be me and you, my husband, and there was Alison, my best friend, and... now you and Alison have a family without me, and that is enraging, but it also seems like if I could have found forgiveness earlier I might have saved myself a lot of heartbreak."

"Aye, it is a hard thing tae change yer heart and ken ye might have changed it earlier."

"There is a lot of regret."

"For me as well."

I said, "I talked to her, did you know?"

"Aye, she told me."

I nodded watching him, a big lump forming in my throat, thinking about how he had gotten to keep Alison, while I had gone away.

But also, going away had been my choice. I had gone back to school, then I had moved to LA. I could have stayed close, but I didn't want to.

I focused on the painting over the couch, an abstract piece in pale earth tones, trying to keep thc cry from coming because it was saddening, maddening to think about how I could have talked things through; even not trusting the rock star, I could have gotten to the point where I could be in the same room with him. It would have helped my mom and my sister, it would have been lovely to have been able to see Alison at the end of her life. To have been a help with Arlo.

He said, “It meant a lot tae her that ye talked. She loved ye verra much.”

“Great.” Tears overfilled my eyes. “Now I’m crying again.” I crossed the room, in my striped pjs, no bra, for a tissue, sat back down and wrapped my white coat around me again for protection. “I really truly wish I hadn’t been so determined to make you pay with my absence, I feel sometimes that I only hurt myself.”

“Ye hurt me as well, Karrie. I deserved it, but it cut deep that ye would never forgive me.”

“It was easier to cut you off than to deal with you being a horrible person.”

“It’s hard tae deal, I ken.”

“Yeah... but what was I doing, wallowing in pain and misery and to what end? My heart was broken, but what... what did I want you to do about it?”

“Ye wanted tae make us feel the pain as well, but the trouble is, ye dinna ken we felt it, ye dinna ken I felt it.”

“Why did you do it?”

His legs jiggled as if he wanted to run from the room. “I daena hae a reason. I took an important phone call and ye and I should hae celebrated, but we were in finals week, so I kept quiet. And I worried about it — I decided tae quit school, but how could I ask ye tae quit? I dinna ken what tae do. I talked tae the band at practice that week, and then everyone kent it but you, and I kept talkin’ m’self out of tellin’ ye. At first it was just a missed conversation, but soon enough I was decidin’ tae leave, without havin’ spoken tae ye.” He shook his head. “It might hae been fear. I wanted tae marry ye, but then I was goin' tae go on tour... I dinna ken how tae do both of those things... any of those things, I daena ken... it was as if I dinna give one thought tae ye, twas only m'self I was thinking on. And there was so much shame—"

"I wasn't really asking about that, I know why you didn't tell me, you were scared of the big changes, we could have worked through it. No... I want to know why you fucked her."

"The best explanation I can come up with is m'cock sabotaged m'heart."

I chuckled. "I wonder why Alison did it."

"I ken why."

"Really?"

"Aye, she felt abandoned. I am nae excusin' her, but she came ontae me so she wouldna feel so deserted. She thought we left her — she made a play tae insert herself in m'life and yers. I think she thought if she had a baby she wouldna be alone. If ye think on it, her brain sabotaged her."

"And I was sabotaged by my broken heart. We're quite a threesome: the cock, the brain, and the heart. It's funny, Tessa was telling me that I have a big heart and a small brain like my mom."

He looked at me, sizing me up. "Ye let Tessa talk tae ye like that? In yer teen years ye would have kicked her arse for it."

"Yeah, now she's being pretty insightful. It's infuriating. Though I do like the idea that I'm like Mom."

"A little. Ye do both love fiercely."

I raised my chin. "How are we different?"

"Yer mum loves unconditionally."

I opened and closed my mouth. "I love conditionally?"

"Aye, ye loved me and then when I wronged ye, ye dinna."

"That's how it's supposed to work. I can't be a doormat. I couldn't let you sleep with my best friend and then just let it go..."

"Aye, I ken, ye couldna trust me again."

"And the truth is, I never stopped loving you, my love *is* unconditional, but... I couldn't let it go."

He jerked his head, a small movement I immediately recognized — he had always done it to mean, 'come along with me,' in thought, conversation, trouble. Alison and I used to tease that once Finch used his head jerk he was impossible to deny. "Ye said a lot there."

"The point is I couldn't let it go."

"Aye, I ken."

He raised his beer. "We lost a great friend. But she taught me that life is verra short and we canna waste it on anger and regret. We have tae strive for our happy endin'."

I raised my beer. "To happy endings."

"Have ye found yers yet, Karrie?"

I shook my head. "No, not really. I mean, I have such a great career, I'm... my boss says I'm indispensable, but no... not sure what I've been doing in the relationship department. I have some good friends though. They would be pissed if they saw this, they instructed me that I was to not, under any circumstances, see you."

"How come no?"

"Because it took so long to get over you. I am though, completely over you, long ago. I mean, it needs to be said."

"Aye, it's good ye are." He looked down at his hands.

"And I'm grateful that I came back this week, that I am here spending time with Mom and Dad. This is a little happiness on top of deep deep sadness."

"Aye, we have tae look for happiness when the whole world is shite." He leaned his forearms on the table. His sleeves were pushed up to the elbow, the tattoos showing. "It's like with Arlo, he deserves so much better than this, ye ken?"

"Yeah, he really does."

He yawned broadly. "Sorry, it was a long day. I think I ought tae go tae sleep. Will ye stay? I will give ye the bed, I can sleep on the convertible sofa."

My mind raced through all the terrible possibilities of letting down my guard to spend the night in Finch Mac's hotel room, but my mouth said, "Sure," before my brain could refuse. Big heart, small brain.

He ran his hands through his hair. "Och, thank ye."

IT DOESN'T MEAN ANYTHING

Karrie

I went into the bathroom and was troubled by what I saw, my face was swollen and tearstained... basically the same colors as my pajamas and it was hard not to see that I looked just like a life-sized muppet. I finger-combed my hair and then finger-brushed my teeth.

When I emerged, ready for bed, Finch had already pulled out the sofa bed and was wearing a comfortable t-shirt and sweats.

I said, "How come you didn't tell me I looked like this?"

"How do ye look? Beautiful? Rumpled like I woke ye up? Like ye used tae look in our apartment back in college? Look at me, I just fought a cop in a yard — if it wasna for yer mum I'd be in jail right now. I daena look m'best either."

"You look like a handsome rock star."

"Do I now?" His little head jerk and a grin. "Ree-Ro thinks I'm pretty."

I climbed into the big comfortable king-sized bed. "I suppose I'll allow you to call me Ree-Ro since you seem *unable* to follow the rules."

"Good, I canna abide by callin' ye Karrie, it daena sound like the girl I grew up with. Does anyone else call ye Ree-Ro?"

I pulled the covers over me. "No, no one else does." The

sheets were too tight so I kicked my legs to get the bottom to loosen up.

Finch said, "Are ye strugglin' in there?"

"Yes, stupid covers." I got settled and could see him moving around the outer room. "I didn't know you had so many tattoos."

He chuckled. "Part of the uniform."

He went into the bathroom to get ready for bed. When he returned he turned out all the lights, leaving a bit of ambient glow coming in through the window. He climbed onto the sofa-bed causing the springs to squeak.

I giggled. "Sounds comfortable."

I could see the side of his face as he stared at the ceiling, not knowing I could see him. I lay with my head on the pillow, unable to look away — the edges of his face, angles and planes, shades of light and darkness.

He said, from his room, "Can we sit together, like we used tae? I winna try anythin', promise, I just wondered if I might hold ye."

I paused for a moment. "You won't try anything?"

"We sat taegether for hours when I was a teen and I never tried anythin'."

I chuckled. "You totally tried things, you tried *everything*... you were just a big bundle of trying things."

He laughed. "Aye, tis true, but now I winna try tae kiss ye on yer neck the way ye like, or run m'hand up yer shirt the way ye canna resist, and I definitely winna kiss yer—"

"Finch, you stop that."

He chuckled. "I am all grown up and I ken better than any of that. And m'back hurts on this forsaken bed. I have an injury, ye ken?"

"Yeah, I remember reading about it in the news. You fell on stage?"

"Aye, the amp wasna bolted down right."

My heart led and I said, "Okay, sure, you can come here, if you promise not to try anything. Nothing at all."

Without a word he climbed from the sofa, dragging a couple of pillows along as he padded into the room. He casually scratched his stomach under his t-shirt, exposing just a smidgen of sexy rock-star abs. I pulled the covers up higher.

He climbed into bed and propped the pillows up behind him, like he used to do, and I wiggled up, to curl up alongside him, my right arm wrapped along his left arm. He entwined his fingers in mine.

His hand was warm and strong and touching him made me feel breathless. "It doesn't mean anything, you know?"

"Aye, I ken... I... there were many nights in college when this was the only way I could sleep. It was comfortable."

I yawned and nestled my cheek against his shoulder. He was right, it was very comfortable.

"Remember when we would sit like this studying for finals?"

"Aye, I remember."

My breathing slowed. I began to drift away, and then I felt it — he pressed his lips against my hairline, and held them there, breathing me in.

STUPID CUDDLING

Karrie

I rose slowly from sleep, becoming aware, first, of the light in the room; second, I was sleeping on my side; third, face pressed into the pillow; fourth, drool down my cheek; and then fifth, a weight on my legs. I moved my arm to glance down. Finch's head was on my hip, his arm thrown across my thighs. Oh.

He was so comfortable and warm and familiar and his shoulders wide and he was vulnerable and sleeping, on me, wrapped around me.

He had promised not to try anything.

And this was everything.

A phone buzzed, I reached for it and tipped it toward my face, without thinking, because that's what normal people did:

1.Check the phone.

2.Glance at the text.

3.Realize it's not my phone.

Too late because I had already seen the text from Jasmine:

```
Hi babe,
when will you be back?
```

My stomach sank. *What was I doing?*

I quietly placed the phone back on the nightstand and stealthily pulled my legs from under him, barely dislodging him. He smacked his lips, turned and, nestling his face into a pillow, went back to sleep. I crept up, grabbed my phone, stuffed it in my coat pocket, put on my coat, and left the room.

I speed-walked to the elevator.

As I pressed the button, Finch emerged from his room, his hair totally tousled, he looked dazed having just woken up. "Ree-Ro, wait up!" He jogged toward me.

I pushed the button. "Why? I um... I need to go... I need to—"

He pulled up in front of me. "Come on, let me drive ye home, give me a minute, I..." He checked where his pockets would be if he was wearing pants with pockets. "Shite, now I have tae go get a room key and... then I'll drive ye home."

I shook my head and jammed my finger on the button again. "I'll call an Uber, this was... this was a *huge* mistake. I'm sorry, Finch, but we need to forget this happened and—" The door slid open and I stepped in, leaving him there, open-mouthed in the hall. "I wish you the best with Arlo, I hope you get to see him today."

He looked completely confused. I pushed the button for the lobby and stepped back while the doors closed, cutting off my view of him.

I kinda felt like a dick, because he would have to wait for an elevator to return to get his room key. But you know what, Mister I-won't-try-anything-but-cuddling-you-to-sleep? You're on your own.

Stupid cuddling.

God I hated him so much.

THAT WAS IN THE PAST

Karrie

When I walked into my house, Tessa had just come down for coffee, and mouthed, "Did you spend the night with Finch?"

"No, I mean, yes, in his hotel, but not *with* with him."

Mom walked in. "Where are you...? Have you been out...? Out with Finch?"

Dad walked in. "With Finch Mac? The chap from the argument yesterday? The one you called dastardly and evil? The one you've been furious with for six years? That seems unlikely." He pulled an egg carton from the fridge.

I smoothed down my hair and poured a cup of coffee. "He has a very big hotel suite, with *rooms*, and he asked me to stay. He slept on the um... the pullout sofa, and I wasn't there... I mean it was not out of friendship or... you know... anything, but out of pity. It was a pity thing. Like a night nurse."

Tessa giggled. "I bet you were night-nursing him."

Mom bit her lips to cover a laugh "Tessa! Your sister was *not* night-nursing him. She doesn't have a nursing license."

She and Tessa cracked up.

"Very funny. You want to have a go, Dad?"

"No, I'm just confused, we're talking about *Finch* Finch? The fella with the guitar? The one who you said you hated with the explosion of a hundred stars?"

Mom patted me on the shoulder. "Sorry dear, this is all just so unexpected."

I sipped from my coffee and huffed. "It's not unexpected. You would sit at someone's bedside if they went through the trauma of the police not letting them see their son. You would hold their hand — I was comforting him."

Tessa chuckled. "I *bet* you were comforting him. Did you fluff his pillows?"

Dad covered his ears. "La-la-la, can't hear you."

I shook my head but I was feeling more relaxed since being home.

But then there was a quick knock and the mudroom door opened. Howard rushed in, tail wagging.

Mom smiled, overly brightly. "That will be Finch, I invited him to come for coffee this morning before church!"

My eyes went wide as I heard him in the mudroom stamping the snow off his boots and rustling as he hung his coat. He entered the kitchen, sheepishly, wearing a suit. "Sorry, I would have given ye a ride if ye would've waited."

I looked away. "I wanted to get back earlier."

They started making a cup of coffee for Finch and I ducked out to get ready.

I came down a while later, as quickly ready for church as I could be, wearing a knit mini-dress in a bold beige and black Argyle pattern with red details and a white collar. I was wearing red sweater-tights with it.

Mom was making eggs, but stopped still and looked me over. "That is spectacular, you are a knockout! Is it Burberry?"

"Yes."

"No one will be able to take their eyes off you."

I blushed. "Finch will be there, no one will notice me."

"Well, the people who love you will notice. Your father and Finch went down to look at a sword Finch loaned your father a few months ago. Will you tell them breakfast is ready?"

I went down to Dad's writing office where he and Finch were holding two ends of a long heavy broadsword. Finch was saying, "...see the markings here? I am told it's m'family's crest, there is a D and a roman numeral I. There is a crown — have ye seen it afore?"

"No, and I was searching for its provenance." Dad added, "I appreciate your letting me hold onto it... are you sure you don't want it back?"

"Nae, I leant it tae ye, it's safer here than anywhere. It's been passed down through m'great-great-grandfather, tae m'father, and m'mum passed it tae me. I canna keep it in m'hotel rooms, seems a sight better tae store it with a historian of the Scots." Finch glanced up noticing me in the doorway.

Dad followed his eyes. "Well, aren't you a beauty?"

I blushed again. "Mom said breakfast is ready."

Finch ran his hand through his hair, looking nervous.

Dad returned the sword to its spot on the wall. He had piles of books on every surface, the broadsword and a couple of smaller swords on the wall, a few locked chests stacked on a table, and some glass-topped cases with fancy jewels and small artifacts inside.

I said, "I hadn't realized you added so much to your collection."

He proudly beamed at it. "I'm becoming one of the premiere historians of the time period, things keep coming to me, estate sales, friends of the family."

Finch said, "M'mum has loads, I'll bring more next time I go tae Scotland."

I said, "You're going to need museum cases and humidity controls." They followed me up the stairs.

We ate breakfast around the table, discussing the events of the night before. None of us knew what was going on with Arlo today, but Mom was able to remind Finch of some of the details. He said, "I was too upset tae listen tae the officer, I canna remember what was said."

He took a big bite of a pile of eggs on toast. "I promised Arlo I would see him last night, how's he goin' tae trust me after all that carryin' on in the yard?" He sipped from his coffee mug.

Mom said, "I could go try to see him, to tell him that—"

Tessa said, "Mom, that's not going to work. Sheryl hates you. You'll end up with a restraining order like Finch."

Finch said, "One at a time the whole Munro family would end up with a restrainin' order."

Mom shrugged. "I don't relish the idea, but someone ought to go over and see if the boy is al—"

I said, "I'll go."

Everyone turned their focus to me.

"Yeah, I'll go. I'll um... I'll take flowers for Sheryl when we get back from church. I haven't paid my respects. I didn't speak to her the other day."

Finch said, with the jerk of his head. "She'll slam the door in your face. You're the root of all her troubles."

"True, but that was in the past. She's probably forgotten how much she hates me since she's focusing on you and Mom now. It can't hurt. Besides, if she does call the police I'm fast, I'll wear my running shoes. I know the secret paths away from her house. I heard Alison explain the escape routes enough times."

AFTER ALL THESE YEARS

Karrie

We all piled in Dad's car and drove to church. The whole time it was like being in a dream — here was my family life, my mom, dad, sister, in our family car, driving from our family home, with one of the world's biggest rock stars inserted into the middle of it.

It was odd really, as we climbed in Dad's eight-year-old SUV, and pulled out of the driveway past Finch's Tesla. Mom put us 'kids' in the back and Tessa sat between us, but I could see Finch's expensive pants stretched across his knees. He wore a different suit from the funeral, this one blue instead of black.

Tessa pushed at my parka. "You are gigantic," she teased.

"I am not, I am properly ratio-ed, big coat, little dress, big boots, tight leggings, check any style guide."

She said, "You can't even wear your hat in the car or you'll get a neck-crick."

I joked, "Mo-om, Tessa is being mean."

Tessa said, "Mo-om, Karrie is being too puffy, and Finch's shoulders are too wide. I'm uncomfortable."

Finch joked, "I canna get any smaller, I am doin' the best I can in this wee car."

Tessa teased, "Dad, Finch's head is too big for your old SUV."

Dad joked, "You kids stop arguing or I'm pulling the car over."

We drove for a few moments, the familiar route to church through town. I glanced at Finch and caught him watching me. He glanced away.

We climbed from the SUV into the freezing cold. Dad and Finch were both wearing long overcoats and it was beginning to sleet as we rushed, slipping and sliding on the sidewalk, up to the church — the rest of the congregation was already inside. We took off our coats and hung them in the coatroom while Mom and Dad briefly spoke to a few people they knew, then we followed them down the aisle to their pew.

Everyone turned to check out Finch, a collective intake of breath at the sight of him, whispering, heads turning, everyone in the church, even the little old ladies couldn't take their eyes off him

I made sure to put Tessa in between me and Finch and settled into my seat and looked around the church at the soaring ceiling and stained glass. I had expected it to seem foreign to be back here, but it seemed familiar even after all these years.

Then Mrs Hart and the choir stood and began to sing. I felt Finch's eyes resting on me but I purposely ignored him. This was what he used to do, bug me in church, to see if he could break me and make me laugh.

He leaned across Tessa to whisper to me, "Remember when we used tae sing this song?"

I nodded, without taking my eyes off the choir.

He whispered, "We were better, they arna singin' it right."

I whispered, "Shhhhh." They hit a high note and not very well.

I bit my lip to keep from giggling.

He said, "I am going tae have tae climb over the pew, run up there, and take over, but Ree-Ro said she winna sing with me — how can I go all by m'self with nae support?"

After the chorus had sung two songs, there was a prayer, and then Mrs Hart waved toward us.

Finch mouthed, "Who me?"

She said to the congregation, "I have asked Finch Mac and Karrie Munro to sing for us and they have graciously agreed." She started clapping and gestured for us to come up.

He looked at me as he stood, "Ye canna make me do it alone, tis unfair."

"Fine, but you're a monster."

Heat rose on my cheeks as I stood, straightened my dress, and began shuffling past everyone on the pew, glancing behind to make sure Finch hadn't deserted me. The whispering rose as the full congregation realized this was indeed Finch Mac and he was about to join their choir.

He pushed his hair from his eyes and grinned and raised a hand to wave.

Mrs Hart sent us to the front of the choir.

We discussed which song, choosing "I Need Thee Every Hour", a piece that was made for a duet.

I whispered, "I haven't sung this in so long."

Finch said, "Aye, me either, if we go down in flames at least we will go down taegether."

And then the pianist began to play, and we both stood in front of the choir, without practicing, and sang.

I rested my hands on the sheet music, my finger trailing on the page so I wouldn't lose my spot, but it came back to me, this piece, with Finch's voice, rising and following mine, a counter melody that met my voice and by the end of the song I was watching the sheet music less and looking out over the audience more and glancing at Finch as our voices rose together.

And then we came to the end.

There was a very large applause and Mrs Hart hugged us

both. Then we awkwardly crept back to the pew for the last of the service.

In the foyer after the service, Finch was quickly surrounded by a crush of people all wanting to speak with him, to ask for his autograph, or photos, so I scooted away to stand beside my parents. Mom said it had been gorgeous as she dabbed at her eyes.

Finch met my eyes across the foyer, and here was the thing, there had always been this feeling with him, a certainty, a way that when I looked up his eyes would meet mine, and it was still happening, even after all these years.

HOW WILL I SURVIVE

Finch

My eyes met her's across the church foyer, over the heads of the crush of fans, she had the high flush she used tae always get when she sang, a way that she tilted her head, kept her eyes cast down, twas a contrast tae her voice, which had always been so lovely, lifted tae the heavens. Her voice had faded from my memory through the years. I was glad that it was in my mind once more.

I only had two recordings of her on m'phone, the first — a voicemail she had left me, when I had a meetin' with a venue manager about havin' a show. She had said, "Finch, I wanted you to know that you got this... don't forget to breathe, are you breathing? In and out, if you pass out from not breathing I will be so mad, it's literally the most important thing and you've been doing it since the day you were born. Do you need me to call to remind you?" Then she added, "I love you, call me when you get the gig."

The second was a video, she was singing "Party in the USA" and laughing as she did.

I had moved the recordings from phone tae phone through the years, the second tae remember the moment: Her parents had been gone for the day and we had snuck intae her room. It had been our first time havin' sex, fraught with embarrassment and fumbling moves. We had been planning it for weeks and thinking about it too much, nae talking about it enough. I was horribly fast.

I lay on the bed with her wrapped in my arms, warm and breathless. I ran my fingers down her shoulder, and had said, "That was fun."

She lifted her head and put her chin on m'chest and said, "It was, it was also very very weird."

"I like ye, I think if we do that every day it winna be as weird, I think it will get even more fun."

She grinned. "I don't know how we will get my parents out of the house every day."

"How will I survive? Now I hae had a taste I think I will need tae do it all the time, tis nae fair."

She laughed. "You'll just have to remember it."

"I canna remember it, I was so nervous I think I blacked out," I laughed.

"Then I need to give you something to remember it by. Give me your phone."

She held it up and snapped a photo of us, our faces were tight in the frame, she had a high color in her cheeks, her hair a mess, ye could tell we were naked because her shoulder was bare. "It's a good photo, but I will remember the moment best if ye sing." I turned on the video camera and put it near her face and she started singing, slow, as if it was a love song...

MALICIOUS MISBEHAVIOR

Karrie

After church, after dropping everyone off at our house, Tessa and I ran some errands to prepare for our mission: See Arlo.

Tessa pulled her car up in front of Sheryl's house, and I took off my seatbelt, and said, "Flowers, check. Gift envelope, check." I looked up at the house. "Courage, check. I probably have courage… but man, she has always scared me."

"Yeah, she's such a nightmare, angry drunk, abusive, was she on other drugs too?"

"I think so, but Mom would never say."

Tessa said, "And now, one hundred percent, she wants custody so she can live off Finch's money. Getting revenge on Mom is an extra added benefit for her, I bet."

I said, "Yeah, you're right about that."

She said, "And we're lucky Mom always dealt with her. We should definitely buy Mom something special."

"Yeah."

"But for now, focus on Arlo."

I got out of the car, walked up to the porch, like a big puffy snowman on a mission, and rang the doorbell.

Alison's sister, Angie, yanked the door open. "What are you doing here?"

"I um, came to see—"

"Mom! That bitch Karrie is here!" She turned away from the door so I took a step forward, getting one giant fur boot onto the door jamb.

Sheryl came around the corner, carrying a whisky glass filled with an amber liquid and ice. "Karrie, who? Oh. What do you want?" She looked unsteady on her feet.

"I um..." I slid my boot forward and shifted my weight so I was basically in their house. "I brought you flowers for your loss." I shoved the flowers forward. I could hear the tv going loudly in a back room. I would need to speak louder.

Sheryl said, "It's cold, you need to get out of my house so we can close the door."

Angie started pushing the door closed.

"I brought you a gift, too." I pushed forward the flowers, and a gift-envelope with a cash bribe inside, and stoppered that damn door with my elbow.

Sheryl came closer to the door. "I don't want anything from you, you and your meddlesome mother. She's always interfering in my life, with my children, the bitch stole Alison from me—"

Angie tapped her foot. "Uh huh, she sure did."

"So I want you out of here before I call the police. Go on, get out of here."

"You're slurring, I can hear it. You're not supposed to be drinking. I want to see Arlo."

Sheryl was forcefully pushing the door closed.

I yelled, "Arlo! Arlo!"

Angie said, "That's it, I'm calling the police!" I saw her dial her phone.

Arlo came into the hallway. The door was closing on the bouquet of flowers. My eyes met Arlo's and I had no idea what to say, so I yelled, "Your dad says he loves you!" Then because that didn't seem like enough, I sang, "Next thing you know, Arlo go low low low..."

From behind me the sound of a loud pneumatic 'Phewp!' and

through the crack in the door above my head a bright orange glove flew end over end into the house.

The door slammed on the bouquet crushing the stems. I yanked them free, shearing all the blooms off — left holding a bunch of stems.

I turned around to see Tessa holding the t-shirt launcher, and wearing a broad smile. "I didn't have a t-shirt, so I sent one of my gloves."

I said, "Well that went well."

She laughed, "We nailed that."

We raced to the car, jumped in, and pulled our seatbelts on, right as a police car pulled up behind our car. The siren sounded, whoot, whoot.

The officer came up to our car window, leaned in, and said, "There's been a lot of activity around this house this weekend... You're related to Finch Mac in some way? He's not allowed on the premises and he's not allowed to make contact."

"We're friends of the family," I said, and held up the stems that I was still holding. "I was trying to deliver flowers, and um, a monetary gift. They slammed the door on me. We're still shocked."

"She called in that there was a projectile shot in through the front door?"

Tessa said, "I shot a mitten in with a t-shirt launcher, it was... um... a family joke."

I added, "There's a custody battle. We came to see if we could check on the little boy. I think she's been drinking, can you send an officer in?"

He went back to his car to call it all in while we waited.

He returned twenty minutes later and handed Tessa a ticket.

She stared down at it, blinking. I glanced over her shoulder to read the details. She was charged with Malicious Misbehavior. She would have to go to court. The officer told us that if he caught us on her property again we would be arrested and taken to the jailhouse.

He left us after saying, "Finch Mac has a case on Monday, right? You know him?"

I nodded.

"Man, I love his latest album. Tell him good luck in court." He strode back to his car, climbed in, and drove away. Tessa backed us out of the driveway.

I REMEMBER HOW TAE LATE-NIGHT LEAVE

Karrie

Mom met us at the door. "Seriously! The t-shirt launcher?"

"Yep, it was brilliant... I don't know, I suddenly remembered I had it in the trunk of my car, and then when Karrie was on the front stoop I thought, 'Why not shoot something into the house?' I thought it would make a good message for Arlo since it was his mom's t-shirt launcher. I realized I didn't have any t-shirts so I decided to send my glove—"

She held up her hands, one in an orange glove, the other bare.

Finch said, "I'll buy ye ten pair in all the colors."

She arched her hand. "I shot it right in, over Karrie's head."

"Then Sheryl slammed the door on me, cutting off the bouquet." I held out the stems.

Mom took the stems, found a vase, filled it with water, and dropped them in. "It's symbolic."

Dad said, "It's weird, is what it is."

I dropped my coat off in the mudroom, pulled off my boots, and went and sat down at the kitchen table. "I managed to keep the money I planned to give her as a bribe, so that's a win."

Tessa and I high-fived each other again.

Finch asked, "It's okay, she already has plenty of money, I send it every month. Did ye see Arlo?"

"Yeah, I saw him, briefly. I yelled, 'Your dad loves you!' And then sang, 'Arlo go low low low,' or something, I was under extreme duress."

Finch chuckled. "No, that's perfect, just right." He scrubbed his hand up and down on his face. "So tomorrow I go to court. I need to make some calls." He stood with his phone in his hand.

Mom asked, "Will you stay for dinner?"

His eyes met mine.

I nodded.

He said, "I need tae go tae m'room tae change, but I would like that, thank ye, Lydia."

As soon as he left Mom said, "So maybe I need you to explain the rules to me again. You hate him with a seething fury?"

"A white hot rage of an exploding star."

Dad said, "That's an improvement, it was a thousand exploding stars or something, right? One versus a thousand has to be better."

I said, "Depends on how big the star is."

Mom said, "But you can be in the same room with him, you will help him, you can spend the night in his hotel?"

"What's going on is that I'm past the 'hate' now. I can be in the same room with him *now* because I don't care about him at all. I can help because I'm a nice person."

Tessa said, "So it's like the golden rule, you're just being charitable?"

I said, "Exactly."

She raised her brow. "I was being facetious."

"Fine, if it's so confusing, tomorrow I'll go back to never seeing him again."

"But tonight, because you already agreed he could come to dinner...?"

I sighed. "He probably hasn't had a home-cooked meal in a while."

Tessa joked, "So tonight you'll make sure he gets well fed, tomorrow you go back to hating him?"

I said, "Have you always had this kind of smart lip?"

Mom, Dad, and Tessa all said, "Yep."

"So when do you leave for your tour?" I asked at dinner.

Finch said, "I need to leave by this coming Saturday, rehearsals start the following Monday, sharp. The tour begins two weeks later."

I asked, "Where are the rehearsals?"

He said, "Sadly, they're scheduled for Vegas. The first leg of the tour begins there and then moves tae the West Coast. It's goin' tae be complicated."

I said, "I was hoping you'd say Orono so you'd be nearby."

"Nae, I winna be nearby."

We ate a big meal and then went down to the rumpus room for hot cocoa in front of the fireplace. I curled up on one side of the couch and Finch sat on the other with Howard between us. Finch was petting Howard, his hands brushing along my blanket-covered legs giving me a bit of a thrill every time. But I hated him, so scratch that, not a thrill, an *unease*.

I tried to understand what I was feeling and decided to define it as: Karrie hadn't had a man in a really long time so this terrible, horrible person was distracting me. It had been months since I had gone out with a regular guy and this was Finch, hot in all the ways I loved — wait, not 'loved,' *desired*.

He was so hot: His dark hair curled around his neck, his rough beard, big biceps, his wide shoulders that stretched the black shirt he was wearing. A silver chain around his neck accentuated the tendons down the side, the planes and angles on his strong jaw, the face that looked like a Greek statue, until he smiled and turned it into a different hotness, the funny, friendly sort of hotness.

The scent of him, his what — cologne? Mixed with smoke from the hearth was nothing short of *potent*.

I watched the tendons and muscles that bound his hands, his grip strong and purposeful. He wore a few leather bracelets, and some chunky silver rings that added to the effect.

He was full of intention. Reflection. His eyes direct.

He stood to move to the fire.

But I was overly warm, thank you very much.

He was wearing vertical striped pants, flared at the bottom, designer, black and white, and they really made his ass look so freaking hot — I flushed thinking about what was under there, last night when his form, his manly, perfect form, had been wrapped around me.

He crouched and built up the fire with a new log, then stood and turned, brushed off his hands, met my eyes and grinned,

Oh god that grin just for me... I glanced away. What had I been thinking about? Oh, right, these marshmallows were delicious. The cocoa was top-notch.

He returned to his seat on the end of the couch but there was a feeling, like he had shifted a bit, a hair's breadth closer.

Cheater.

He promised not to try anything and here he was, moving in, *trying*.

But then the warmth enveloped me. My fingers combing through Howard's fur, my father told us a story about his life pre-children, and Tessa had her laptop out, "Just doing homework, but no big deal, keep going Dad." Mom was painting one of her paper towel holders on a small table. I fished another marshmallow out of my cocoa and popped it in my mouth, but then felt Finch's eyes on me, hard.

The night was full of long lingering glances and uncomfortable too-closenesses.

We played Finch's playlist on Spotify and along with every band he had an anecdotal story, a long crazy tale about meeting the musicians and what they were like. Mom asked a million questions, and it was a really great evening — then Dad yawned.

"I'm sorry everyone, I'm going to head to bed. Last night I was up worrying about mayhem in the night and today worrying about my daughter and her arrest for malicious misbehavior."

Tessa folded up the laptop. "It was a misdemeanor, Dad, a ticket. I'll be fine."

He pretended to wipe his eyes, "My baby's first brush with the law, so, so proud."

Tessa cocked her head. "Are you, Dad? Cause that's kinda bad parenting."

"It was for a good cause, and it's a great story. You launched a bright orange glove into a house, we ought to write an epic poem that we recite on the anniversary."

He stood, "You coming, dear?"

Mom dropped her brush into water. "Yes, I'm exhausted." To Finch she said, "We have the guest room if you need it."

"Thank you, Lydia, but I'll go back to the hotel, I want to be fresh tomorrow. I meet first with the lawyer and then he's going to accompany me to the courthouse."

Dad said, "You have a suit?"

Finch said, "Aye, Joe."

I asked, "Why do you ask, Dad? You've seen him in three suits!"

"Oh yes, I suppose you're right, that's just the traditional question — an elder, on hearing a young man must go to court, should ask, 'Do you have a good suit?' I have somehow become the wizened elder in this scenario."

"Phew, I thought you were offering to loan him one of yours."

"I have one suit for church, and it would be way too short."

I rolled my eyes. "Also, beyond fit, Finch's suits are probably very expensive, he wears designer suits."

Dad said, "Well la-di-da, I've never worn designer in my life, unless you count the art your mother painted on the back of my leather jacket."

I said, "Actually that is sort of designer."

Mom said, "You don't wear designer because you don't need to — you don't have millions of young women ogling your buttocks up on a stage."

Dad laughed as they went up the stairs. "Do young women really ogle Finch's butt?"

We could hear Mom teasing, "It's half the point of rock and roll, you're not so old, you remember."

Tessa stood and tucked the laptop and books under her arm. "Good night..." She stopped at the end of the couch. "But wait...." She narrowed her eyes. "Do you need a chaperone? I will stay down here if you want me to..."

I said, "You can go to bed."

It was just me, Howard, and Finch and a crackling fire. I concentrated on the mug of cocoa feeling the heat rise in my cheeks as I realized he was watching me, his elbow on the arm of the couch, leaned comfortably, his gaze leveled.

I met his eyes.

He jerked his head back, ever so slightly, "Remember how yer mum and dad used tae go up tae their room at night, just like that, and they would leave us down here?" His eyes sparkled.

"Boy do I, them was fun times."

"I used tae try how far under yer shirt I could go knowin' yer dad could come down the stairs and bust me, it was exhilaratin'."

"I remember. They *trusted* us." I teased, "It was so cruel of them."

He chuckled. "If they had said, Finch go on up tae Ree-Ro's

bedroom, I might have collapsed on the floor, a chill runnin' through me. I wouldna been able tae do anythin'."

I chuckled too, but then my face fell, thinking about how fresh and trusting I had been, and...

He said, "I'm sorry tae mention it, I was just rememberin' and there is a fondness in the memories. I miss those days when we were new tae the world and in love with each other, ye ken?"

"I do know, but..." I put down the mug and yawned. "I think I need to go to bed."

He stood. "Howard, it was good sittin' on the couch with ye, old man. On another night I might stay over and keep ye warm on the couch like I used tae years ago afore yer gray hair, but now I have a date with a judge t'morrow. I canna have dog fur all over me."

The whole time he spoke Howard cocked his head back and forth as if he were really listening.

I stood up. "Actually I think Howard can sleep with me and keep me warm. It's getting cold tonight. I'm an LA girl, these temps are cra-zy."

Finch looked at me, "...An LA girl? I daena think so, Karrie, I have met LA girls they are no'nearly as interestin'."

"Thank you." I moved to the stairs and he followed me up to the kitchen.

I said to Howard, "As long as you promise not to bark, right Howard? No random barking in the night. Mom and Dad are used to it, they can sleep through it, but I can't."

His tail wagged.

I said to Finch, "Let yourself out, don't forget to lock up."

"I remember how tae late-night-leave the house of Joe and Lydia Munro, g'night, Ree-Ro."

UNEMPLOYED

Karrie

Brushing my teeth for bed, thinking about LA, I texted Blakely:

Hey boss!
How was the premiere?

There were three dots for longer than I was comfortable. I spit toothpaste and drank some tap water.

Then her text:

It was perfect,
everything went really well,
the reviews have been great.

I texted back:
That is great.
Saw your man showed up.
He's hot!

I rubbed a mascara remover on my lashes while I waited.
She returned with a happy emoji.

Then:

```
He swept me off my feet.
It's been an amazing
couple of days.
Thank you for everything you did to help me
get ready.
Jess is taking all the credit
I know it was mostly you.
```

I sat there for a long time trying to figure out how to ask what I needed to know, but then I finally just wrote:

```
                                So, I need to ask,
                            do I still have a job?
```

Then I couldn't take my eyes away from the three dots as they moved on the screen. Finally, this text:

```
Things are a little crazy
right now
while I figure this out,
the short answer is: yes. Probably.
But just do what you need to do there,
take all the time you need.
```

Great.

Take all the time I need? I had a dog and an apartment three thousand miles away. Take all the time I needed?

I sighed.

I had gone from signaling that I had moved on, that I didn't think about him at all, that I had a fabulous life, to being unemployed, to living in my childhood bedroom.

And somehow spending *way* too much time with him.

That was going to stop, right now.

I rubbed a washcloth over my face, splashed water to rinse it, and patted dry in a towel.

Tomorrow was a new day and it would not, absolutely not be a day focused around Finch.

A TEENY WEENY LITTLE BIT OF WHY

Karrie

I found Tessa waiting for me on my bed with Howard beside her.

"Hi, you, whatcha need?"

"Something going on with you and Finch?"

I balked. "Me and Finch? No, absolutely not, no way. What... what would make you think...?"

"Um, the spending the night with him last night, singing at church with him this morning, helping him today with Arlo, the long lingering glances, the bright red cheeks, the stammering right now, all of it." She waved her hands in a circle. "All the all of it, your face hasn't been a normal color all day. You keep saying you hate him but there is nothing about you that makes me think it's true."

I rubbed my face and smoothed back my hair, attempting to look normal. "Ugh, great, but no, not at all, you don't need to worry about—"

"You think I'm worried about it?"

"Of course. You're not? Wait... is this because you're a fan? You want something to happen because he's a rock star?"

"I'll have you know that since Alison went into the hospital he's practically a part of the family — he loves Mom and vice versa and, *whatever,* if this was about being a fan I wouldn't need you. He's already over here all the time."

"True. So..." I huffed, "what's your point?"

"You seem happy, or not happy really, but more like content, I don't know, I always thought you two were going to be together, but then you weren't. And we kept seeing him, or Arlo, or Alison, but not you, and it was really sad around here because of that, and even when I saw you it seemed like you were the broken half of yourself."

I put my hand on my hip. "Are you literally saying that he completes me, that I am broken without him?"

"I am repeating all the endless things you used to say about him: 'I'm going to love him forever and ever,' and, 'I'm going to marry him,' or, 'we are family.' Sound familiar?"

"Yeah, it sounds familiar. But first, no, there is nothing going on with me and Finch beyond becoming comfortable with being in the same room with each other. You and Alison urged me to be comfortable with it, so I'm working on it. And Finch and I are different people now so..."

She said, "Here's a direct quote," she made her voice higher, "'I want to grow up with him, we will *always* be the same.'"

I rolled my eyes and slumped onto the bed. "You can't hold that against me. I was young. I was naive. I loved him with all my heart, *past tense*. Now I suffer him. And we can be in the same room together. This is a good thing." I rolled on my side and slung my arm across her lap. Howard licked my face. "But I love you and I'm proud of how you turned out. You're awesome. Even when you're kinda being a dick — can you stop being a dick? Maybe tell me something super immature about yourself so I won't feel so embarrassed about being the kind of person who needs to be lectured all the time."

"Well, let's see... Okay..." She looked sheepish. "Probably a teeny weeny little bit of why I'm being pushy *is* because Finch is a hot rock star and I would have so, so, so, so very much street cred if he was hooked up with my older sister."

I laughed. "I *knew* it."

She said, "It's totally different from 'he's a friend of the family'. If he's dating my *sister* it would make me kinda desirable too." She pulled the bedcovers over us, and we kept our voices quiet because Mom and Dad were asleep,

"And you like Mitchell, that's who you're dating?"

She sighed. "I do, but I wonder... is there someone better? I don't want to decide too young, you know?"

I said, "I totally know, you're talking to the queen of 'too young'. What do you like about him?"

"He adores me. He makes me laugh. He wants to make me happy."

"Those are all pretty great, how about your feelings for him?"

"I think I love him, scratch that, I know I love him."

I grinned. "Really? My little sister loves Mitchell?"

She nodded.

I said, "Now I wish I had been nicer."

"That's okay, he gets it, he knows. Everyone takes your side in it." She added, "Even Finch."

Oh.

She said, "I gotta go to bed."

"Yeah me too, we have to be busy tomorrow while Finch is in court. I hope it goes okay."

She said, "Not me, I have class, senior year, almost Finals Week."

"Oh! I forgot, you should get some sleep! But this was fun."

"It was, I'm really glad you're home."

UNTENABLE

Karrie

In the morning I texted Finch:

Good morning.
I really hope your day goes well.

He texted back:
Thank you.

Then he texted:
Now I'm 4 for 4
with the Munro Family.

Oh, did we all text you?

Aye.

He sent a gif of a dancing monkey that made me laugh.

Then we waited for news.

Dad wrote in his office.

I helped Mom with her website and her social media while she worked on one of her new projects.

Tessa went to classes.

We ate our meals and puttered around.

Then I got a text around 5:30, the night already dark.

Finch:
`Are ye at home?`

Me:
`Yes, are you done?`

Finch:
`Aye,`
`on my way.`

We all stood around the kitchen waiting for him to arrive.

When he blustered into the mudroom, Mom asked, "What happened?"

Howard jumped on him trying to get his attention.

He stood there, wearing his snow clothes, wet and bedraggled — his face fell and he began to cry.

Mom said, "Oh, honey!" She wrapped him in her arms and we all kind of backed out of the room so that Mom could comfort Finch about whatever had happened in court.

Finally he emerged from the mudroom and slumped into a chair at the table with his boots and coat still on, his hat in his hand.

I asked, "So what happened?"

He met my eyes. "I got visitation rights. The judge kent I was tae go on a world tour, he kent m'situation would be untenable, it's the word he used tae me — untenable. He allowed me tae see Arlo today, I have just seen him in the visitation room of the court. And when I am home from the tour I am allowed visits."

He tapped the table. "I am his father, but I am tae be his visitin' relative? I will only get tae see him on holidays? *That* is 'untenable.'"

My mother patted his hand. "I am so sorry."

"I'm goin' tae be dealin' with that woman his whole life."

Mom said, "We will help, we'll do anything to help. I have a file, I will go to court, we can..."

His red-rimmed eyes were locked on me.

"Ree-Ro, can we go for a drink? Just... I daena ken, tae the pub, just tae talk?"

"Oh um... sure."

I stood. He stood. He was already dressed for the weather. I on the other hand had to layer up with a sweater, tug on furry boots, put on my big white coat, my tall white hat and my mittens, while he stood distractedly waiting, flapping his hat against his other hand. Once I was ready he tugged his hat onto his head and holding the door open, we called, "Bye!" and then went out into the night.

AN IMPOSSIBLE PROBLEM

Karrie

He drove me to McLoonie's.

He let me out and parked and then, because I hadn't been sure where to sit with a world-famous rock star, I waited for him right inside the door.

He waved at the bartender, pointed at the back table, and ignored all the patrons who had turned to watch, whisper, and film as we wove through the pub. Finch whispered, "Daena look at them, once someone makes eye-contact they'll all rush me."

The table was a booth that partially blocked him from the view of the room, but as Finch hung his overcoat and suit jacket on the peg beside it, a young man approached. "Hey, Finch Mac, I am a *huge* fan, I like, totally can't believe I saw you here, can I get a photo?"

"Sure."

Finch put his arm around the kid, and smiled while I took their photo, then, by the time we were done, three more people had gathered around the table. Finch signed autographs and posed for more photos, until the bartender headed over to disperse the fans. Finch stood and announced, "Thank ye kindly for making me feel so welcome, but I am havin' a private conversation — a round is on me."

A cheer went up and Finch sat down. "That ought tae hold them."

He ran his hand through his hair, loosened his tie, and unbuttoned the top button of his collar as he ordered us two beers. It was an incredibly hot move, but that wasn't why we were here — we were not here to objectify him, but to help him with this distressing business.

And he was very distressed.

He sat looking at me across the space, elbows on the table, hands folded, pointer fingers pressed against his lips, I knew all of this, noticed it, because he was intense, and his stare was constant, pressing, and lengthy, plenty of time for me to squirm and note his position.

He looked like he had something to say but didn't know where to begin. He opened his mouth, then closed it, narrowed his eyes and then shook his head, then opened his mouth, but stopped himself.

I sighed.

And it broke the tension.

"I need ye tae marry me."

I nervously laughed. "What the...?"

He picked at something invisible on the table. "I need ye tae marry me."

"I heard you the first time, and my response is still 'what the...?' Because that is the only response that makes sense."

He chewed his lip.

I narrowed my eyes. "*Seriously?*"

"I have never been more serious about anythin' in my life, I need ye tae marry me. M'lawyer said as much, he said—"

"Your lawyer told you to go get married on your way home from court? That doesn't sound like a very good lawyer."

"It wasna like that — he said that I would have done better in court if I had been married. He said..." Finch made his voice higher, "'Well, Mr Mac, it's the best we could do when ye daena have a wife or a home tae speak of.' I have a home! I have a home in Scotland. I also have a home in New York. And I can buy a home wherever else I want. Ye ken all that. But I canna prove tae the judge that I can *make* a home, no' when I am away on tour. M'only option is tae leave Arlo here. Now, because I canna make a home for Arlo, I have tae ask Sheryl for permission tae see Arlo, and ye ken, Karrie, that she is going tae make m'life miserable."

"I know."

"And yer mum could help, she told me she would take Arlo whenever she could. She helped Alison all the time, though this would be different — I would be gone for weeks at a time. It's a great deal tae ask, but she daena have any connection tae Arlo. There is nae case tae be made for her tae have custody, or even visitation, and there is nae reasoning with Sheryl. She will fight yer mother, she winna want tae give Arlo over, even for visits. It's a mess."

"Mom always regretted not legally fighting for custody of Alison, she could have fostered her. Then this wouldn't be an issue."

"Aye, she regrets it verra much. She tells me all the time, but it inna helpful, I need solutions, no 'what ifs...' Sheryl is Arlo's grandmother, she lives here. The judge sees her as a stable presence in his life."

"That is a nightmare—"

A waitress came up, blushing. "I'm a huge fan, huge huge fan, can I get you an appetizer?"

She never even looked at me, even when I ordered mozzarella sticks. Finch ordered us sliders and fries.

As soon as she left, I asked, "Alison didn't have a will? Or instructions saying who should have Arlo?"

"Aye, she had one, but they arna abidin' by it! " He leaned forward. "See, Ree-Ro, this is why marryin' ye is a good idea. Alison wanted Arlo tae be with me, but Sheryl has stepped in and was helping Alison and Arlo in the final months while I was away. He has a room there, it looks verra regular, and because I have a reputation, the judge daena believe I am 'regular' enough. The judge is ignoring Alison's wishes and my own parental rights, because he canna ignore that I am goin' tae be on a world tour for the next nine months. If he gives me custody who would care for Arlo while I am on tour?"

I was chewing my lip now. "So your lawyer said if you were married it would be better...?"

"Aye, all but said it, but like most normal people m'lawyer dinna ken I had someone in m'life who might be willing tae help by marrying me."

I shook my head. "Literally two days ago I was still wondering if I could ever *tentatively* trust you again and now you want me to marry you? You must think I'm the biggest idiot in the world."

He scowled. "I daena think ye're an idjit, no'at all."

I shook my head. "This is too big. I want to help, but this is too much, I... There must be some other way. Isn't there someone else you could marry or who—"

He winced. "Och! Karrie Munro is goin' tae recommend that Finch Mac marry some random woman? Ye're bein' unreasonable."

"Unreasonable! I'm not the one saying we ought to marry out of the—"

Our food was delivered to the table. The waitress flirtatiously flipped her hair and laughed about nothing at all. It would have been hilarious if I hadn't been totally freaking out.

When she left, Finch said, "Either ye are being unreasonable or yer hatred of me has made ye cruel."

"You think me cruel?'

He pushed his plate away. "This conversation is gettin' too far away from us..."

I said, "Yes, but also, you think I'm cruel?"

"Nae, but I think ye have lost sight of me, of yer life, yer family, and ye are so set on makin' me pay for what I did that ye are losin' sight of what is important. Please give me the benefit of the doubt, I had a shite day, and I am tryin' tae solve an impossible problem, and Arlo is important."

"Fine, yes, you're right, Arlo is the most important. Let's just, for one moment, think of all the, must be, *millions* of other ideas."

I pulled two mozzarella sticks onto my plate and a slider. "How long is your tour?"

"Nine months."

"Oh. And downtime?"

"I begin with shows in Vegas, then a couple of weeks down for Christmas, then, beginnin' in January, I have shows continuously until May. A few days off here and there, but most weekends are booked solid in different parts of the country."

"Oh, and then you get a break in May?"

"We have a wee bit of time afore the next leg, the European part of the tour over the summer."

"Wow, that's a lot." I exhaled. "So if there were no judge involved, and you could do whatever you wanted with Arlo, let's just say, what would you do?"

"His mother just died, I... I think he needs somethin' stable... I daena ken... I canna bring him on tour with me. It would be long hours in a hotel. I would have tae hire someone tae care for him and who would I trust? He ought tae stay here in his school... I canna take him tae Scotland, he has only met m'mum once. I guess if I had m'way, if it were just up tae me tae decide, I would ask yer mum tae take him in while I was gone."

"Oh. And she would probably do it, but... I mean, she is running a business. I don't think she wants to be a full-time mom again. She'll do it, but it's a lot to ask."

"Aye." He popped a jalapeño popper in his mouth and chewed and swallowed. "I am between a rock and a hard place."

"Keeping in mind that no idea is a bad idea — can you postpone your tour until this is figured out?"

"I have already postponed dates. I pushed it back because of Alison's treatments, tae be here for Arlo. This tour is a huge enterprise, it brings in millions of dollars, and employs many people, I canna just let them down."

"You're right, this is an impossible problem." I glanced around the restaurant. Two different people had their phones up, facing us, probably photographing us, but pretending not to be. How did he ever get used to this?

He followed my eyes to the table closest. The girl dropped the phone and pretended to be talking about something else.

He said, "And one of the issues is tae hire someone tae care for Arlo, I would have tae trust them. I canna trust many people. Ye ken — ye are wondering if ye can trust me and ye have known me for years. We grew up taegether. Ye are wondering, though I have been tae yer house, I love yer family, I am a part of yer life, but I am tae look out on all the strangers in the world and pick someone and trust them? It is..." He shook his head.

"I can see it. I can see how difficult it is."

"The only solution is tae allow Sheryl tae watch over him."

"And that is an awful thing. I really thought she would have gotten treatment, or turned her life around by now."

"Alison's sister is worse, and she has a new boyfriend who has been hanging around. He is a piece of shite. Do ye remember Kyle? He was two years above us in school?"

"Juvie Kyle? She's dating *Juvie* Kyle?"

"Aye."

IT IS NO' A GAME

Karrie

We looked at each other while the bartender sent over two more beers and the waitress refilled our waters.

He did that little jerk of his head — ugh he was such a player, but also, he had once been the love of my life, and Alison had asked me to help him. He needed me, and Arlo needed me. He said, "Ye can think on it as a business decision if ye want. I ken ye hae a job—"

I shook my head.

"Ye daena hae a job, Ree-Ro? I thought ye had an important career and—"

"I didn't want to admit it, I don't have a job right now. It's all..."

"So ye are between things, that's good, daena ye see? — I will give ye everything ye need, a house, wherever ye want. Ye would be m'business partner. Ye tell me what ye want, I will do it for ye."

"And what do I do in return?"

He shrugged. "Ye go tae court with me and we tell the judge that ye are goin' tae pick m'son up from school every day and give him a warm dinner at night and tuck him in tae sleep."

My chin trembled. "When you put it that way it really does seem the least I can—"

Right then another older woman came up to the table. "I'm so sorry, I know you're in conversation, I just wanted you to know what a big fan I am, I love your music so much."

Finch said, "Thank ye, kindly."

"You're welcome, I saw you in Boston, two years ago..." She leaned on the table as if she was getting comfortable.

I concentrated on eating my slider and blinking to keep from crying, but still had to wipe my tears.

The woman never even noticed, she finally returned to her own table.

I put down my burger and wiped my hands on my napkin. "My parents are going to think I've gone insane to even consider this."

"I daena ken why. I ken they want ye tae be safe and happy, but I believe they value forgiveness and a good redemption story more than they care about yer revenge hate of me."

"I don't revenge hate you."

"Good. And if ye think about it, ye are still the girl who promised me she would marry me." He gave me a sad smile. "What's it been, Ree-Ro, about fourteen years?"

"Yeah, when I was twelve we made some crazy pledge to get married." I picked up a mozzarella stick and dragged it through the marinara sauce.

He narrowed his eyes. "But it wasna quite like that, was it, Ree-Ro? It began when ye were twelve years old, but it went on and on, we were goin' tae be married every day for years, for *years* we promised each other. It was planned out even when we went tae college taegether. Ye canna ignore the fact that we promised tae do it and now I need ye tae keep that promise and... it's poetic."

I chuckled. "Poetic doesn't usually include business arrangements."

"This is true." He raised his beer and tilted it toward me.

We sat staring at each other for a long long time.

Occasionally taking bites of our food.

Finally, I said, "I know this is going to sound weird, but who is Jasmine?"

"Who... what, *Jasmine?*"

"The other morning I saw she texted you. I just... I need to talk about the particulars of marrying each other. Are we going to have an open relationship? If it's just business, am I to be like the nanny? I mean, that's fine, right? This is just business, I just need to know all the particulars."

"Och, do ye hear yerself? Yer a fine distance from the girl who used tae love me so that she would never be so rational."

I raised my chin, "Who is Jasmine?"

"Jasmine is m'housekeeper. She is the sister of my drummer. She stays at m'house when I am away and takes care of m'things. In case ye read one of her comments, she inna anyone but a friend, but she always calls me 'Babe.' It's her nickname for me. I am no' seein' anyone."

"What about the models — you had someone on your lap. One of the TMZ photos had a model." I snapped my fingers. "I can't remember her name. She was hugging you."

"The most recent photo of a girl in m'lap was a fan photo. Some barely clothed girl asked if she could take a photo, I said, 'Aye,' and she sat down right on m'lap. And the model, Zoey A, was huggin' me because I had just told her about Alison. We used tae date, now we are just friends. M'last girlfriend was Maya Morgan. We broke up because we disagreed on everything, that was about a year ago. I went out with some women since. I slept with some, none that I saw a second time."

"Oh, that's very forthcoming. Not sure how I think about all of that. So... Remember how when you had shows you used to get so hot for me, you would rush off the stage and we would find the closest place and just go to town and... Do you do um... *that*? I mean, are there groupies — do I have to worry about it?"

"Nae, Ree-Ro, ye ken, when I used tae get so hot for ye, after the show, it wasna the 'show' — it was you, backstage waitin' for me. And I was young and new tae performin'. If I had tae fuck every time I left the stage I would be a mess. It's nae how it works—"

"But if we marry, and it's a business relationship, will you be, um... seeing other people?"

His jaw clenched. "Nae. Whether we marry for love or business, tis a contract. A promise, I winna break it." He exhaled. "I winna do it tae ye, Ree-Ro, I promise."

"Because I felt like such a fool, and this would be like... so bad... I would be a fool on the world's stage. It would break me. We need... you have to promise that you would always be honest."

He leaned forward and took my hand in both of his. "Ye are no' a fool. Ye are the love of m'life. If ye bestowed on me a second chance I wouldna squander it, Ree-Ro, I hae lived without ye, I daena want tae be without ye anymore."

I rubbed my thumb along his knuckles, the strength held there in his hands. Then I pulled my hand from his. "But that's not what this is, right? This is *business*. Because I'm not there on the whole 'love of your life.' We barely know each other." I added, "Anymore."

He leaned back in his chair. "Aye, tis true, Ree-Ro, but won't we have fun gettin' tae know each other again?"

I shook my head. "No, and this is a really good point, we are practically strangers!"

"But we arna strangers."

"But let's be honest, tell me one thing about yourself, now that you've grown so very old—"

"I'm no' that old."

"So *very* old, tell me something that I might not like about you."

He picked at the edge of his napkin. "I think if it is possible, I might have a much bigger opinion of m'self than I used tae."

"Oh really," I teased, "is that because of the stadium shows?"

"Aye, and the cameras always pointin' m'way."

"That would do it."

"How have ye changed? Something that I winna like."

"Well... I don't know... oh, how about this, I never listen to Finch Mac's music, and I make people turn it off if I'm in the room."

He put his hand on his heart. "Och, ye are a terrible person."

I grinned.

He said, "But the good thing is, yer 'thing I daena like' might help bring down m'opinion of m'self — ye will like that." He smiled and then jerked his head back. "Yer missin' out though, since most of m'songs are about ye."

I shook my head. "I don't believe you."

"It's true! Daena worry, I will show ye."

I sighed. "What are you thinking, Finch? This is crazy."

He shrugged. "I daena ken what I am thinkin', I was drivin' home from court and this idea formed, I daena ken anythin'."

My eyes went wide. "Would we *sleep* together?"

"I just want ye tae marry me, we will figure out the rest. I mean — I think ye got confused about it when I said it was a business decision. I dinna mean it was tae be like a job. I meant ye ought tae think about the business side of it, but I daena want ye tae think it is *only* about business. It is more than that. We ought tae get married because we always meant tae. It's a business decision but I believe it is also important."

"This is not one bit how I imagined it when I first thought about us getting married."

"Ye thought we were going tae begin at the beginnin' but we arna at the beginnin' anymore. We are older and wiser and there is a wee braw boy who needs us. This is far different from how ye imagined, but it might be better."

"I had such little girl dreams of romance and—"

He stood up from the booth, causing a stir and commotion from the surrounding tables. He took my hand and pulled me up to standing, facing him, and then he knelt down on one knee and took my hand.

There were at least four phones aimed at us.

"Finch, you don't need to—"

"Aye, I do, I canna let the moment pass us by, Ree-Ro."

He looked up earnestly into my eyes. "We have a chance within us tae do this over, tae fix what I broke so many years ago, and I ken it is a great deal tae ask that ye no'only forgive me but that ye help me pick up the pieces of what I broke, but I must ask ye, because I need ye... I truly need ye, and Arlo needs ye, and... Will ye marry me, Ree-Ro?"

I stared down into his eyes, looking there for proof and promise and certainty, finding the eyes of my Finch looking up at me from inside the depth of the past years — he was familiar and family.

I nodded. "Yes, Finch, I will marry you."

He stood and hugged me and fellow customers all around the pub cheered.

We didn't kiss.

We sat down and finished our meals. I felt dazed. "Are we really doing this?"

He answered, "Aye," the most comforting of his words.

Then having paid the bill, which was very high since he bought rounds of drinks for everyone in the pub, he said, "We ought tae get our story straight for yer parents."

"Och," I joked, "I forgot about m'parents."

He grinned.

I glanced at my phone, checking the time. "They're probably still up, waiting for news."

"Can I be there tae tell them my side of it?"

"Of course. It will definitely take two of us to get them to understand. And *another* thing, if we're going to do this, from a business perspective, to get custody of Arlo, we need to make it public and very family-friendly — by the way, that getting down on your knees thing was very smart. This is what you need from a public relations point of view."

"Ye are goin' tae be m'public relations management?"

"Well, so far you haven't been managing your public relations very well."

"M'persona is a drunken belligerent rock star, I think I have managed it verra well."

"Now you're going for the persona of father and family man, from this moment."

He nodded, and we slid out from the booth and pulled on our coats, hats, and gloves. A few fans approached but Finch shook his head, and a woman from a corner table called out, "Finch Mac, did you ask her to marry you?"

Finch said, "Aye, I did, and she has agreed tae it. I am a lucky man."

I whispered, "Well done you're a master at the game."

He held the door for me. "Ree-Ro, it is no'a game, it is the truth."

The cold hit me in the face as we left the pub.

STICKY

Karrie

My mother and father and Tessa were downstairs in the rumpus room.

When we arrived downstairs, the show they were watching, *Brooklyn 99*, was paused. Mom asked, "What's going on?"

I got settled on the couch with Howard beside me, and said, "I'm going to marry Finch."

My mother's eyes went wide.

Tessa clapped, then squealed, covering her mouth.

Dad said, "Jesus, are we time traveling? It's like we've gone back — you were twelve years old, standing here in the middle of the rumpus room." He made his voice high, "'Dad, I'm going to marry Finch.' You sounded crazy then too."

"Very funny, Dad, I know how it sounds, but we talked it—"

Finch said, "Sir—"

Dad's brow went up. "Who me? I'm 'sir' now? Okay, interesting take, but I'll allow it."

"...I got down on my knee in the pub and asked her tae marry me."

Tessa squealed again.

"...Ye can imagine, she had reservations, but we have

discussed them and we ken it is what we need, what we um... want tae do."

My mother's eyes went even bigger. "Karrie! This goes against everything you have stated for years and reiterated just a few hours ago — you do not have any positive feelings toward Finch. You were adamant. And now he's using 'we'? Did he brainwash you? Are you joining his cult?"

I stood up. "Mom! You love Finch!"

"Of course I do, but you're my daughter! You swore you were never going to involve yourself with him again, then you go to a pub for what...?" She looked at her phone. "Ninety minutes and now you're going to get married to him? I need a better explanation than: 'We decided.'"

Finch and I looked at each other.

I said, "It's a business decision. It's for Arlo. Finch's lawyer told him that if he had had a wife, a stable home, he might have gotten custody."

Mom said, "Marriage has to be much more than a business decision."

I said, "Not really, not in most of the world, there are millions of people who get married for business arrangements."

Mom said, "But *you* were going to marry for love."

"I was going to marry Finch for love, now I'm going to marry him for business. It's still Finch, at least I'm consistent." I grinned.

Mom threw her hands up in the air and turned to Dad. "What are we supposed to do about this cockamamie story?"

Dad had his arms crossed, his mouth resting on his hand. "I have no idea. They're being ridiculous. You can't build a marriage or a lifelong business arrangement on a ninety minute negotiation."

I rolled my eyes. "We are right here. We can hear you talking about us."

Mom said, "Karrie, marriage isn't to be entered into lightly, this is before God, an oath before God. It's bigger than... anything, but it would help Arlo?"

I gulped. "Yes, we'll marry tomorrow, then Finch will have a new court date. He'll get custody, and then when Finch goes on his tour I will be the one responsible for Arlo. You'll get to see him every day."

She said to my dad, "I do like the sound of that."

Then she returned to looking at me, "But you didn't answer about the other stuff. The most important part, the oath before—"

Finch joined me standing, still wearing his dress pants and his dress shirt with the loosened tie. He said, "Mr and Mrs Munro, I have been in love with Karrie since I was young lad. I ken it's no'traditional, it's no'the usual way, but I have always loved her. I need her tae help me gain custody of Arlo, but I also want tae marry her because I love her, and will always strive tae make her happy."

I watched his face the whole time, he looked really really earnest.

I drew my eyes from Finch to my parents who looked shocked.

Mom said, "Well shit, this is unexpected." She huffed. "Karrie, do you love Finch?"

I swallowed down the lump in my throat. "I think I have loved him my whole life, I hated him for a while there too, and now I'm kinda confused about the whole thing, but also... we have a time constraint, and..." I glanced at Finch's face, his jaw clenched, color rising on his cheeks. "I think I can..." I exhaled again. "I think that when I was young and I decided to marry Finch, I was naive and believed that my life was just going to be a big happily ever after. But marriages are hard work and so I think that's what I'm saying... I married Finch in my heart a long time ago and then I stopped working on it, because he... but... I've decided to work on my marriage."

Mom gave me a sad frown. "Marriages don't usually start with 'working on them,' marriages can be long and — can you both sit down? I feel like I'm lecturing you and you are two grown-ass people who don't need to ask us for permission for anything."

I said, "This is true. Why didn't we just elope?"

Finch and I sat down on the couch, dislodging Howard who stood, turned a sleepy circle, and then plopped down with his head on Finch's dress pants.

Mom shook her head. "Thank heavens you didn't elope, I might have had to cut you out of my life."

Dad said, "Ha! You'd only be able to cut her out of your life for what, twenty minutes?"

She said, "Probably, though that might be too long. Empty threats aside, to continue, marriages take a lot of work. There are ups and downs and though I dearly, constantly, love your father, there have been long stretches where I am irritated by his whole..." she waved her hand around in a circle, "vibe."

"Right back at you, my love," said Dad. "And I think, insults aside, usually when someone decides to marry we want them to be way up high on love, like at the tip top of the high dive of love, springing even higher, spring, spring, then deep diving into the endless morass of marriage."

He waved a finger at Tessa, "Are you writing that down? Someone write that down. I'm adding that to my philosophy book: *Talking to You People About Reality*."

I said, "But Dad, you both just admitted that there are highs and lows in every marriage, plus, you said that years ago I stood here and told you that I was going to marry Finch. I wasn't allowed to marry him then—"

"Thankfully!" said Mom.

"...But, let's say I did, let's say I was..." I turned to Finch. "Remember our oath?"

"Aye, I told ye that I was goin' tae marry ye and ye told me that ye were mine always."

My mother rolled her eyes.

"...So, if you think about it, maybe we are just in one of our low periods, it's not really fair to judge a whole twelve years of marriage on our low period."

"Your low period has had you living apart, hating each other, for six years."

Finch said, "I never hated her."

"Well, my dear, she hated you."

I said, "...While this may be true, if a married couple decides to work on their marriage who are you to tell them not to? Isn't marriage forever?" My face grew hot with all the eyes on me, especially Finch's.

I said, "Another point, did I tell you that Alison asked me to? I mean, she didn't tell me to marry him, but she asked me to forgive him and to help him. She was right, I need to...because... I don't know, it's hard to put into words..."

I folded my arms and huffed, thinking. "When I stopped coming home I had to convince myself that it was for righteous reasons. One of the things I told myself was that I didn't want to be stuck. Stuck in a small town, stuck in a messy family, stuck about people that hurt me, and, I'm sorry to say, stuck like you, Mom, stuck helping everyone and putting your needs last, so I left and I've been living a fabulous life in LA, basically alone, and unstuck. But I think what's come to me is that you aren't stuck, you're the glue. You glue us all together, including Alison and her son, and therefore Finch and me and Tessa and Dad, and all the people who buy your art and... people count on you. And you're the glue that holds it all together and I don't know... I think I really want to stop being unstuck and I'd like to try my hand at being proper glue for once. Like you."

I wiped my eyes. "I want to step up and help Finch keep his son. For Arlo, and Alison, and you, because you have done it for me, and for Finch, because I made an oath that I would always love him. Forever. That's why I'm marrying him, because of an oath I made to be glue, and I can't say today how I feel about him, because I need a little time, but I can keep my oath anyway."

Mom frown smiled. “That was really beautiful, my love. You think I’m glue?”

“I know you’re glue, you’re the stickiest glue in the world.”

“Damn it, now you made me cry!” She put out her arms and I crossed the room to sit on the couch and be held by my mom.

Dad picked up a box of Kleenex and passed it to Mom. “Now you’re all sticky.”

She blew her nose. “It’s my kids, they make me all kinds of sticky, it’s terrible.”

Tessa said, “Now I need to get in there!” She climbed onto Mom’s lap too so that we were all hugging. Howard climbed off the couch, crossed the room, and jumped awkwardly onto us.

Dad said, “Well we are a big pile of Munros—”

Mom said, “Poor Finch, all by himself over there.”

I kissed Mom on the cheek. “See what you do? Always worrying about other people when this was specifically your hug.”

She dabbed at her eyes with a tissue. “True, I do do that.”

Dad teased, “You said do-do.”

And Tessa giggled like she used to when she was three and Dad made that joke for the first time.

AND NOW LOOK!

Karrie

I climbed off the pile and went back to the couch and called Howard over to sit between me and Finch. I joked to Finch. "We were wrong, that wasn't hard at all."

He laughed.

Mom said, "Well, I suppose your father and I are giving you our blessing, not that you needed it, but I will help, whatever you need."

Dad nodded, then clapped his hands together. "So we get to keep the rock star in the family? This is awesome news. Do I get an automatic invite to the Grammy awards? Or does it depend on how nice my tux is?"

Mom laughed. "You would wear a tux?"

"Heck yeah, if I were invited to an award show? I'd be in a black tux with a satin cummerbund and the ruffled shirt, you know the kind, a little velvety? — so fast it would make your head spin."

We all laughed.

I said, "Tessa, how do you feel about this?"

"Besides all the other stuff, can I meet Billie Eilish?"

Finch said, "Ye ken Finch Mac, but ye want tae meet Billie?"

"She's much more famous than you."

He chuckled. "I'll see what I can do."

Mom said, "Besides all that, what is the practical side of this — when do you get married?"

Finch and I both said, "Tomorrow," at the same time.

Finch finished, "Then I will call m'lawyer and ask tae have a new hearin' in front of the judge. That might take a while, but..."

Mom said to me, "And that's another thing, my love, are you *sure* you're ready to not only take on being a stepmother to Arlo, but you'll have to deal with Sheryl, plus court custody battles, this is a lot to take on."

"Yeah, I'm ready." I joked, "I'm jumping off the high dive into the swimming pool of responsibility glue. Splash!"

She said, "Don't drown."

"I won't."

Finch said, "Besides, I'm certified in CPR."

Dad said, "Well that was a perfect, well-timed husband joke, I think these kids are going to be all right."

We sat for a moment, then Finch said, "Tessa, do ye still have the old guitar?"

"Yes! Are you going to play?"

He said, "Aye, I wanted tae prove a point."

Tessa ran up the steps.

I said, "What are you...?"

"Ye will see."

Tessa returned with an acoustic guitar. Finch perched on the edge of the couch and tuned it for a moment. It gave me a thrill to watch him, the way he focused on the strings, his lashes on his cheeks, his brow drawn in concentration. Then he paused his hands, before he began to play. Four notes in, Tessa clapped, "I love this one!"

He played without singing, humming a bit, until he sang, "... *ye told me once there was naethin' that I couldna do... ye told me twice there was naethin' tae keep me from you...* and it goes on," he continued playing while he said, "do ye remember, Ree-Ro, when ye told me that? We were in our meetin' place over in the woods and I had just played ye my first song."

"I do, I remember that."

"How about this one..." He began playing another tune, humming along, then sang, "...findin' ye in forever... losin' ye in the night..."

Tessa said, "Wait, that's from your album, *Playground*, I love that song too."

He kept playing a bit longer, then changed to a third tune, more upbeat, and hummed for a moment, then sang, "*...the bright blue yarn, punk tee, shag carpet, soft skin, hair twisted round m'fingers...*"

Tessa's eyes went wide. "Wait, is that about..." She looked around the room. "Is that about this room?" She said, "Are those songs about Karrie?"

"Aye." He jerked his head back at me, "Did I prove m'point?"

"Those songs are really about me?"

"Ye ought tae have been listening, I was singin' tae ye all these years."

"Wow, that is very..."

He grinned and put down the guitar.

Mom looked at her phone. "If the show is over... Look at the time! We have a wedding tomorrow! I declare bedtime!"

She gestured for Dad and Tessa to go up, and asked, "Are you going to spend the night in...um... the guest room, Finch?"

Dad laughed, "Nice how you worked that."

He said, "I ought tae spend the night at m'hotel, it's bad luck tae see the bride, as ye ken, and I have a few things tae handle in the mornin'."

"All right, goodnight Finch, I'm pleased you're joining the family, *officially*."

They all climbed the stairs.

Finch and I faced forward on the couch, side by side, with Howard sitting between us.

And for some unknown reason I burst into tears.

"Och, why are ye cryin'?"

"Because I just... I don't know! I think... that was really hard and I feel so overwhelmed by it all."

He turned to face me on the couch and took my hand and frowned. "I'm sorry Ree-Ro, it has been a lot tae put on yer shoulders."

I looked deep into his blue eyes, my sight blurry with tears. He reached over Howard, and pushed a strand of hair from my eyes. He clasped my hand, his finger stroked back and forth on my knuckles, his body weight on my legs as he leaned close.

My mother came down the stairs, "My apologies! I forgot something!"

We stayed in the position but I laughed through my tears. "Remember when she used to do that all the time, forget things so she could come down and check we weren't making out?"

She laughed. "I *used* to do that, but this time I honestly forgot something. And..." she put her hands on her hips. "Honestly seeing you like this is really assuaging my worries. I'm really looking forward to..." She got another tissue and dabbed her eyes again. "Seeing you two together, married, I don't think I've ever been happier," she sobbed.

Then she added, "And Arlo will really be my grandson — just like that! A grandmother! At fifty!"

Finch and I laughed. He said, "Aye, just like that ye are a grandmother."

"That is just the best news." She sobbed again.

Dad's voice called down from upstairs. "Honey, are you bothering them?"

"No! I'm just standing here crying!"

To us she said, "Love you both," and jogged up the stairs.

He trailed his fingers along my cheek. "Are ye still overwhelmed?"

"More so."

"Are ye second guessin' our decision?"

I shook my head. “No, not at all.”

I ran my thumb down the side of his face. “It’s scratchy. I remember when your cheek was so soft. And then your first beard. And I remember going into the drugstore to buy you shaving cream when we were in college together. I’ve known you for so long.”

“Ye met me when I was just a boy.” He pressed forward and gave me a kiss, my cheeks wet, it was my Finch’s lips pressed to mine, the weight of him along my body, on the couch of my childhood home. He was heavy, present, insistent, real, a breath between us — and then he pulled away...

He ran his hands through his hair and said, “I ought tae go tae m’hotel.”

I nodded.

He stood up, checking his pocket for his keys and phone. “Tomorrow ye will marry me, Ree-Ro?”

“Yes.”

“Tomorrow ye will become Arlo’s step-mum?”

“Yes.”

“Ye have made me a verra happy man.” Then he climbed the steps, two at a time and a few moments later I heard him leave through the mudroom.

I looked down at Howard. “I blame you, I was perfectly happy visiting, but no, you had to sit on my legs like you missed me. You drew me in and got me involved and now look! I’m getting married to Finch Mac!” He raised his head and his tail wagged.

I scratched his head. “I know. You’re happy because we get to keep him.”

JUST TO HEAR YOU SAY YES

Karrie

Finch wasn't around all morning. I called the courthouse for an appointment to get our license, and planned that we would meet after lunch. We decided all of this by text.

But then, midmorning, I called him.

"Hi."

"Hi Ree-Ro, I was just thinkin' about ye."

"Were you?"

"Aye."

"Sometimes I think I ask you questions just to hear you say yes to me."

"Aye, I ken ye do."

I smiled into the phone.

"I called because I needed to tell you something."

"What?"

"I forgot to tell you that I have a wee little dog. His name is Zippy, and he's a total jerk but I love him a lot and he's so cute... I'm sorry I didn't mention him, I hope he's not a deal breaker."

He scoffed. "I'm goin' tae be yer husband but I might say, 'never mind' because ye hae the cutest of the dogs? Is he very wee?"

“He is so wee. Mom embroidered a sweater for him with Big Fat Jerk on it.”

“He sounds perfect, he daena break the deal.”

“Are we really doing this?”

He chuckled. “Aye, we are doin’ this, we might be the two most daft people in the world.”

“I agree, we barely know each other, totally daft, who does this?”

He asked, “When was the last time ye hated me?”

“I don’t know, like a day and a half ago? When was the last time you thought I might forgive you?”

“Like six years ago?”

“We are such a mess.”

“I kissed ye though.”

“That you did... that was...”

“Was what...?”

“Really nice.”

“I thought so too, verra braw. I will kiss ye again at our wedding.”

“Promise?”

“Aye.”

“I got you to say it again.”

He chuckled.

I said, “Are we making a mistake?”

“Nae, Ree-Ro, I said it before and I will say it again, I have made many mistakes but lovin’ ye is no’ one of them.”

“Thank you. I’ll see you at the courthouse at one o’clock sharp.”

“See ye then.”

WILL YOU HOLD MY HAND?

Karrie

For my dress Mom and I picked a blue, vintage, tea-dress that had been my great-grandmother's and had been stored for decades in Mom's closet. I looked down. It was too busty. "Once again my lack of breasts is totally disappointing."

Mom clutched and folded the back. "How about... hold on, let me get my sewing kit."

She returned a few minutes later and put stitches up the back of the dress while I was wearing it. Then she cut the thread, and stood back, cocked her head, and appraised her work. "It looks great, truly beautiful, but you can't take it off. You should take these scissors in your purse so Finch can cut the stitches to get the dress off you tonight."

I moaned. "That seems unlucky on a wedding night."

She laughed. "I've wondered... you once told me that you and Finch were going to save yourselves for marriage, when did you finally...?"

I grinned. "We managed to wait until senior year. We were so freaking horny for each other."

Mom laughed.

She said, "I used to see it in his eyes, he's always been desperate for you." She put the thread and needle back in her kit. "I'm seeing that look in him again, desperation, I think the stitches will slow him down. You'll thank me later."

I muttered, "None of this is applicable, it's business."

She raised her brow. "Sure, of course it is, but whether you sleep with him or sleep alone, you'll want to take it off to put on your pajamas."

I nodded, looking in the mirror. "Yes, I'll take the scissors. But just to change into pajamas, because this is totally a business arrangement."

Dad drove to the courthouse, Mom beside him, me and Tessa in the backseat. I muttered, "You people like living like this? It's freezing! It's absolutely ridiculous."

Dad looked at me through the rear-view mirror. "You nervous?"

"Why should I be nervous, because I'm marrying a dude I barely know, a guy I've hated for years, and becoming a stepmom in the middle of a custody battle? Oh and I probably don't have a job anymore? That why?"

He said, "Yeah, for all those reasons."

"I'm not nervous at all, this is great." I smoothed back my hair. I was wearing the gigantic bright white parka, which finally made sense going to a wedding. My hair was smooshed under my fur hat, but Tessa had a bag of brushes, mirrors, hairspray, and emergency makeup with her. We pulled up in front of the courthouse.

Dad said, "There he is."

Finch was standing on the steps, in his dark suit, a long overcoat, looking incredibly handsome. He was surrounded by about eight people all asking for photos, but when he saw our car pull up, he jogged down to meet us.

Dad said, "This is where you get out, we'll meet you at the church."

I couldn't hear him over the roar in my ears, panic overtaking my brain. I just sat there, my hand on the door handle.

Finch opened the door and leaned in. "Ye ready, Ree-Ro?"

"I'm.... I'm kinda freaking out."

He crouched down and held my hands.

"What's happenin'?" He pushed a bit of my hair back from my cheek. "Ye scared?"

I nodded.

He clutched both my hands in his. "Are ye too scared tae marry me, or too scared tae take the next step tae walk up the stairs beside me?"

I said, "The second one, I think..."

He said, "I daena think it will be that frightenin' if ye think of it in steps. We are only goin' tae go up tae the office tae get our license. Ye daena have tae be scared of it. It'll be a bureaucratic nightmare, but it winna be scary. Then I will drive ye tae the church and Pastor Simon, ye have known him since ye were wee, he is goin' tae marry us. Yer family will be in the church. How can ye be scared of it?"

I nodded.

"And ye can change yer mind at any time, ye can, I winna hold it against ye, but I want ye tae ken that I will do everythin' in m'power tae make this work, so that when ye look back on this day ye winna have regret; ye will remember it as our first day, a good day. I will do m'best."

I said, "I won't change my mind, have you met me? I always do what I say I'm going to do... case in point... this."

"Aye, ye are resolute, unyielding, and loyal." He leaned forward and kissed me, his warm lips pressed against mine. Then he pulled away. "I also believe ye ought tae follow yer heart."

I nodded.

Dad said, "This is very sweet, but it's also freezing with the car door open."

Tessa said, "Dad, she's having a panic attack."

"I know, everyone feels panic on their wedding day. I'm

supportive of all forms of being mental, I'm also supportive of heat."

Finch stood, and gently pulled my hand bringing me up out of the car.

He closed the door behind me. Then he looked down in my eyes. "How ye doin' Ree-Ro?"

"Better, but will you hold my hand?"

"Aye, the whole time."

We climbed the stairs, hand in hand, through a gathered crowd. Someone called out, "Hey Finch Mac, why are you going into city hall?"

I looked over my shoulder at no fewer than eight phones aimed at us.

He said, "Gettin' a marriage license," as he steered me into the building.

He was right, it wasn't too scary. All the employees were thrilled by his presence and helped us get what we needed, then soon enough we were in the backseat of his car, Mitchell driving us down the street to the church.

FINCH'S EYES ON ME

Karrie

We met my parents in one of the small rooms behind the chapel. Mom helped me out of my coat. "We get the main chapel for twenty minutes, as a favor to me, so I hope you don't mind that it will be fast..."

My attention shifted, because Finch was on the phone at the other side of the room. He was listening mostly, and I could tell from his stance, and his hand in his hair, that he was concentrating and distressed. By his voice I could tell he was talking to someone official, about Arlo.

I wandered over and stood beside him... He put out his arm and I wrapped around it, tucked my cheek to his shoulder and he kissed my hairline.

Then he said, "Aye, I understand, ye'll file the paperwork? Aye... I'll speak tae ye tomorrow."

He hung up and looked down at the phone. "M'lawyer has found out that the social worker — is that what they are called?"

I nodded.

He continued, "They visited Sheryl's house and have decided tae take Arlo from the home. M'lawyer said the judge will allow my new application in the mornin'."

My heart raced. "Where will Arlo be tonight?"

"He winna be removed until the mornin'."

Mom said, "Well, this is bullshit. Excuse me, my apologies." She brushed off Finch's shoulder and straightened his coat. "But you do not worry, he will be fine. The judge will be ready to listen in the morning and you will present all the new facts. I will go with you. I have a file folder I have been keeping for years, just for the record, but I will be breaking that out tomorrow. This is all going to be good."

She smiled. "But now, it's time for a wedding!"

Tessa sprayed a cloud of hairspray over me, and was brushing color on my cheeks and wiping concealer around my nose and making me stand still long enough to brush my brows and put some mascara on my lashes until I was made up like a bride, face-wise.

Mom pressed a multicolored bouquet in my hands. I lifted it to smell. It was lovely and fragrant. We did this all on one side of the room while Finch sat on the couch, turned away, on the other side of the room, until finally Tessa said, "I declare you perfect."

Mom and Dad and Tessa went to sit down with Mitchell in the chapel.

Finch asked, "Is it all right tae turn around?"

"Yes."

He came around the couch and just looked at me, and said, "Ye are such a beauty, Ree-Ro. I am relieved the boy I once was dinna ken ye would grow up like this, or he might have been too frightened tae speak tae ye."

"I'm glad you weren't too frightened."

"Aye, me too."

I looked down at my dress. "The dress is okay? I didn't have time to buy a new dress, a new white dress, though that was my dream when I was thirteen. I was planning to get married in a long white dress in a big wedding, with a veil over my face, and..."

"The dress is perfect, Ree-Ro, we will have an even better story, that ye dinna even have time for a wedding dress because ye were so selfless for Arlo, and instead ye wore a blue dress, m'favorite color, and ye were the most beautiful woman I have ever seen."

I smiled. "Thank you, Finch. I think that story might actually be better."

Then Finch and I walked into the chapel of the church where, when we were young, we had sung together, and we walked up to the altar. Halfway, under his breath, Finch said, "I dinna go tae church for five years, daena tell yer mum, and now I have been three times in a week."

"A funeral, singing in a choir, and a wedding, those are all big things, too. I haven't gone either, not in years, don't tell Mom."

"I was hopin' ye would remind me how tae do it."

"Neither of us have been married, we haven't rehearsed, I think we have to figure this out the hard way."

He said, "At least we are taegether."

Pastor Simon was waiting for us at the altar. We let go of each other's hands, and stood side by side, our arms a hair's breadth away, a tremble and sway in our stillness.

The scent of church was mingling with the fragrance of the bouquet and the scent of Finch's aftershave, a hint of sandalwood and leather.

I lost my focus for a moment, but the mingling scents calmed me and brought me back to the present. I wanted to pay attention, so I would remember — Pastor Simon welcoming us, the soaring ceiling, the echoing words. We lowered our heads and repeated a prayer, and then Finch, staring straight ahead at the minister, gave a very slight tug on my skirt. I dropped my right hand and found his, and his fingers entwined mine, and as the minister continued speaking, Finch and I held onto each other, for support and strength.

Then we turned to each other and repeated our vows. Finch's deep voice, promising to love and honor me until death do us part. I was surprised when he brought rings from his pocket and I trembled as I gave him my hand and he slid a gold band into place around my finger.

I was dazzled by that ring, and how its sudden appearance somehow made this all much more real.

I lifted my chin and promised Finch that I would love and honor him until death do us part and then pulled his hand to my chest and held it there, crying and trembling.

Finch said, "Ree-Ro, here is a ring for ye tae put on m'hand."

"Oh, really? You thought of it all?"

"Aye."

Mom rushed up with a tissue and took away my bouquet so I could dab at my eyes.

Tessa loudly whispered from her pew, "You're messing up your makeup."

Finch whispered over his shoulder, "Wheesht, we are tryin' tae be solemn." He handed me the ring and then held out his finger and I slid it over his knuckle into place. Then I clutched his hand to my heart again.

The minister said, "I now pronounce you husband and wife."

Tessa stood, cheering and applauding then looked at Mitchell, "What? Not allowed to clap? I've been literally waiting for this my whole life. You better get up and join me." Mitchell, Mom, and Dad stood up and joined Tessa in applause.

Our hands still holding each other Finch pulled me close and gave me a sweet kiss in front of the altar, a short one, a pressing but then... the edge of his lips against mine, he whispered, "Did ye just marry me, Ree-Ro?"

I laugh-cried because I was ridiculous and put my arms around his neck and whispered, "I promised I would."

And we were down the steps, leaving the altar, with Dad

saying a little bit too loudly, "This whole thing looks like a lot more than a business arrangement."

We had no plan.

We decided to go back to the pub; we knew they would help us have a little privacy and that, as Finch put it, "I can buy a round of drinks and pretend like everyone else at the pub are m'guests."

We had one big long table down the middle of McLoonie's and drinks were had and food ordered and conversations happened around the table about the wedding and other things. Tessa and Mitchell held hands and she smiled happily. It was mostly jovial and lighthearted, except, in the pauses, Finch's eyes were on me, and he grew quiet, seeming thoughtful.

I leaned in. "How are you?"

"I'm worried about Arlo." He reached out and tucked a piece of my hair behind my ear, his fingers lingering on my cheek.

"Me too, are you ready to leave?"

He said, "Once we sing—"

"Sing?"

"Aye, there is a microphone, there in the corner, do ye see? A stool for a musician, do ye think there is a guitar?"

I smiled.

He jerked his head back. "Will ye sing with me on our wedding day?"

It took a moment to get set up, then he and I were sitting on chairs in the corner and he was tuning a guitar. He said, into the microphone, "What will we sing, Ree-Ro?"

I leaned in and said, "Up to you, rock star."

He chuckled, then said to the guests, as he strummed the guitar. "M'wife, Ree-Ro has told me she daena listen tae m'songs, but I ken she is teasin' me. I think she remembers all the words tae m'first song because she helped me write it and I sang it tae her all the time. Do ye remember?"

I nodded. "Yes, I do."

He began to play his first song, the one that had made his career. *...I'm stan-din'... I'm staan-din'... I'm staannn-dinnn'... waitin' for ye tae come home...*

And I remembered every word.

When we were done with the song, after the applause died down, he said, "I wanted tae make a toast tae m'wife."

I blushed as he held up his beer. "Remember the first time I asked ye tae marry me, durin' PE class in eighth year?"

I teased, "I don't remember you asking me, I think I asked you."

He put down his beer and strummed the guitar. "Is that how it went, ye asked *me*? We were sittin' on the field, restin' after a run."

I leaned into the microphone. "And I said, 'We could get married, Finch...'"

"And I said, 'Aye, and we—' Och! Ye did ask me!" The audience laughed.

I said, "It was the most romantic of your 'ayes' — you agreed with me, it was a very lovely thing..."

His eyes gleamed in the dim light. "Whoever asked first, however we came tae be, Ree-Ro, ye were right, it was a verra lovely thing. Thank ye for suggestin' it many long years ago, and thank ye for agreein' tae finally do it."

He strummed a few more notes. "Ye are the most beautiful woman in the world, when I look at ye, from the first time I saw ye, tae now, I am breathless, how am I so lucky tae hae ye love me?"

I blushed and took a sip from my beer, then said, "Mr Mac, I truly believe you have this confused, how are you the lucky one?"

He shook his head slowly, strumming the strings of the guitar. "Yer forgiveness is a gift, Ree-Ro, I broke our hearts and ye are gluin' them back taegether. Ye are taking me and Arlo in and helping us become a family, ye are the beat of my heart. I am just a man who can play guitar, ye are the song."

I tear rolled down my cheek.

"That was so beautiful."

"I love ye, I canna wait for many long years lovin' ye."

Tessa called up, "Here's to Mr and Mrs Mac."

He raised his beer again and our guests raised their glasses and cheered.

He hugged me and kissed me. Then he said, "His forehead pressed tae my cheek. Ye ready tae go?"

BLOWING PAST BUSINESS

Karrie

Mitchell drove us to my house in Finch's Tesla and I ran in and packed a bag while Finch waited in the car, because I had mentally collided with the wedding and hadn't thought past it. Now I was sort of standing on the other side of the wall dazed about what had just happened, surprised to have ended up here.

I stuffed a t-shirt and sweatpants in a bag and looked down at the ring on my hand.

Wow.

Ree-Ro was married to Finch Mac. And this morning I was convinced it was a business arrangement, but now...

It felt like so much more.

I tossed toiletries into a case, shoved it into a larger bag, threw some more random clothes in on top, and looked around the room.

What the hell was I doing?

What did I need? I grabbed more socks for some unknown reason, a pair of heels, a bottle of perfume, ten different hair products.

Funny that when I was young and first thought I would marry Finch, I had a room full of photos of us together, but now... there wasn't a photo of him, no proof that young Finch existed except in my memories or tucked away in guest-room drawers.

This was grown up Finch.

I was going to a hotel room with my new husband.

I was so stressed I kind of thought I might faint.

But also... I said out loud, "Here you go, Karrie, this is all your dreams come true." I was packed, ready — I tossed the bag on my shoulder and left my childhood room.

In the car we were quiet. Finch's shoulder against mine, we leaned together. Occasional kisses.

Mitchell drove, and was quiet, but then I noticed he was smiling.

I said, "What's up, Mitchell?"

He said, "I'm happy for you two, kinda think I helped a little bit."

I laughed. "You're sure about that? That's not how I remember it."

"Think about it, since you met me, I was so irritating that you forgot all your ill-feelings toward Finch. I was so bad at my job, you were worried about him."

Finch chuckled.

I said, "When you put it that way I guess it was kind of helpful." I kissed Finch.

Then I said, "Mitchell, remember our conversation about assigning me a 'code name'? Did you and Finch ever do that?"

His brow went up. His eyes met Finch's in the rearview mirror. He said, "Yep, we did."

"Tell me, what was my code name?"

He said, "LOL. I came up with it."

I tried to think why. "What did it mean?"

He met Finch's eyes again. Finch nodded. Mitchell said, "I

asked him what to call you and he said," Mitchell lowered his voice. "'The love of m'life.'"

I said, "That was before...?"

"Yep, that was right after we left the grocery store."

I kissed Finch on the cheek.

"Thank you for thinking the best of me even when we were so far apart."

"Ye're welcome."

Finch let us into our hotel room.

I dropped my bag on the floor and watched him as he loosened his tie and unbuttoned his collar. He sat down at the table with his head in his hands.

"I ken this is supposed to be a happy occasion, but I am verra worried about Arlo, Ree-Ro."

I cocked my head. "I never noticed how much my nickname and Arlo's name matched before."

"I like the sound of it."

I sat down beside him and wrapped my hands around both of his.

"I daena understand — if they ken he inna safe in her care, how can they wait until tomorrow tae take him away?"

"I don't know."

"He just lost his mother and now his grandmother has a restraining order on me. I promised him I would see him, how is he going to tru..."

He shook his head, not wanting to say it: trust, reminding us both of my trust issues.

He let go of my hands to tug off his boots and socks. "He is probably verra scared. Do ye think they told him they are goin' tae move him in the mornin'?"

"I have no idea, but your lawyer has filed for a new review of your case?"

"Aye."

"Good, when they move him from Sheryl's house, your petition to have custody, along with your proof that you're going to have a stable home for him, will all be in a pile on a judge's desk. I truly do think this is going to be okay."

He nodded. And took a deep breath and seemed to relax.

I said, "Would you like a beer or a glass of wine?"

"Champagne."

"Oooh! Can I call room service?"

I sat on the bed while I called, and then he crawled on the bed beside me and pulled me back onto the bed.

I looked up at him with my eyes wide, and sort of half-joking said, "Finch, are we going to um...?"

"Aye, we are going tae 'um'... we are man and wife, it's a thing we have tae do for the long line of tradition and the sanctity of marriage." He grinned. "Ye haena been thinkin' on it?"

"No! I hadn't even thought about it, I don't know why... you've been thinking about it?"

His arm was heavy across my waist, his face against my side. "Besides Arlo, I haena thought of anything else since we decided tae marry."

"Ha!" I laughed. "I'm impressed you remembered to buy rings."

"They are symbolic of the act, so the rings were on m'mind—"

"Wait, rings are symbolic of the—?" I looked at my ring on my finger. "Oh, yeah, that makes sense."

"I have an engagement ring for ye too."

"You do, where?"

"It's in Scotland, it belonged tae m'mum and I had it engraved for ye, years ago. I was plannin' tae give it tae ye. It's in the safe there."

"Oh, what does it say?"

"Forever."

I looked up in his eyes. "I can't wait, that's... I love that."

"I'm glad it will be on yer finger, where it belongs." He raised up on his elbow and watched his hand trail down my arm. "Ye have had many lovers since we were taegether, Ree-Ro?"

"Three, four if I have to count Ted, ugh, I don't like to count Ted."

"Och, I daena count Ted either. I daena ken him, but whatever he did, he deserves an arse-whipping. What did he do?"

"He told me he had 'fun' and that he was 'surprised' because he usually liked 'big-breasted women' and wondered if I had considered a breast augmentation."

"He dinna!" His hand went to my breast and lay on it, cupping it. "Ted is such an arse."

A knock on the door announced our champagne delivery and Finch jumped up to answer it. I watched him as he posed for a photo with the steward, but the conversation kept going and going, so I went up behind him, took the bottle and popped the cork in the bar area. The steward left.

I poured two glasses of champagne and met Finch in the middle of the room. He swept me up in a one-armed hug and raised his glass. "Tae us, Mr and Mrs Mac."

I feigned surprise. "I can't believe that's my name!"

"Och, ye ken, ye wrote Mrs Karrie Mac over and over when ye were wee, ye were such a bonny young lass if no' a wee bit mental."

I grinned and we both took a sip of champagne. Then he pulled me close and kissed me, his lips tasting of champagne and sparkles, his tongue licking my lips, with small flicks but then deepening as his hand pulled my back close and closer and oh so so so much closer, pressing against me, his mouth moved down my jaw to my neck and then he pulled away and drew me by the hand to the bed.

"Finch Mac, this feels a great deal more than a business arrangement."

"Karrie Mac, it's verra much more. Ye canna argue with it, Ree-Ro, we thought it would be about business but that only lasted for a day. We love each other too much, I canna argue with yer love for me, it's too strong."

"My love for you?"

"Aye, it's in every fiber of yer being, ye are telling me ye had sex with three other men, since me, not Ted, he dinna count, but the three others ye mentioned and I could tell ye never loved a one of them."

He sat down on the bed and put down our champagne flutes.

I said, because I was nervous, "So we're just blowing past business and going straight to..."

"Straight tae the moment when I get tae see Ree-Ro completely undressed again, it has been a verra long time."

"That's going to be kind of tricky." I crossed the room for my bag, fished through it and returned with the scissors. "You'll need to cut me from the dress, but carefully, it was my great-grandmother's." I turned around and raised the back of my hair.

He set to work, carefully snipping at threads, and joked, "Och, this will slow me down."

I laughed.

PRESSED MY LIPS AGAINST HIS TEMPLE

Karrie

When he got the final stitch loose, he pushed open the back of the dress so that the sleeves slid down my arms and then the full dress dropped to the floor. His hands rested on my hips and then his fingers slid under the waistband of my tights. It felt so sexy and tantalizing the way he was taking them off so-o-o-o-o slowly, I rocked my hips back and forth, to help, and heard a groan erupt from him. He pressed his lips to the small of my back as he pushed them all the way to the ground. I stepped free of them and waited while he hugged around my waist, a long pause in my-his-our excitement.

He chuckled, his lips against my skin. "It's as if I opened a present and I'm too excited tae look inside."

"And you only opened it halfway. I'm still in my panties and bra."

He chuckled and unlatched the back of my bra. "I have tae pace m'self."

I let the bra slide down my arms to the ground, then turned in his arms, his lips following around me until they were pressed to my stomach.

I counted, "One, two, three..."

He drew away and looked at me, awkwardly standing before him, in nothing but my panties.

He teased, "Damn, Ree-Ro, ye're even more beautiful than before."

"So I lived up to your memories?"

"Och aye." His eyes were wide as he cupped my breasts. "Hello m'mates, ye ken I haena seen ye in a verra long time. Did ye miss me? I missed ye verra much."

I laughed. "I forgot you called them 'm'mates'."

"I dinna forget. How would I forget them? They are perfection."

"Thank you."

"It's braw tae have them in m'hands again." He lay back and pulled me toward him and helped me get a knee over so I was straddling his lap. I unbuttoned his shirt. "Dear God."

"Ye have been wantin' tae get me undressed as well? I might hae saved ye the trouble of waitin'."

"I have always wanted to get your clothes off."

"Really, Ree-Ro, that's how ye remember it? In my memory ye were battin' my hands away, and pulling yer shirt down and..." His voice trailed off as he pulled forward so he could push his shirt off his arms and toss it to the side.

He smiled up at me, then tapped his lips, and jerked his head, drawing me in.

I placed an elbow beside each of his ears and kissed him, warm breath and tingles through me as his hand caressed and fondled my breasts driving me to excitement as my tongue licked his and I began to lose my mind a bit, scratch that, a lot—

He interrupted, "We ought tae drink more champagne. I am about tae lose m'mind and I need ye tae help me slow down."

"Yes, absolutely..." I rolled off him. "I agree... you really remember all the things that get me going."

"How could I forget? I was studyin' ye for a long time."

"I'll get the champagne." I climbed off the bed, and as I walked to the kitchen, wiggled my hips.

Finch cheered and whistled. "Woo-hoo!"

I laughed. "You like that?"

He turned off all the lights except one lamp by the bed, dimmed for intimacy.

I said, "Nice touch." And carried the bottle to the bed but Finch blocked me by lying spread-eagled.

"Ye canna come on until ye pay the panty tax."

I feigned outrage. "What if I'm all 'Down with taxes!'"

"Then ye canna come on the bed — please, please pay the panty tax." He folded his hands and batted his eyes.

I said, "You'll have to collect my taxes."

"I like this game!" He leapt off the bed and slowly pulled them down my legs while I poured some more champagne in our glasses, stepped from the panties, passed him his glass, and then drank a sip.

He was flushed, drinking from his champagne flute, his eyes on me. "I am tryin' tae be sophisticated, but I am verra close tae yer privates after a long time of thinkin' I would never see them again. And ye arna wearin' any clothes."

I sipped from my glass, deposited it on the end table, and climbed onto the bed. "Now you can't come over here until *you're* undressed too."

He ran his hand through his hair, put down the glass and unbuckled and unzipped his pants, and dropped all the layers to the ground, exposing his full glorious fully-at-attention—

"Whoa, Finch, I had forgotten how majestic you are." His body was a marvel, all tattoos and wide shoulders, powerful thighs under his perfect ass.

He smiled wide. "Majestic! Ye are an awesome wife. I like it when ye call me that." He crawled beside me with his head resting on his hand.

I lay on my back and we watched each other in the dim light of the room, trailing our fingertips up and down each other's skin, tantalizingly slow and delicious. His focus was intense. We were bare and vulnerable as we explored each other's body, reminding ourselves about each other, relearning our pleasures. I grew so excited I didn't think I could bear the inches away he was, but then he leaned forward and kissed me and I lost time in his kisses.

I inhaled against his ear, drawing in the scent of his cologne, musk and leather and sandalwood. Then he pulled away again and concentrated as his finger trailed down my body once more, and I slowly, so slowly, arched to meet his fingertips, writhing as his finger drew close between my legs and then dove and played there. His lips met mine again and I moaned from the pleasure of it — a moan low and growing. His lips on my cheek he teased, "Remember when we were young and I would try this and ye would bat m'hand away?"

I laughed. "And remember once I let you, when you would start I would say, 'More, more, more...'?"

"I remember, I wrote a song about it."

I drew my head away and searched his eyes. "Truly?"

He nodded. "Say it again."

"More."

His mouth nestled against my throat, licking and kissing and sucking, until I was almost out of my mind—

More... more... more...

I trailed my hand down his chest, the planes of his abs and ribs, the tautness under his skin, the curves of his biceps and fine fine ass, and then down to his cock and around it and then trailing back up his skin, hardness covering his softnesses. *More.*

I had forgotten about those soft spaces through the years, and he was so strong now, long past the young man he once was.

I whispered, "I think that I was so enamored with our plan, that over time it became all I saw, all I knew. I stopped seeing you before me, and I didn't see how you changed. I'm sorry I didn't see you."

His lips hovered enticingly close to mine, and we breathed together, sharing the air. "Do ye see me now?"

"Yes," I gasped, "and I want more."

He used his knee to push my legs apart and rolled onto me and gathered me up, and pulled me close and entered me for the first time in so long. My breath caught as he filled me. He held me, on me and in me—

wait...

and he stilled...

His breath, long draws in and out, his heartbeat against my chest, the pulsing of his skin, the thrum of him, held back, but about to burst forth. It felt as if our breaths matched, echoing in the darkness, our hearts synchronized.

inhale... exhale... inhale...

I clutched his hands and pulled them over my head, meeting his eyes, we lost ourselves, but then he closed them, pressed his cheek to mine—

Please...I canna wait any...

I moaned, my legs wrapped around his waist pulling him deeper, and we began to push and pull against each other.

He groaned as we built in intensity, and my groans met his as our climax hit, his last few powerful thrusts breathlessly rocking my whole wide world.

Then his arms relaxed, and he collapsed down heavy on me, grown weighty, close, his sweaty brow damp against my lips. He exhaled and his body relaxed. He whispered, "Am I too heavy for ye?"

"No," I whispered, "you're just the right amount of heavy." It was a lovely long lingering intimacy, holding him, caressing him, the full weight of him, on and in me, as we caught our breaths and our heartbeats slowed.

He chuckled, vibrating against my shoulder, "That went well, I think we remembered how tae do it. It was quicker than I wanted, but on our next run I will do m'best tae be more deliberate."

I giggled.

He addressed my breasts, "Well done, m'mates, I am ever so fond of ye, but now I remember Madame V between Ree-Ro's legs. I daena want tae play favorites, but I have tae, I did miss Madame V terribly."

I laughed again and looked down at my breasts. "I'm sorry he's playing favorites. He misses you plenty, don't worry."

He said, "Madame V is just awe-inspirin'."

"'Awe-inspiring'?"

He nodded, seriously. "I forgot how she makes me feel, I want tae bow down tae her. I will definitely need tae work on m'manners—"

"Speaking for Madame V, she has no expectations of 'manners', she has a bit of a wild side."

His eyes went wide. "A wild side! I canna wait for her tae introduce Mister Colossal Cock tae her new wild side."

I giggled. "I missed Mister Colossal Cock so much — he and Madame V are married now?"

"Aye."

He kissed me. "Do ye have someplace ye need tae be?"

"No, what do you mean, why?"

"I was thinking if I crawl down and make it up tae m'mates for that insult earlier," he began fondling a breast, "that in a few minutes we might be able tae go round a second time. It's important tae have some proper marital practice."

"There's nowhere else I need to be."

I ran my fingers through his hair as he kissed and caressed my... my *everything,* a slow build up and a trembling desire for him, kissing and licking him in return, exploring his taste and form, trying to see how much of him existed for me, wanted me, could fill me. He panted with desire and finally took me again, this time slower, and after a long unhurried deliberate (as he had promised) fucking, with hot wet lips and gentle pants in my ears and caresses and gentle loving kisses, he climbed off the bed, grasped me by the ankles, his expression half-out-of-his mind, and drew me toward him. He turned me, and bent me over the bed — he lay on me, his breath bringing heat to the back of my neck. His hands wrapped around mine, drawing my hand between my legs to rub there while he focused on a taking of me that was full and present and deep and rough. I was drawn up into a climax that roared through my body as he continued on, plowing into me until he groaned, and shook, and rode his own climax — and collapsed, trembling on me.

He nestled into my hair.

There was a long quiet time, when our breaths calmed, our hearts slowed, our grip relaxed, his arm went around my waist and he lifted me, carrying me, my back to his front, and crawled us onto the bed and dropped my head down on the pillow. He curled up behind me, his arms sheltering me.

"Ye smell good." He inhaled. "Ye always have. I had forgotten, but it has come rushin' back."

I said, "What do I smell like? I've definitely changed shampoo since high school..."

"It's no' yer shampoo, ye smell verra...I daena ken how tae describe it. But everythin' about ye feels familiar and comfortable."

I turned in his arms and held his head against my chest and breathed him in, his wide shoulders around me, his arms tight and bound, the rest of him soft and weakened from the effort... "I feel it too. I know we have a lot to relearn about each other, but it feels like I already know all I need to know. Like this," I trailed my fingers down his arm, "being in bed with you again, after so long, I should be so nervous but I'm not. I just remember you so well."

He nodded, his beard against my chest. "Aye, Ree-Ro, ye were m'friend, then m'lover, m'enemy, and now m'wife. Ye have been everything tae me."

I sighed, and pressed my lips against his temple feeling there the thrum of his pulse.

TESSA'S ORANGE GLOVE

Karrie

I woke just before dawn and listened to his breathing. I squiggled close and spooned against his back breathing in his scent. He was so vulnerable, here in bed beside me, spent from all the rambunctious sex, deeply sleeping beside me — I was his wife.

From now on this would be how we would wake up.

I kissed his shoulder and then texted Tessa:

Hey, you sleeping?

A minute later she responded:

Yeah.
But whatcha need?

I have an idea.
Can you come pick me up?

After I gave her a list of things I needed, I snuck out of our hotel room and met Tessa as she pulled up in front of the lobby doors.

She handed me a coffee as I climbed into her car. "Mom made it for us." She drove us away from the hotel.

"Mom was up too?"

"Yep, she helped me pick out your court outfit, she would've come, but needed to get ready, she'll meet you and Finch and his lawyer at the courthouse with her file folder."

"Good."

"Was Finch awake?"

"Not yet, I left him a note."

"How was the honeymoon last night?" She took a sip of her coffee.

I glanced out of the corner of my eye. "How old are you now?"

"Twenty-one."

"Well then, I'll say, he fucked me very well."

She sprayed coffee out of her nose. "Oh my god!"

I laughed. "He was amazing."

She asked, "So it's more than just a business arrangement?"

I looked at the homes going by in the quiet, still, darkness just before dawn."It is so *so* much more."

"You love him?"

"I love him so much it is making my heart hurt for all those moments I lost."

She pulled her car up across the street from Sheryl's house.

"Maybe it was necessary, you know, he needed to leave college to start a career, he needed to father Arlo, and to help Alison. He was young. He probably made some stupid decisions. He probably acted like an ass. He probably, scratch that, ***likely***, spent some time being someone you wouldn't like at all. And then Alison went into the hospital and he had to focus on that.

He's gone through a lot in the past year. If you think about it, maybe he had to grow up so you could love him."

I nodded. "And I had to remember what was important, thank you for saying that, I think you're right."

We looked up at Sheryl's house, still dark. Tessa said, "I brought blankets and lawn chairs. It might be fun to tailgate."

We unfolded the chairs on the sidewalk across the street from the house and bundled up in blankets and got comfortable as the sun rose. She said, "The only thing I forgot was new gloves, this coat had the one orange glove in the pocket."

"I still can't believe you sent yours flying into the house."

We waved at everyone who drove by.

Then Finch called, his voice rough and deep as if he just woke up. "What are ye doin'?"

"Good morning."

"Good mornin', Ree-Ro, what are ye doin'?"

"If someone comes to pick up Arlo, I figure he's going to be scared, so me and Tessa are going to wave at him, so he knows he's not alone."

He chuckled. "That's weird but inspired. Our meetin' is in an hour and a half."

"I will be there."

We sat there for so long.

At one point Tessa joked, "And what was our logic with this, why did we think they would do it at dawn? They're bureaucrats!"

I burst out laughing. "Yeah, this is idiotic."

She giggled. "We're like, if we get up at five a.m. we won't miss anything — two hours later, we still won't miss anything."

I said, "Ugh, I have to pee."

She said, "Concentrate on desert animals."

"What the hell are desert animals, like snakes?"

"Yes, and dust and dry leaves."

"Hmmm. Okay, that's kinda working."

She scrolled through her phone. "Oh! There are wedding photos!!!"

"Of who...?"

"You and Finch!"

"You're kidding, who took photos? What in the...?"

She turned the phone toward me and there I was, walking out of the church beside Finch. He was holding my hand. He was beaming at me, kissing my cheek.

I got a notification from Instagram that I had thousands of new followers and the number was climbing up in real time. "What do I do?"

"You're the agent's assistant, you tell me."

Then it was just me watching my insta followers go up and up and up and going through my posts to see if I needed to cull any photos that weren't my brand: rock star wife.

Was I a rock star wife?

What do rock star wives do? Who was my role model?

Around eight, a car pulled up to the house. A woman in a business suit looked at us for a moment. We waved.

Then she went up and knocked on the door.

A few moments later Arlo emerged from the house, he was wearing a parka and had a backpack on his shoulder.

Tessa and I waved.

He grinned and held up Tessa's orange glove and waved it back at us.

Tessa waved her bare hand and her gloved hand and he gave her a thumbs-up as the woman opened the car door and he slid his small body into the car.

The car drove away.

Tessa said, "Well, we've done all we can do."

FINCH MAC'S WIFE

Karrie

While Tessa drove across town, I changed into a dress from mom's closet. Tessa said, "You look like one of the middle-aged women from church."

I buttoned up the front.

"I can't believe Mom has so many boring dresses." I finger combed my hair and then said, "Cover your eyes," and sprayed hair spray on my hair.

"It's *Mom*, she can wear literally any boring dress and still she's the artiest person any of these ladies know."

She drove into the courthouse parking lot as I applied lipstick.

"You nervous?"

I puckered my lips in the mirror. "So nervous, so freaking nervous. If this doesn't work the whole marriage thing will have been for nothing."

"Ha! I saw Finch looking at you, big sis, it won't be for nothing, this custody is just icing on the cake."

She dropped me off at the front and for the second time in two days I walked up the steps.

. . .

Finch was waiting for me. "Hi gorgeous."

I beamed.

He took my hand and led me toward my mother and the man I assumed was our lawyer standing outside a room at the end of the hall.

My mother said, "Sheryl is already inside."

The lawyer held the door open, my mother walked in, then Finch, and holding his hand, me. The room was a small courtroom, a judge on the bench, two tables in front. As my eyes swept the room they landed on Sheryl, whose face fell when she saw me.

I turned away and directed my most confident smile at the judge. I felt Finch's hand shake. We all stood while the judge explained that as he had interviewed Arlo last time he was not going to subject him to more of it. Arlo would remain in the conference room while we discussed the 'new information'. We all sat. My mother looked nervous, she was clutching a thick file folder and the lawyer accompanied her up to the judge's bench to discuss it.

The judge put on his reading glasses and flipped through the folder, then he pulled the glasses to the end of his nose and tilted his head to ask Finch's lawyer why he was only seeing the folder now.

The lawyer explained the timeline, Finch didn't know during the last court day that the folder was necessary, Finch thought Sheryl had stopped drinking, while Mom stood stiffly, nodding.

The judge told my mother she could return to her seat. Mom asked, "Will the folder be returned to me...? It's um... some of it is important, it's... with Alison gone I would like the photos, even the ones that are painful to look at."

The judge nodded, kindly, "We will return the folder." I squeezed Finch's hand. The judge looked like he had just taken mom's side.

The judge asked Sheryl some questions, including, after he looked at another file, "When was the last AA meeting you attended?"

She scowled, "A week ago."

He asked, "Do you have a witness that you are attending meetings, that you are not drinking?" He flipped through the file. "You attended rehab in... June 2019? Have you been drinking since?"

She angrily said, "My daughter was dying, I haven't had time to attend meetings."

The judge tilted his head to look at her over his reading glasses. "But you had a young boy in your home, you didn't make time to go to your meetings?" He flipped through the folder again.

He looked at my mother, "Are you willing to sign an affidavit that you witnessed Sheryl Parker drinking?"

Mom said, "I didn't witness her drinking, I believe she was drunk."

He squinted.

I raised my hand. He asked, "You are?"

"I am Karrie Mac, Finch Mac's wife, and—"

He flipped through the paperwork. "I didn't realize Finch Mac had a wife."

"We were married yesterday."

He blinked.

Finch said, "Yer honor, we are only just now married, but I asked her tae marry me a decade ago."

My mother said, "I have a letter there in the folder that my daughter signed, ten years ago, a pledge that she was going to marry Finch."

"All right, Mrs Mac, what did you want to add?"

"I saw Sheryl Parker drinking. I went to her house a week ago to give her flowers after the loss of my friend, Alison." He flipped through some pages, I assumed he was making the connection: Karrie and Finch were engaged a decade ago, Alison and Finch made a baby six years ago.

I thought to myself, *I know, I agree, it's fucking complicated.*

I continued, "And I wanted to check on Arlo. Sheryl was carrying a lowball glass that looked like it had a whisky and coke in it, on ice, she was swirling it, and she was slurring."

He asked, gesturing down at the paper. "This is the incident with the t-shirt shooter?"

"Yes, your honor, my sister got carried away by the moment."

"You're lucky no one was hurt. The boy, Arlo, was there at the home at the time of the incident?" He started out the question looking at me, but by the end had directed the question at Sheryl.

"Who...? Me, oh um, yes, and I wasn't drinking, that was just a coke—"

I said, "In a whisky glass."

Sheryl said, "You don't know anything."

The judge said, matter-of-factly, "The police report and the social worker's report, both state that you had been drinking."

He turned to a final page. "I have already asked Finch Mac these questions, now I will ask you, Mrs Finch Mac, do you have a plan for Arlo's living arrangements?"

I said, "Yes, your honor, Finch and I want Arlo to have a stable home. He just lost his mother, we will help him with the loss and... keep him in school... and..."

He narrowed his eyes. "Finch Mac has a tour, how would you keep Arlo in school?"

"My parents live here, near his school, they go to church here, we want him to have as much stability and—"

He interrupted. "This doesn't sound like a very concrete plan."

I gulped.

I glanced at Sheryl, who had a smug look on her face. My hands trembled.

This was too important, I couldn't screw it up. I raised my chin. "My apologies, your honor, it's not, we all just lost Alison, Finch has a tour coming up, and we're newly married. We haven't made a plan, but we will make a home. He will have his father. And Arlo will be our number one priority in every decision we make."

The judge nodded, closed the folders and said, "I grant custody of Arlo Mac to his father, Finch Mac."

My mother raised her fist to the sky and said, "Yes!"

Finch was called forward to speak to the judge.

I wiped my eyes. And glanced over my shoulder at Sheryl. She was glowering as she gathered her things.

I gave her my most haughty glare:

You deserved all of this, you terrible person.

You abused Alison, you didn't protect her from her step-dad.

You're a fucking alcoholic, and you thought you were going to get custody of this little boy?

Finch Mac's son?

Well, guess what, bitch? I'm his step-mom now, you'll have to get through me.

GREATEST THING EVER

Karrie

We went into a conference room where I hugged Mom, and then Finch swept me up in his arms. "Ye did it, Ree-Ro, ye did it! Och, Alison would be so grateful. Thank ye. I love ye."

I said, "I love you too." And his eyes went wide but we were interrupted by a stack of papers to fill out.

Then Arlo was shown into the room and he hugged mom and Finch. He and I fist-bumped. "That was a long confusing experience, right?"

He nodded. "But I had Tessa's mitten."

I grinned. "Perfect, did you understand what she meant?"

"It meant my dad was going to come get me."

I said, "She will be so psyched, that t-shirt gun was the greatest thing ever, Alison was so right about it."

Finch said, "Well, that's it, we're done, I have custody of ye, Arlo, little man, we get tae take ye home now."

"To Nan's house?"

We all said sure.

I AM A 'WITH'

Karrie

Finch and Arlo drove by themselves so Finch could explain that he had married me.

That made sense because I had no idea how a six-year-old would react to his dad getting married while he was not there and just a couple of weeks after his mom passed away.

They were a little late coming home because they had stopped at the Starbucks for drinks and pastries.

When they walked in Arlo was sheepish around me. And frankly I felt sheepish around him, too.

But then Finch said, while everyone was busy doing something else, "Hey Arlo, will ye come down tae the rumpus room with me and Karrie?"

Finch threw him over his shoulder, and carried him downstairs, dropped him on the couch, and said, "Arlo, I gave ye big news earlier, big big news. I ken ye already met her, but I want tae make it official... this is Karrie, or Ree-Ro, she's goin' tae be yer stepmum."

I collapsed onto the couch. "A stepmom? Whaaaat? Like one of those stepmoms in the movies? Really?"

Finch jerked his head back. "Verra funny, Ree-Ro, ye ken ye are it."

I exhaled and sat up straight. "Here's the thing, Arlo, my name is Karrie, your dad also calls me Ree-Ro, it's a combo of Karrie and Munro, get it?"

He nodded.

"You can call me either, anything you want. And I knew your mom, and she was a beautiful, wonderful person and I am honored to have known her. I would never ever want to replace her. So... wait! Wait right here, I will be right back." I jogged up the steps to the guest bedroom, dug through the drawer, grabbed what I wanted, and raced back downstairs. He thought it was funny that I was out of breath, so I really played it up, doubling over, breathing heavily, while he and Finch laughed and laughed.

Finally I held up the locket. "I want to give you this..."

I sat down beside him on the couch. "See this little button on the side? If you press it..."

I showed him the photo. "This is your mom, me, and then your dad. This day was one of the happiest days of my life before yesterday, when I married your dad. I want you to have this locket because I want you to know that I am not an 'instead', your mom and I have our arms around each other, I am a 'with'. Does that make sense?"

He nodded.

I sighed as I looked down on it. "I thought it would be more fitting for you, but now I see it's kind of girly, sorry about that—"

"I like it."

"Good, and I think this photo is meaningful, but if you get tired of it and you want one that has just your mom in it, and... or we can get you another locket that has a photo of just your mom, or, I am truly sorry, I'm nervous and I babble when I'm nervous."

I clasped it around his neck. "If you want to you can wear it under your shirt or hang it on your wall or something, I mean, in your room..." My voice trailed off because — where was his room? Where were we going to live? It was freaking me out that there was so much changing at once.

He asked, "Why are you nervous?"

"Because this is a big big day. Lots of big things happening."

He narrowed his eyes, looking a great deal like his dad and a little like Alison too. "It's going to be okay."

"Is it?"

My step-son said, "Aye."

THE CRINKLE AT THE EDGE OF HIS EYES

Karrie

I began receiving texts mid-afternoon from LA.

Blakely:

```
Did you get married?
OH MY GOD
did you marry Finch Mac?!!!
```

Jay-Dog texted:

```
Ha ha ha ha ha ha ha ha!
You weren't trying to make him jealous?
Ha ha ha, you're welcome!
```

Blair:

```
DUUUUUUDDDDDE.
What happened?
You married him, how, what, how.
What?
```

Vi:

```
Seriously?
```

I want all the details.

Dani:
I guess the shopping worked.

I thought, *hell yeah, believe me now?*

We all had dinner at my family's house. After dinner Tessa pulled up a YouTube video that was all about Finch's wedding to a mysterious woman, a former public relations assistant, named Karrie Munro. There were street-interviews. Young women saying, "That sucks, he's so hot," and, "She's so lucky!" And, "She's not even that pretty."

I pretended to be outraged.

An anonymous source said that insiders reported that Finch Mac married me as 'a decoy to add respectability to his brand.' Finch squeezed my hand.

I said, "It's fine. No worries."

He said, "I'm troubled by what I'm draggin' ye intae."

"I got this, I'm in this business arrangement with my eyes wide-open."

But I was nervous about the evening — where would we go? What were we to do with Arlo? I had my eyes wide-open but this was all so big.

Thankfully Mom broke through the worry by asking, "Arlo, will you stay with us here tonight? We can all watch a movie, eat popcorn, and then when your Dad and Karrie go to their hotel, we can have a sleepover. Sound good?"

He nodded.

Mom winked.

So after dinner I put on my pajama pants and a sweatshirt and we watched *Ant-Man* and ate popcorn, with Arlo half-on half-off Finch's lap, Howard, between us, and Finch and I holding hands on the back of the couch.

My mother occasionally looked over, grinning. At one point she paused the movie to say, "I just want you to know that I am so thrilled to have you here, Arlo."

He said, "Thank you Nan, please turn the movie back on."

We all laughed.

When the movie was over, Finch kissed and hugged Arlo goodbye. And he and I left and held hands while he drove us to the hotel. As we walked from the parking spot to the lobby he said, "Och, we accomplished a great deal in twenty-four hours."

"I'm exhausted. If you think about it, we got married, honeymooned, *twice* last night, won your son back, celebrated as a family..." I yawned.

"Och aye, I am exhausted too, but also, I might try tae do better tonight, three times seems necessary."

"Necessary?"

"Aye, once because ye are new tae me, twice because I love ye, three times tae show off that I can..."

I laughed as he led me through the lobby, a couple with their phones out filming us.

When we got upstairs, I said, "It's going to be a busy night, sex three times, and so much planning — where are we going to live, and when do you leave?"

From the bathroom, he stuck his head out with the toothbrush in his teeth.

I grinned. "Are you brushing your teeth without me?" I rushed in, squeezed toothpaste on my brush, and began brushing my teeth beside him, both of us looking at each other in the mirror. "Och, ye are sexy when ye do it."

Toothpaste dribbled down my chin. "Do what, this...?" I spit in the sink.

"Och!" He picked me up and sat me on the bathroom counter and I wrapped my legs around him. He was already fully wanting me.

"How'd you do that?"

"It's no' m'fault, ye are wearing such scanty clothes!"

I looked down at my sweats. "Ha!"

He put his brush in his mouth and pulled my layers of shirts off and threw them out of the bathroom. "See? Ye daena have a shirt on!"

I pulled his shirt off and tossed it and then we fondled and caressed each other while we finished brushing, driving me to distraction.

I wriggled past him, stripped my pants off and let them fall as I bounded from the bathroom to the bedroom. "Last one to the bed with clothes on is a gigantic loser."

He raced after me, but he had buttons and zippers so he was still removing stuff when he got to the bed.

I put my hand in the loser L on my forehead.

He said, "I am goin' tae have tae redeem m'self by winnin' in bed then."

As I shifted up to the pillows, he crawled on, following me.

"And how, Mr Mac do you win in bed?"

"Well, Mrs Mac, first one tae climax is the loser."

"Mrs Mac is not thinking that's how orgasms work." I moaned as he nestled in between my legs kissing and sending me very quickly through rocking pleasure straight over into a climax that shook my world. The kind of soul-rocking climax, the kind where I pulled him up, wrapped my legs around him, clung to him, trembling and out of my mind as he pulled himself up and in and on and turned us over so that I was on him, riding him, bringing him along with me to his own orgasm.

Spent, I collapsed on him, as he grew soft and weakened. I held onto his head and he held me tight and we kissed and kissed until it was time to pull away. He splayed his arms and legs out and said, "Phew!"

I dropped down beside him, sprawled on my back.

He said, "That was fantastic."

I moaned, "Yes, yes it was."

"I think ye like me, Ree-Ro."

"I do, I like you so much."

"Do ye ken, earlier, ye said ye loved me — ye love me?"

I turned on my side and looked in his eyes. "I love you so very much."

He grinned, the wide smile in his dark beard, the crinkle at the edge of his eyes.

There weren't three times of sex, there was just the one, because we were exhausted — instead we talked, getting to know each other again. He asked, "Do ye sing verra often, Ree-Ro?"

"Never, this week was the most in a long, long time."

"I am glad I was there for it."

I raised my head and looked down on him. "That is so nice of you to say as you're arguably one of the most famous singers in the world." I put my head down and drew circles with my fingertips on his chest. "What's that like, being a rock star? Do you love it?"

"What do ye think?"

"Well... knowing young Finch I think you struggle with it. I think you love having fans of your work, but you have trouble with the adulation."

He nodded. "Aye, ye ken me verra well."

"I do, we grew up together."

"Do ye miss singing, do ye wish ye had been the one with the music career?"

I shook my head. "No... I mean, I do love singing with you, but I liked singing with you at the pub after our wedding, the ease of that, you and the guitar — it's the 'you' of it, you know?"

He said, "I liked singing with ye too, I missed that a lot. Scale of one tae ten, how much do ye want a music career?"

I said, "I think now I am a one on the scale. The PR work really showed me how difficult it is."

"Aye, tis difficult, but being married tae me inna gonna make it any less difficult, ye hae entered the eye of the storm."

"So many young women want to destroy me for taking you."

He kissed my forehead. "Ye ken what I missed?"

"What?" I raised my head again.

"I missed havin' ye be a writing partner on m'songs."

"Really? I mean, you became a world famous rock star *after* we broke up, I wondered if you needed me at all."

"Och, I needed ye every day. Remember when we would sit at the piano in our old apartment?"

"For hours — you would play, we would sing, writing lyrics and music down, ordering pizza, staying up all night."

"I still have those notebooks, ye ken, a whole shelf of them."

"Do you? That's cool. Who helps you now — who do you write with?"

"I daena hae anyone who is as good as ye were. Ye had a way of wordin' yer advice, Ree-Ro, everyone else who tries just pisses me off. It's like they're all tryin' tae get me tae sing *their* song. When ye used tae write with me ye just wanted tae help me get the best song." He kissed my brow. "I was verra lonely without ye."

"Were you?"

"Aye, and I... I wanted tae call ye, tae ask if ye were okay. I would sit with m'phone in m'hands wanting tae hear yer voice, tae hear ye tell me ye were okay."

"Really?"

"Aye."

"I wanted you to ask me if I was okay. I wasn't, not for a long time."

He exhaled. "I ought tae hae done it then. Yet another thing I regret."

"You know, regret... we have to let go of that, I think. We lost time, but we have each other now, and Arlo is here... we have to think of the time away as a necessary growing period or something."

He rolled me over and wrapped around me, tightly, his head at my breast. He nodded. "Aye." He was clinging to me, almost as if in desperation. His voice quiet as he asked, "Are ye okay now? Have I made it better?"

My cheek nestled on top of his head. "Yes, you have, and I am okay, Finch, I love you, thank you for asking."

"I did call ye once, I was stuck on a lyric, really stuck, and I got intae a big row with the band over it and that night I thought if I called ye that ye might help me through it. I let it ring and ring, but then I got yer voicemail and decided no' tae leave ye a message, but ye almost got a midnight call from Finch Mac beggin' ye tae help me finish the chorus."

"You didn't talk to me, so what did you decide to do?"

He grinned. "We filled in the time with a guitar solo."

I laughed, and we kissed and there was some fine cuddling as we fell asleep. I woke a bit later and simply listened: to his sounds, his breathing, and his turning. Then his hand found its way to my hip, his head nestled against my side, and then I was sleeping again, before he rolled away.

A GOOD TEAM

His phone buzzed on the nightstand.

Mmmfmmffffmm.

I glanced at it, a call from my mom.

I nudged his shoulder until he roused enough to answer. I heard the crying faintly in the background and mom's voice sounding frantic.

He said, "Uh huh, yeah, can you put him on...?" Then "Hey little man, it's me, I'm putting on my clothes..."

I leapt from the bed and started tugging my clothes on too. He tucked the phone between his ear and his shoulder while he tugged on his pants and then, "You're alright, little man, and I am really close by and I'm comin' right now..."

He gestured, so I held the phone near his ear while he pulled two shirts over his head and then ran a hand through his hair. "I'm coming... me and Ree-Ro will be there in just a minute..."

I passed him his coat and began pulling mine on. I grabbed the hotel room key.

"Do ye want me tae stay on the phone? Sounds good, please calm down... I ken... Arlo, I ken ye're scared...." I grabbed his keys and his wallet and dropped them down in his pocket as we rushed out the door to the car.

. . .

In the car, I drove, while he kept the phone to his ear. "I ken ye are… I'm sorry we left for the night…"

I lamented, "Why did we leave, we should have known…"

He put his hand over the phone, "Aye, I thought he was…" He went back to talking into the phone.

It took twenty minutes to get to my house. It was three a.m.

He jumped out of the car as I was parking and got up the front steps of the house as the door opened and Mom passed a crying Arlo into his arms.

"Och… ye are a big boy and ye are verra sad…" I followed them into the house, hugging Mom and Tessa as Finch carried Arlo upstairs to the guest room.

I frowned. "We need a roof over our head, all of us together, really soon."

Mom patted me on the back and gave me a glass of milk to carry up for Arlo.

I climbed the stairs after my husband.

He was on the bed, pillows propped behind his back, Arlo curled up on his side, doing that little stutter cry that meant he was almost done — he looked exhausted. I whispered, "Do you want some milk? It will help you sleep."

While Arlo gulped down the milk, Finch took off his parka and boots.

I said, "Mind if I curl up on your other side?"

Finch smiled and patted the bed.

Arlo curled up on one side of Finch, I curled up around his arm, with my head against his strong shoulder, his lips pressed against my forehead. I watched Arlo slowly fall asleep, his face worried and distressed then becoming calm and then fully relaxed.

Finch whispered. "Even after all those years we make a good team."

The next morning Arlo went down to breakfast first while Finch used the bathroom and then he opened the door to ask, "So Ree-Ro, are we back tae bein' a 'share the bathroom' couple or are we all grown up and a 'private bathroom' couple?"

"Probably share...?"

"Good, because we will hae tae spend time in hotels while I'm on tour, so it will be a lot easier..."

I lowered my pants and peed, smiling happily at him while he brushed his teeth. Then I joined him, standing in front of him, he watched me in the mirror. "Have ye ever been more sexy?"

"Sexy, this? You said the same thing last night and it got me all kinda hot. Is it the potentiality? Is it because I'm right here? All yours?"

"Absolutely, it's all of it." He hugged around my back, pressing against me, playing with my breasts.

I said, "Mister... what was your cock's name again?"

He chuckled. "Mr Colossal Cock, clearly ye need a reminder—"

There was a knock on the door. We looked at each other in comical horror, stifling our laughter.

Tessa's voice through the door, "Um... hey...waiting for the bathroom, just wanted you to know that I'm literally standing right outside the door."

Finch and I both burst into laughter, finished brushing our teeth, and left the bathroom.

Tessa was chuckling when we passed her. "Don't get me wrong, that was hilarious, I totally shouldn't have interrupted."

"Well, we are on our honeymoon. That could've turned in an instant into something you did not want to hear. Consider yourself warned."

Dad came from his room, padding down the hall. "What are you kids talking about?"

Tessa said, "Dad, Karrie is warning me that we ought to be careful if we surprise her and Finch as they are *honeymooning* all the time."

Finch groaned.

Dad joked, "Dear God! Just don't honeymoon in the hallways."

Finch said, "No sir, of course not, sir."

But then as we went down the stairs he grabbed my ass and tugged me close to kiss and we made out a little bit there on the steps.

I whispered, "Dad just told you not to..." As he nibbled and kissed me behind my ear.

"He's an old punk, he'd understand — I'm defyin' authority."

Then he joked, "Just please daena tell him."

I laughed and we went downstairs.

YOU'RE THE GLUE

Tessa left for school, but the rest of us were at breakfast. Mom asked, "When does your tour start, Finch?"

He glanced at Arlo who was watching us all carefully. Finch said, "I must leave in three days."

Mom said, "That is not enough time."

Arlo's face twisted up. Mom patted the back of his hand. "We have to talk all of this through, just bear with us." To the rest of us she said, "He needs continuity."

I said, "Arlo has school, is that continuity?"

Mom said, "He was very worried last night without Finch." She smiled at Arlo. "That is completely normal, you need your Dad close by for a little while, right?"

Arlo said, "Yes."

Finch scrubbed his hands up and down on his face.

I said, "And your tour starts in Vegas?"

"Yes, we have a sound stage starting..." He glanced at his phone, then tossed it down. "I daena ken why I am checkin', I hae been worryin' about the dates for months. It starts in three days."

"You'll be practicing all day every day?"

"Ten tae twelve hour days."

"Okay, so hear me out... we rent a house in Vegas. Arlo and I will be there. He can take two weeks off school, then we come back here for Christmas break, and then we... we decide."

Finch just looked at me.

"What...?"

He jerked his head. "It means a great deal tae me that ye are saying 'we', Ree-Ro."

Mom patted his arm. "It's been a long time of worry, hasn't it?"

"I dinna ken how I was going tae do it. I am verra grateful."

I gave him a sad smile. "Well it's part of our business arrangement, right?"

He said to Arlo, "Daena let that bother ye, little man, she is just teasin' about the business arrangement, she loves us desperately."

"This is true."

I saw my parents' eyes meet with a smile.

Finch said, "All right, we'll get a house with a pool."

Arlo said, "It will be cold!"

I said, "It's hot in Vegas. And my house is close by in LA. Maybe when your dad has a day off we can go see my house, too. And I'll show you my favorite beach."

Mom narrowed her eyes. "But during his work, it will be long days of just you two doing..."

I gulped. "Um... swimming... and I'm sure there are plenty of fun family friendly things to do in Vegas—"

Mom said, "I don't mean to overstep, but I could use a change of scenery and if it would be okay, I would love to come. I can be the helpful Nan."

Arlo clapped.

I grinned. "You would do that for us?"

"Absolutely. And maybe Tessa too. She's done with finals early next week, we can fly her in right after."

Dad said, "I will stay here with Howard, you're welcome, he's too old for Vegas."

I looked at Finch. "So we have a plan and it includes almost my whole family. You cool with it?"

"Absolutely, they're my family too."

Finch and I moved out of the hotel and into my family home and Arlo stopped needing us to sleep with him. He chilled out a little, and by the third day he was enjoying the fun of going on a trip, packing his belongings into a suitcase, and excited about the vacation. He got a visitation with Sheryl for a few hours on the last day

I drove him over and waited outside the whole time, texting back and forth with Mom:

How'd you bear to do this
with Alison so many times?

Mom texted:

It was never easy.
She was older though,
I had no rights,
I had to accept it and drive away.

I texted:

I would never be able to.

She returned with:

That's because you're his stepmother now,
you're embracing the role,
do you need me to bring you a coffee?

I wrote:

No I'm good.
I'm just here reading.

What are you doing?

She wrote:
Packing my art supplies
for our big holiday in Vegas
with my new grandson and the rock star!

I joked:
And me.

She texted:
Of course,
you're the glue holding us all together now.

ALL THIS EXTRA LOVELY WONDERFUL BAGGAGE

Karrie

The next day we were through airport security, and at the gate Finch got a call and was talking for a while. He covered the phone and mouthed, "M'mum."

I whispered, "Tell her I said hi."

He said, "Ree-Ro says hello."

Then they talked longer while I helped Arlo get a drink and my mom helped him get his earbuds to the right level. Finch was completely oblivious to all the people standing around staring at him, lurking to listen to his call, waiting to ask for his autograph. I heard Finch say, "Mum, he inna coming back, I told ye... he has moved on... ye need tae find someone ye like who can..."

Our flight was called and Finch led me and Arlo and my mom to First Class seats and then finally I heard him say, "Right, Mum, I need tae go, I'm on m'flight... Right, I'll call next week."

He sank down in his seat and pulled his baseball cap down to partially cover his face, though he had on a dark shirt open at the neck, showing off his tats, and his black and white striped pants and boots, looking absolute hotness.

My mom's seat was in the row behind us. She happily waved goodbye as she settled down to watch movies the whole flight.

I said to Arlo as we settled in the plush leather seats, "This is awesome right? So fancy."

He shrugged.

Finch teased, "Arlo's flown First Class before."

People came on the plane and started photographing him. He hung his head, trying to hide, but almost everyone coming down the aisle had their camera pointing at him anyway, or were nudging and staring, some bold enough to say, "Dude, love your music."

"Thanks."

I said, "This is going to take some getting used to."

"It's pretty chill in Maine, it gets pretty crazy in other places..."

The flight attendant came by to lean over and ask if Finch needed anything, he said, without any prodding. "M'wife would like Coke, m'son would like an apple juice."

She said, "Oh... of course," and backed away.

I said, "That's nice, I think I can get used to you calling me 'm'wife'."

"It's m'new superhero shield, I say, 'm'wife...' and the crowds of fans disperse." He grinned.

I helped Arlo get settled and comfortable, stored his backpack under the seat in front of him, and then settled in myself.

The fasten seatbelts light went on. I asked,"What's going on with your mom?"

"She's upset... m'father was such a piece of shite."

Arlo looked around me with his eyes wide. "What?"

Finch said, "Sorry Arlo, but it's true, m'mum thought he was verra charmin' as he bossed her around like a barbarian, and filled her house with all this antique junk. Somehow she still thinks he's goin' tae marry her, and claim me as his son, and take her tae live in his fancy home somewhere—" He ran his hand through his hair.

Arlo asked, "Have I ever met him?"

"Nae, and yer lucky, yer grandfather, Donnan, is the king of

— m'apologies — dobshite wankers. I think he is gone for good, and just between us, we are grateful for it." He grinned to cut the sting. "But yer grandmother in Scotland sends her love tae ye, Arlo, and tae ye too, Ree-Ro." He kissed me sweetly.

I whispered to Finch, "When I flew into Maine two weeks ago, I did not think I would have all this extra lovely wonderful baggage when I left."

Our plane pulled from the gate. I put out both my hands and Finch and Arlo both put their hands in mine.

SO FREAKING IMPORTANT

Finch

We had a fine house with a swimmin' pool and plenty of room for all of us. It was gated for security and Mitchell drove me back and forth tae the sound stages where the band and I were workin' on the show.

It had been a busy week, long hours of practicin', and then coming home tae a new wife, a new family, a rental home, and helpin' Arlo acclimate tae our new circumstances, living in Vegas, and all of us suffering because of the loss of Alison, but there were also laughs, swimmin' in the pool, watchin' shows. We were becoming a family and though it was difficult at times, it felt like we were growin' taegether and it was going tae be good.

One day I had tae meet the band early as we had a meetin' and so I got up with the dawn and showered and got ready for my day, then crept tae the bedside. Arlo had had a nightmare, and had come tae our room in the night, sleeping in the middle, legs splayed, a heavy sleepy arm across Karrie's face.

I knelt beside the bed.

Karrie mumbled, "You going to work?"

"Aye." I kissed her cheek, then paused tae look at her.

Her eyes closed she smiled and whispered, "Are you thinking about how much you love me, because I love you, too."

"Aye, I do love ye, Ree-Ro, I couldna hae done any of this without ye."

She said, "I know, I'm so freaking important, I love being important."

I kissed her again, and kissed Arlo's sweaty brow, and tiptoed out of the room.

I'M IMPERFECT

Karrie

Arlo and I got along great, except... sometimes he melted down. I didn't hold it against him, this was hard what we were doing, blending a family, getting used to my little jerk of a dog who had joined us in Vegas, and supporting our beloved rock star's career, while spending twenty-four-seven with each other.

Mom helped. But still it was me and Arlo a lot of the hours and we were very new to each other.

And he was in grief.

Kids grieve in interesting ways. For Arlo it was long moments of 'nothing is wrong' and then a meltdown of epic proportions.

Often in our first few days, in our mansion with a pool in Vegas, the meltdowns would be directed at me. I understood. It was also really hard.

He told me that he hated me, he blamed me, and I was at my wits end, so I said, "You know what, Arlo, I am imperfect."

He narrowed his eyes and stormed off to sulk.

Later he came to the kitchen while I was making us a snack and pretended like nothing was wrong, climbing up on the barstool and asking for a juice box.

The next day, he had a sulk again, and he got testy with me. I again said, with a shrug. "Well, what are we going to do? I'm imperfect."

Third time I said it he asked, "What do you mean, Ree-Ro?"

I said, "It's shorthand for saying you want your mom and she would be perfect for you and I'm not her, but I am doing my best to be right for you. Not perfect, but right. And I'm going to always be here for you. I'm always trying." I gave him a sad-smile. "Imperfect, it's a word that means a lot more."

And then the next day, a better day, I was sitting by the pool and he was floating staring at the sky. I asked, "Whatcha thinking about Arlo?"

And he sighed, a very grownup kind of sigh, and said, "I'm imperfect too."

And that's when I knew we were going to be okay, eventually.

I got a text from Finch:

```
I'm asking Mitchell
to pick up food and bring you and Arlo,
I'll be done in a bit.
```

I grinned at Arlo. "Let's get dressed! Your dad invited us to see him at work!"

We raced around getting dressed, kissed Nan goodbye, since she was giving me lots of opportunities to be alone with Arlo, and loaded up in the car to be driven across Vegas.

I said, "Mitchell, you excited that Tessa will be here tomorrow?"

"Yep, really excited. I like her a lot."

I laughed. "Yeah I could tell."

He said, "Mind if I pick her up at the airport?"

"Don't mind at all."

He passed a stack of magazines back: People, Star, Us Weekly... "What's this?" But I could see, Finch was on the cover of all of them.

"Thought you might like to see them. I don't know what to do."

I flipped through. They were all about his meltdowns, his suspiciously sudden marriage, his arrival in court. "Finch needs a story on his terms, I think I ought to set up an interview, I know Stacy over at O magazine..."

My voice trailed off when I saw the crowds, hundreds of people, milling around the guard gates at the sound studios. "Whoa..."

Mitchell said, "They've been here for days."

The crowd filled in around the Escalade, yelling, "Finch! Finch Mac!"

Arlo's eyes went wide. "Are they going to come in?"

"No, not." But there was a bang on the side.

"Finch! Finch Mac!" Someone knocked on the window.

I joked to Mitchell, "Should we open the window, let them know Finch isn't back here?"

"Hell no! Wait — did you just ask that?"

I laughed. "I was just seeing if you were paying attention." Our vehicle rolled slowly through the crowd.

Arlo said, "Why do they think dad is in here?"

I said, "Well, the windows are tinted, but you'd think they could tell by the shape of our heads that he's not back here, unless they think he's ducking below the seat."

He giggled. "When they go to his concerts Dad is very tiny up on the stage, maybe they think he's in here, he's just really short."

I laughed. "That's hilarious, maybe they think he's a very short rock star, we keep him in a toddler car seat."

He giggled again.

We finally made it to the guard gate, where Mitchell announced, “It’s Finch Mac’s wife and son.” Behind us the crowd stopped clamoring as the news filtered back — *It’s not Finch Mac, it’s just his wife.*

Mitchell drove us through the gates and up to the front of the soundstage.

We could hear Finch’s band rocking inside. Mitchell had to park, so I filled my arms with the bags of food to deliver, and yelled to Arlo, “Cover your ears, it’s loud!”

A moment later one of the stage workers rushed over with some ear protection for him, because it was *crazy* loud. The bags of food were carried to a table to be unpackaged and Arlo and I moved up to the front of the stage.

Finch was playing the last song, his biggest hit, his show closer, and the whole band was jamming, hard. Finch waved when he saw us, and smiled down at us while he sang, singing to us, for us. And Arlo and I danced at the front of the stage at our own almost private concert.

When the song ended, Arlo and I cheered and cheered, while Finch passed his guitar to a member of his crew and dropped off the stage right in front of us.

“What did ye think?” He mopped his face.

Arlo said, “That’s my favorite song.”

I said, “Me too. I loved it! It sounded so great.”

Finch jerked his head back. “Ye almost sound like a fan, Ree-Ro.”

“I am such a huge fan.” We walked over to the food table together.

Arlo said, “Ree-Ro listens to your music all the time.”

Finch said, “Does she now? Verra interestin’.”

“I don’t know if you know this, Finch Mac, but all those songs are about me.”

“I told ye, Ree-Ro, it’s *always* been about ye.”

I folded up in his arms, in a big hug, with Arlo in the middle, putting his arms around our waist and we all held on. I whispered to Finch, “Is this what a happy ending feels like?”

He kissed my hairline. “Aye, it’s also what a new beginnin’ feels like.”

LAST NIGHT OF THE TOUR

Karrie

The stadium was thundering. I was standing backstage as the band headed out for their encore.

I had been in Maine for a few weeks, with Arlo back in school, but now we were with Finch as he finished this leg of the tour.

He was illuminated in the glow at the front of the stage as he spoke to the audience. I couldn't hear him from here, over the thunderous clamor of the sold out show, but I guessed what he was about to do... he had said, as he passed, "Next song is ours, Ree-Ro."

I had joked, "Only a monster would call me on stage without a proper practice this week."

He had laughed. "We sing it taegether all the time, ye practice plenty."

Now he was on stage, and slowly he turned and put out a hand toward me.

I stepped onto the stage. The roar was even more deafening from here.

A stagehand waved me toward a microphone. The lights so bright it took a moment to get an idea of where I was. He announced the next song, "It's one I've been workin' on, with m'wife, it's about how forgiveness can be a gift."

The song began and I focused on Finch, trying not to look out at the dark sea of my husband's uproarious fans. I reminded myself, *they aren't here for you, all you have to do is sing to Finch, he's the one... he's always been the one.*

We began singing. Facing each other, a smile at the edge of his lips, beads of sweat on his brow, he was at home up here while I was terrified, but it was okay — I felt safe as he held my eyes and sang for me.

As wide as the deep sea, as long as your silence, a gapin' rift... your forgiveness is a gift...

The song ended, I waved and left the stage as he and the band started the next song, the show closer, the one that would get everyone up, cheering, losing their minds.

I couldn't take my eyes off him, he was a fucking rock star, all our dreams come true.

When the song was over, he raised his guitar victoriously above his head, passed it to a stagehand, and headed right toward me, hot sweaty sexy, his eyes gleamed as he took my hand. "Ye want tae go tae m'dressing room, Ree-Ro?"

"Oh yes, I do, I really really do, Arlo is with Nan, we have..." I checked my watch. "Twenty minutes before the after party, and I am so hot for you."

He led me through the dark backstage and opened the door of his dressing room. "Ye said it's yer time?"

I whipped my shirt off over my head. "Yep, ovulating today." I joked, "Why are you still wearing your clothes?"

He grinned, unbuttoning his pants and peeling them down. "We goin' tae make a wee rock star, Ree-Ro?"

"Heck yeah." He held me in his arms and I wrapped my legs around his waist and we rocked each other's world.

Because there was something true and real about these moments, in the sweaty hot aftermath of a concert, we had always been meant to be — here we were moment after moment, singing along with each other, and building trust, a family, a life together, finally.

THANK YOU

This is the second edition of Finch Mac's story, I went back and added chapters from Finch's point of view. I don't know why I decided to, but I wanted to hear from him, and I'm so happy now, I love hearing his side.

This is *(probably!)* a stand-alone story, but it's book one of the Campbell Sons series.

Also, within it there were some overlaps with my other books.

Firstly, some of Karrie's father's research seems to be skirting very close to some of the mysteries in Kaitlyn and the Highlander: Mag Mòr, the Earl of Breadalbane, and the swords and other artifacts in Joe Munro's office (keep these in mind!) are all nods to that other world.

And if you're a fan of Kaitlyn and the Highlander, you've definitely heard the name Donnan before. Oh. Yes. You. Have.

So if you haven't started reading Kaitlyn and the Highlander yet, what's stopping you?

It's a bestselling series, contemporary with a mix of history, a bit of comedy, a lot of drama, adventure, swoon, and a lot of fun.

You can jump on the Magnus train here:

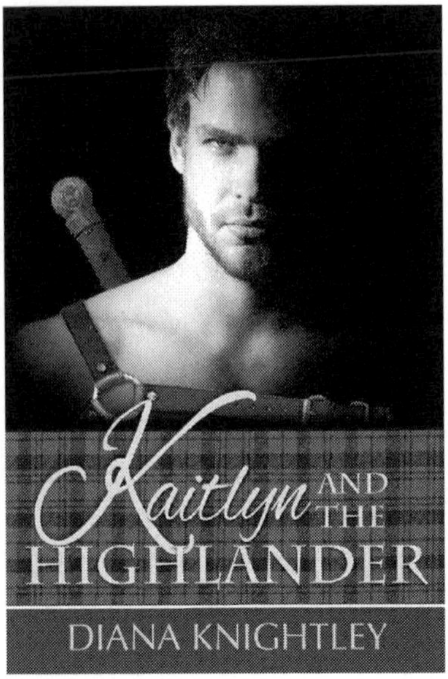

And secondly, Karrie and the Rock Star took place in the world of Liam and Blakely. If you'd like to read their ongoing contemporary, rom-com, hot Scottish hero, story it's here, being told episodically on Vella:

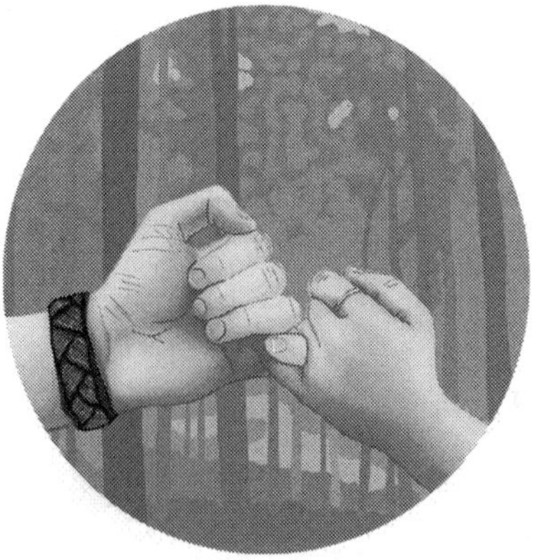

Liam and Blakely on Vella

Thank you for taking the time to read this book. The world is full of entertainment and I appreciate that you chose to spend some time with Finch and Karrie.

I fell in love with Finch when I was writing him, and I hope you fell in love a little bit too.

And if you want to come talk to me about this, or any of my stories, there are 7k of us in a FB group here: Kaitlyn and the Highlander We talk about love and casting and books and Scotland and stories and Heroes.

I would love it if you would follow my Substack, here:
Diana Knightley's Stories

And my TikTok too: @Diana_Knightley_author

ACKNOWLEDGMENTS

Thank you to Isobel for being the seed that started this story. I told you I wanted to write a rom com and you worked the question like a mad lib, filling in all the blanks: Rock Star! Widower! Baby-Mama! Second Chances! I love the way it turned out, thank you for your ideas.

Thank you to Fiona for the beautiful hot rock star on the cover. Thank you for all your time and attention and for making him just what I wanted.

And thank you so much Cynthia Tyler, for your bountiful notes, for reading through thrice, as you do — for your edits, notes, thoughts, the proofing, and the compliments. I love working with you.

Thank you to David Sutton for your notes and for going above and beyond by asking a sheriff's department in Maine about the crime of shooting a t-shirt launcher into a private home! That was wonderful.

Thank you to Kristen Schoenmann De Haan for your notes and for telling me that you like the way I write moms. (My answer: my mom was the best so I have experience with one.)

And thank you to Jessica Fox for saying: I fully support any and all future mashups between your stories. I was so excited about the crossover and was glad you approved.

And huge thanks to Jackie Malecki and Angelique Mahfood for being admins of the big and growing FB group. Over 7K members at the time of publication! Your energy and positivity and humor and spirit, your calm demeanor when we need it, all the things you do and say and bring to the conversation fill me with gratitude.

I have a new venture, Patreon, and thank you to those of you that followed me there whether it's fan level or 'I love Liam and Blakely' tier, or both. Thank you for being a part of the magic, Amber D Fine, Tasha Sandhu, Jackie, Angelique, Paula Seeley Fairbairn, Diane Porter, Anna Spain, Kathi Ross, and Sandy Hambrick for being the very first.

And, over in the Facebook group, a huge thank you to every single member of Kaitlyn and the Highlander group. If I could thank you individually I would, I do try. Thank you for every day, in every way, sharing your thoughts, joys, and loves with me. It's so amazing, thank you. You inspire me to try harder.

And for the most of the posts, comments and discussions, thank you — Mariposa Flatts, Anna Shallenberger, Kathleen Fullerton, Debra Walter, Lori Balise, Vickie Denton, Lauren Scarlett-Johnson, Alysa Isenhower Hill, Mitzy Roberts, Makaylla Alexander, Dawn Underferth, Cindy Straniero, Sandy Hambrick, Anna Spain, Dorothy Chafin Hobbs, Rochelle Hopkins Fitzpatrick, Cynthia Tyler, Karen Scott, Christie Louise White Sanders, Christine Ann, Madeline Benjamin Gonzalez, Joann

Splonskowski, Carol Wossidlo Leslie, Holly Bowlby, Marie Smith, Enza Ciaccia, Kaye Bonner Eicher, Harley Moore, Elaine Brown, Maria Schell, Nite Skye, Hannah Ziegeler, Margo Machnik, Teresa Gibbs Stout, Debi Mahle O'Keefe, Stephanie Laite Lanham Summers, Jessica Blasek, Ginger Duke, Diane M Porter, Tina Rox, Kathy Ann Harper, Dianna Schmidt, Lillian Llewellyn, Liz Rains Johnson, Shannon McNamara Sellstrom, Jennifer Goerke, Jenny Thomas, Jackie Briggs, and Azucena Uctum. You all help keep it interesting over there!

Thank you to Alison Caudle for playing the suggest a name for a character game. I picked 'Alison' for Alison's name.

And to Margo Machnik for sending me a direct message wishing that she knew more... It got me thinking and it got Finch talking, telling his side of the story, and then the second edition was born.

I love it so much more... thank you for the seed.

If I have somehow forgotten to add your name, or didn't remember your contribution, please forgive me. I am now back to writing book 16 of Magnus and Kaitlyn and it is hard some days to come up for air.

I mean to always say truthfully, thank you. Thank you.

Thank you to *Kevin Dowdee* for being there for me in the real world as I submerge into this world to write these love stories. I've loved you almost my whole life and joy of joys you've loved me back. You're the freaking best.

Thank you to my kids, *Ean, Gwyneth, Fiona,* and *Isobel*, for listening to me go on and on about my books, advising me whenever you can, and accepting my characters as real parts of our lives. I love you.

KAITLYN AND THE HIGHLANDER

Kaitlyn and the Highlander (Book 1)
Time and Space Between Us (Book 2)
Warrior of My Own (Book 3)
Begin Where We Are (Book 4)
Entangled with You (Book 5)
Magnus and a Love Beyond Words (Book 6)
Under the Same Sky (book 7)
Nothing But Dust (book 8)
Again My Love (book 9)
Our Shared Horizon (book 10)
Son and Throne (book 11)
The Wellspring (book 12)
Lady Mairead (book 13)
The Guardian (book 14)
Magnus the First (book 15)
Only a Breath Away (book 16)

Kaitlyn AND THE
HIGHLANDER
DIANA KNIGHTLEY

Time AND SPACE
BETWEEN US
BOOK 2 of KAITLYN AND THE HIGHLANDER
DIANA KNIGHTLEY

Warrior
OF MY OWN
BOOK 3 of KAITLYN AND THE HIGHLANDER
DIANA KNIGHTLEY

A POST-APOCALYPTIC LOVE STORY BY DIANA KNIGHTLEY

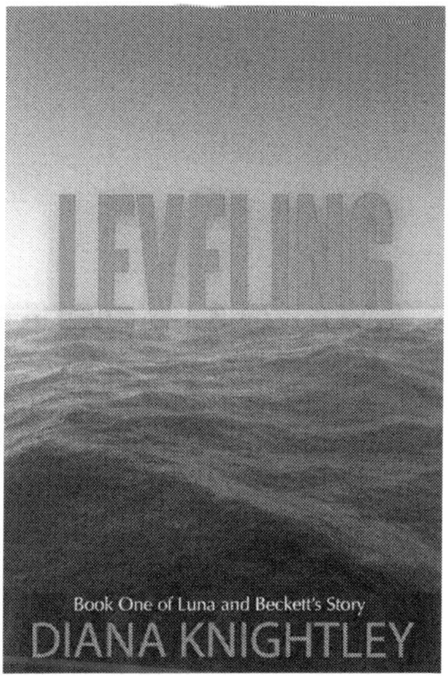

Can he see to the depths of her mystery before it's too late?

The oceans cover everything, the apocalypse is behind them. Before them is just water, leveling. And in the middle — they find each other.

On a desolate, military-run Outpost, Beckett is waiting.

Then Luna bumps her paddleboard up to the glass windows and disrupts his everything.

And soon Beckett has something and someone to live for. Finally. But their survival depends on discovering what she's hiding, what she won't tell him.

Because some things are too painful to speak out loud.

With the clock ticking, the water rising, and the storms growing, hang on while

Beckett and Luna desperately try to rescue each other in Leveling, the epic, steamy, and suspenseful first book of the trilogy, Luna's Story:

Leveling: Book One of Luna's Story

Under: Book Two of Luna's Story

Deep: Book Three of Luna's Story

ABOUT ME, DIANA KNIGHTLEY

I write about heroes and tragedies and magical whisperings and always forever happily ever afters. I love that scene where the two are desperate to be together but can't because of war or apocalyptic-stuff or (scientifically sound!) time-jumping and he is begging the universe with a plea in his heart and she is distraught (yet still strong) and somehow, through kisses and steamy more and hope and heaps and piles of true love, they manage to come out on the other side.

My couples so far include Beckett and Luna, who battle their fear to find each other during an apocalypse of rising waters. Liam and Blakely, who find each other at the edge of a trail leading to big changes. Karrie and Finch Mac, who find a second chance at true love. And Magnus and Kaitlyn, who find themselves traveling through time to be together.

I write under two pen names, this one here, Diana Knightley, and another one, H. D. Knightley, where I write books for Young Adults. (They are still romantic and fun and sometimes steamy though because love is grand at any age.)

DianaKnightley.com
Diana@dianaknightley.com
Substack: Diana Knightley's Stories

ALSO BY H. D. KNIGHTLEY (MY YA PEN NAME)

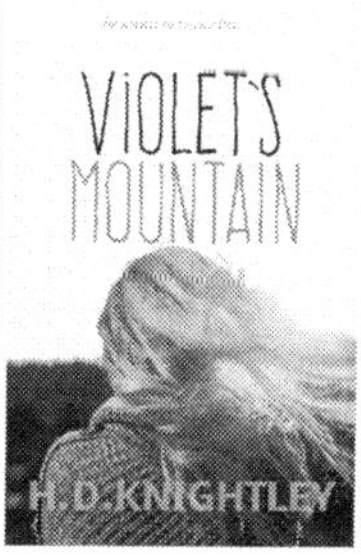

Bright (Book One of The Estelle Series)

Beyond (Book Two of The Estelle Series)

Belief (Book Three of The Estelle Series)

Fly; The Light Princess Retold

Violet's Mountain

Sid and Teddy

Made in United States
Orlando, FL
21 July 2023

35336097R00167